PETALS & PUNCHES

LORI THORN

Copyright © 2024 by Lori Thorn

All rights reserved.

No part of this book may be reproduced in any form or by any electronic or mechanical means, including information storage and retrieval systems, without written permission from the author, except for the use of brief quotations in a book review.

❦ Created with Vellum

This book is dedicated to all those who try to live nobly.

1

BET

If you ask me, the cemetery is an ideal place to do yoga. The grass is lush, and the atmosphere is peaceful, but have you seen the shade? It's the best part. These oaks deserve to be paid overtime for the impressive coverage they provide.

Not that anyone would ask me. I can't imagine someone seeing me in Warrior Three and interrupting with, "I beg your pardon, but why are you doing yoga *here?*" I smile at the thought and transition to Mountain Pose. A bead of sweat slides down my back beneath my shirt. It's June, and it is scorching in the small bayside town of Haven Cove. So hot I wouldn't usually practice outside today at all, except my last delivery was here, and I desperately need the break.

In the distance, I know there's a funeral party gathered around a casket. Their outlines are small from here; many wear white instead of dark hues. Strange. The flowers I delivered to them were also unique. Lily had taken the order, and when I saw it written in her sprawling script, I wondered if she had gotten it mixed up. She's a great boss and has managed the shop for as long as anyone can remember, but she is a little... kooky. When I asked her if she was sure, she sang from the cooler, "Of course I'm sure. You can *Bet* on it!" Then laughed at using my name in the same pun she's used at least two thousand nine hundred and eighty-six times. Still, a black, red, and gold casket spray is unusual. It reminded me more of our school-related orders: homecoming or graduation bouquets, boutonnières, and corsages.

It's not really a downside, but one thing to be extra careful about (if you decide to practice yoga in a cemetery) is respectfulness. I take pains to respect the place and the visitors and bring a small snatch of flowers from work and lay it on a different headstone each time. My spot today is in an older part of Grant Memorial Park and far from the gathering I delivered to, ensuring there's no chance I could distract from it. Out of an abundance of caution, I've positioned myself behind the largest tree on this side of the grounds. I'm down to 15 minutes until I return to Daisy's Daisies & Other Flowers. As Lily's only full-time employee, I can't leave her hanging for long.

I step one foot down at a time from my L-pose, and then the shouting begins. Uniform at first. I peek over at the ceremony. The people are reciting (yelling!) some chant or cheer with a moving depth of emotion. Are they a religious organization? The words are muddled, and I can't completely make out what they're saying, but when the group stops, a single voice rings out. I hear them, clear as day. "Or *some* of us are." I am too far away to see the man who said it, but I can tell he's sneering from his tone. There is sudden movement between some of the white figures. People standing beside the movement intervene, and the commotion ends.

Fighting at a funeral is not terribly uncommon; I know this, yet I'm still holding my breath. Being a florist for five years has taught me some surprising lessons. For example, any situation with heightened emotions, whether mournful or joyous, is ripe for arguments that otherwise might never occur. Whatever this outburst was, it does seem to have calmed. I put on my shoes, pluck my keys from the grass they nestled into, and head back to the shop.

2

TED

"Fifty percent? The tuition is going up that much?" Mrs. Woods's expression says it all. The news I was forced to deliver had knocked the air out of her. "This goes into effect in January?"

I swallow and try not to hate myself for saying the following words. "Yes, Ma'am. Julie has been attending for a couple of years, so you know we haven't implemented any tuition change in that time. We actually haven't adjusted tuition in six years, but the costs of running the school have increased, so now we have to take action." It was *technically* true. We hadn't changed our tuition, and we did need to… but by this much? Phil would have never.

Mrs. Woods glances at the floor before looking back at me. "I'm not sure we can afford it. I'll have to talk with my husband and see."

"I understand. Julie has been doing great. I hope you can stay on." I hesitate on the way to open the door for her. I shouldn't say it, but I can't stop the words from falling out. Just before she's in the parking lot, I add, "Mrs. Woods, I'm sure we could work it out somehow if you hit trouble." A smile spreads across her lips. "Thanks, Ted. I know you've got a lot on your shoulders. You're doing a good job, you know?" I nod. Her heels click against the pavement as she goes to her car.

Every conversation has been the same. Or worse. And I don't have any options or understand why this is happening. Everything is falling apart.

It all started when Phil died. Or before? It's funny how the accumulation of time has the effect of blending everything.

Phil. I loved Phil.

When my dad passed, Phil saw me struggle, and I don't know why he decided to take an interest in me, but he did. He started giving me free private lessons, talking to me, and listening. I got increasingly involved with his school, eventually joining the demo team for community outreach when I was old enough. I earned my fourth-degree black belt after graduating high school. When I asked if I could teach at Noble Martial Arts, he brought me on as an equal and taught me about the business side of running the school. It was perfect. Even though we weren't blood-related, it felt like a family business, and I treasured it. It was like a dream come true that I never knew I had. I know everything about Noble. Every crack in the wall and every student who has stepped on the mat. It's all sacred to me. It *is* my life.

When Phil got sick, he'd told me... A lot of things. But I can't think about that. It doesn't matter because that's not what happened. Phil is gone, and before I could even process the loss, his brother, Mark, started texting me about Noble. I've never even seen Mark before. Through our interactions, I have gleaned that he doesn't understand martial arts, Haven Cove, entrepreneurship, or even how to be a decent human. The things he's said to me are disgraceful, yet he is the proprietor now. I can't - won't - leave my community, yet I can barely stand working with him. The school won't last if he continues.

"Good evening, Ted. Are... are you okay?" I've been frozen, staring out the window since Mrs. Woods left, but Delia's voice snaps me out of it.

"Yes, sorry. Guess I got lost in thought there. You ready for a great class?" I force a smile. The rest of the Advanced Class starts to file in, and I make a mental note to let Delia know about the tuition hike after we dismiss. She'd probably be one of the easier conversations, and I can't take another rough one. Not now.

3

BET

Lily and I are chatting behind the register, enjoying a rare quiet moment when my phone buzzes in my back pocket. I fish it out and, seeing the screen, announce, "Mom."

"Better take it," Lily smirks. Thanks to the long work hours we'd spent together, Lily understood my relationship with my parents more than most. Don't get me wrong. It's not bad. I love my folks, and they love me, but we have different ideas about what's good for me. Before I can answer, the chime on the door announces a new customer. I slide my phone back into my pocket, but Lily nods toward the cooler.

"You sure?" I ask.

"Yeah, I've got him."

I slip into the flower cooler and try to answer but don't make it before the call ends. Phone tag. Mom answers after one ring, her bright voice practically singing her greeting. "Hey, Mom, I don't have long. I'm at work." I swat at the long gladiolus stems stretching out of their buckets, tickling my arm.

"Well, this is already a convenient segue. If you'd just settle down, you wouldn't have to work so hard all the time, and I'm calling because I've found you a date." I open my mouth to reply, but only a short, manic laugh comes out. "Bethany, don't say no. It's hard for me to arrange anything for you now that you've moved so far away."

"Mom. You don't have to set me up with anyone. I get dates on my own. Please don't feel obligated to..." but she cuts me off.

"You get dates on your own? When was the last time?"

Silence.

"We're worried about you, Bethany. Since the incident, it's like you aren't even trying. Worse, it's like you're purposefully running men off. Couldn't you let your hair grow out and wear a nice dress? You're such a beautiful girl!"

"The way I look is not to please men. It's to please me. Wouldn't you want me to be with someone who likes how I look when I'm being myself?"

Mom's turn for silence.

These types of conversations offer a lot of awkward pauses as we try not to step on each other's feelings. Mom goes for ignoring my question completely this time. "So, will you meet him? David is his name. He's a little bit older than you, 32, I think. A lawyer. One of the Sloan cousins. Very handsome."

I pinch the bridge of my nose and inhale. "Is he going to call me Bet or Bethany?"

"I'm so glad you agree. He knows you by your birth name, of course. I'll never understand why you can't go by it, or at least Beth! He knows you're free Sunday and will text you later."

"You already gave him my number?!"

"You're going to love him!" She's singing again.

"Thanks, Mom. Love you, I gotta go." I hang up and open Messages to text Emma with furious speed.

Bet Greene

> Guess I have a date Sunday, but don't get excited, it's brought-to-you-by-Mom™
> 11:53 AM

EMMA WILL REPLY with the immediacy of a bestie who unabashedly lives vicariously through my dating life. Still, I shove my phone into my back pocket and hustle to help Lily at the counter. The lunch rush is starting, and she's already put a caller on hold while she continues to assist the gentleman in person.

I'M FINALLY on my way home, fingers stiff from dethorning a Rose Bowl float worth of roses, when I get to check up on my texts. As expected, Emma's numerous replies have me laughing out loud.

EMMA BEST BEST Bestie

> Oh? 11:53 AM

LORI THORN

EMMA BEST BEST Bestie

> It's too late. I'm already excited and will need to know everything. 11:54 AM

EMMA BEST BEST Bestie

> Can we trademark that? I feel like it's a solid investment. 11:54 AM

EMMA BEST BEST Bestie

> Who is he? 11:55 AM

EMMA BEST BEST Bestie

> With whom? 11:55 AM

EMMA BEST BEST Bestie

> I know you're working but... I MUST KNOW THE NAME OF THE SUITOR! 11:55 AM

EMMA BEST BEST Bestie

> What do you think you'll wear? 12:05 PM

EMMA BEST BEST Bestie

> What does he do? Is he a doctor? He is, isn't he? *swoons* 12:10 PM

EMMA BEST BEST Bestie

> Since he's a doctor you should wear something classy on top but paired with a short skirt to show off those gams. #gamsfordays 12:10 PM

EMMA BEST BEST Bestie

> Charlie says hi. Tell me more about the thoracic surgeon when you're home. 12:15 PM

IT'S ALWAYS a toss-up between showering when I get home or after I bake. Ideally, I would wash the day off, but there's a real risk I'll end up covered in flour. Flowers and Flour. My life in three words. Today, I decide to delay the shower until after baking. I've got all the ingredients out and ready, and my phone propped up against a stack of cookbooks. I press the button to FaceTime Emma and am greeted by a too-close forehead and a shock of blonde hair.

"Hi Charlie, how are you, sweetheart?"

"Aunt Bethy?" The words are round in the mouth of a 3-year-old.

"Hey Bud! Is your mom around?"

He pulls away from the camera, and I see a flash of his full profile as he shouts, "Mama! Mama! Aunt Bethy!"

The camera moves into a sensical position, and Emma smiles at me. Her sandy-colored hair is up in a messy bun with strands hither and thither. I can tell she's tired from the day, but her eyes are bright, and she leans against the counter before saying a single word. "Details."

"Maybe you can tell me some. He's a Sloan cousin. David?"

Emma presses her lips together and looks at the ceiling. "Mmmm. The Sloans are handsome, but I don't know a cousin David."

I pause, measuring the almond flour. "Don't know, as in you know there isn't a cousin David, or don't know, as in you aren't familiar with their family tree?" It's a fair question. Haven Cove is a cozy town, but it's positively bustling compared to Marysville, where Emma and I grew up. Where she still lives. Where everyone knows everyone.

"I'm sure there's a cousin David. Who doesn't have a cousin, David? I just don't know him. Probably escaped."

"Mom says he's a lawyer."

"Oh! He definitely escaped, then. Where did he graduate from?"

"I don't really know anything about him. Just that he's 32 and will reach out to me." Her unresponsiveness causes me to look up from the Orange Cake batter. Emma is so focused on me it's as if she's in the same room. "What?"

"Don't count him out because it's a Mom setup. Maybe he's the perfect match for you." I try not to roll my eyes, but an expression must have escaped because Emma insists, "I'm serious!"

It's time to change the subject. "I won't bring any prejudgement. I agreed to go out with him, didn't I? Anyway, enough about mystery-David. How are you? What have you been up to?"

As if the question is a reminder that there's a roaming toddler somewhere behind her, Emma turns on her heel quickly to spot him. "He's playing with his blocks. Phew, okay. Realized it was quiet."

"Charlie's good then?"

Hesitation. Then, a careful "Yes."

"But…" I prompt her.

Emma sighs heavily, and her shoulders slump. "It's harder than I expected with Chad away so often. I thought, well," She breathes in before spitting out, "At first, I thought it wouldn't be too bad because I do most everything with Charlie and the house chores and stuff to begin with, but it's nonstop. When he's gone, I have to be on all the time. I didn't realize how valuable taking a shower alone was. Even if I try to sneak in when Charlie's asleep, I worry about him waking up and not being able to hear him over the water."

"That does sound hard. When does he get back?"

"We're halfway done; it'll be another two weeks before he's back."

I nod at my counter and turn on the food processor to blend the orange into a paste. The brief loudness allows me to think about what I'll answer. I want to ask if there's anything good about Fucking Chad's absence. When he started taking long-distance work assignments, I hoped the space would, I don't know, inspire Emma. Give her a glimpse of life without the constant jabs and undercurrent of inadequacy. I once heard Chad ask her why she doesn't dress up for him anymore, and it sent me such a flood of protective adrenaline my body buzzed the entire day. The blender stops whirring. In the end, I'm worried about her happiness. "If you need his help, will he stop taking these assignments?"

Emma rubs her eyes. "I don't know. It's a lot more money."

"Could you hire a part-time nanny or something?"

She shakes her head and looks down, and though she doesn't say it, I know that means Chad said no. Emma tries to keep the relationship between Chad and me peaceful, and we grudgingly comply. He must love her at least that much. "What are you baking today?"

"Vegan Orange Cake. It's a traditional recipe, new to me. You use an entire orange, peel and all." I hold up a spoon of orange puree to the camera.

"Ooh! Sounds so good. I miss your baking!"

"I miss you and Charlie. I wish we were closer and I could help you more. I'd bring you baked goods every day." The declaration earns a weary smile. "Seriously, you're always welcome to visit me. Stay here for a little while. At least text me anytime!"

"I *do* text you… all the time." She giggles, and I shrug.

"Even more then!"

THE WEEK HAS GIVEN way to Sunday, my one full day off. I had started thinking David may not reach out, but late Saturday evening brought his call. It was a short exchange but easier and more comfortable than it could have been. Maybe he wasn't so bad. Now, I'm sitting at the bar of Marco's Italian Restaurant, where we agreed to meet. I'd chosen my least-comfortable-but-best-ass-factor maroon pants, a cream-colored satiny boat neck blouse, and simple black pumps. Even my short hair got some tousling attention. It's so dark, and one note that styling it can be a challenge, but let the record show an attempt was made.

The salt crystals of my margarita just touch my lips when

I hear a throat clear behind me. "Nice rim job there! Uh... You must be Bethany?"

Were those the first words he said to me? I twist on the stool, and my expression must have been scathing because he backpedals at full speed. "Oh, I... I'm sorry, that wasn't tasteful." He looks down and says more to himself than me, "I'm so nervous."

He looks it. David is wearing old-fashioned-looking brown pants and a jacket. It fits poorly in the shoulders, like he's wearing his father's suit. He is not the overconfident shark lawyer I expected to meet, contributing to his mystery. I pat the stool next to me and ease my expression. "It's okay. I'm nervous too, and you can call me Bet. Only my parents call me Bethany."

David pulls the stool out to sit, but before his butt meets the pleather, a waiter appears and asks if we're ready to move to a table. David jumps up as if he discovered he was going to sit on a tack. I stand to follow, and David's head follows mine- up, up, up. I'm taller than him in my heels and wonder if it will be a problem. It wouldn't be the first time. Come on, David, don't have small dick energy. I'm internally rooting for him, and I'm not sure why. Something about him is... approachable.

The gangly teenage waiter leads us to our table. As I'm arranging myself, I swear I catch David giving him a look that asks, oh-my-god-what-is-happening? Hiding the smirk trying to surface on my lips, I throw him an easy question, "I don't know much about you except you're a lawyer and a Sloan cousin. Care to fill in some blanks?"

David chuckles, and the corner of his eyes crinkle. "I feel like that's a lot of blanks, and for some reason, I'm struggling to come up with details." He scratches his beard and inspects the lighting above. "Um, I fish a lot on the weekends. I have a little boat I like to take out on Lake Henry. Do you, ah, fish?"

I can't resist the smile this time. "No. My dad used to take me out occasionally when I was little, but I never got into it. Where is Lake Henry?"

While reading the menu, David replies, "It's on the outskirts of Newberry. Where I live. Newberry is right outside of Gainesville, so I have plenty of work there."

"That's quite a distance away. I didn't realize you weren't more local, I guess."

"Yeah, it's a three-hour drive."

"Ready to order?" Our favorite teen has returned with a golf pencil and notepad in hand. He's looking at David, but I answer as I hand him the menu. "Chicken Picatta and the house red for me, please."

David hasn't looked up from the menu yet but points swiftly and announces, "The stuffed snapper, and I'll do the asparagus on the side."

The pencil scratches against paper. "And what to drink?"

"Oh! Uh, sweet tea would be great."

Our waiter scurries away, and I'm left wondering why David didn't order alcohol. Whatever reason he has is fine; I'm curious though, and now I feel a little bad for ordering first. Does my drinking bother him? "So you live in Newberry. What brings you here?"

"I had some business. You know the McAffertys?" I nod. They're one of the most prominent families in Marysville. "They're close to my family and have been going through a hard time. I'm helping them prepare for Thomas Senior's end of life. Mrs. Greene, your mom, was at a luncheon last week, and we started talking, and…"

"And she roped you into going on a date with her wayward daughter?"

David flushes, red rising high into the visible part of his cheeks. "She was very complimentary about you."

I wink at him, and he relaxes again. "So, is that what you

do for work? I thought lawyers were all courtroom objection types?"

"Mmhmm. I'm an Estate Attorney. I help people prepare for what happens at the end of their lives. Things like appointing power of attorney, establishing trusts, naming beneficiaries, and preparing wills. That sort of thing."

"Helping plan a person's exit from this existence seems hard. Is it depressing?"

David explains he doesn't view it that way. It's fulfilling to help someone go peacefully without worrying about what happens to their family after they're gone. I can tell he's settling into the conversation a little more. Our food is served, and he turns the tables on me. "How about you?"

"I'm the assistant florist at Daisy's Daisies and Other Flowers and…"

David interrupts, "What a name!"

"Yeah, the owner's name isn't even Daisy. She's named after another flower. Dare to guess?"

He swallows a gulp of tea. "Rose?"

"She would hate that you guessed that. Lily, actually."

"This will sound like a wild question, but why not Lily's Lilies and Other Flowers?" David is eating this up. His eyebrows are doing a veritable dance across his forehead.

"She thought lilies were too pretentious for a shop name." David laughs, and it's warm and genuine. A little knot of regret starts pulling in my stomach—something to unravel later. "I know, I love her. It's a demanding job with just the two of us. Especially during the holiday months, we work a lot of hours. At night, I bake a few batches of vegan goodies for the cafe next door and try to squeeze in some yoga whenever possible. Me in a nutshell." I wave my fork in the air to punctuate the thought.

"Why vegan? I mean," He gestures toward my plate of chicken, "You're not vegan."

"A couple reasons. Even if I'm not, some people are, and vegan baking is even more delicious than traditional." David shoots me a skeptical look. "Think about it. Bakers used eggs for years and years because they were what was available. Vegan bakers have been scientifically choosing alternatives and, through that process, have found even tastier replacements."

"People think it's healthier." Why is he challenging me on this?

"Some people do. It's not always healthier at all. Some people think steak and potatoes are healthiest, too."

David shrugs. "I can't understand the egg hate."

"You would deny someone allergic to albumin a delicious fluffy pumpkin cookie?"

He tuts and says, "Allergies are different."

I shrug. This isn't the first time I've had this conversation. "To me, it's important to respect another person's choices. I understand why people adopt certain diets, but I don't have to understand to be unbothered by it. Even supportive." I squint toward David. We're suddenly on uneven ground. Things were going so well! Besides him living so far away, which makes it impossible to date in the first place. I try to lighten the mood when he doesn't reply. "You clearly haven't tried my confections. I think I have some key lime pie left if you want to taste a piece."

His brows shoot up in surprise, and it takes me a second, but oh gods, does he think key lime pie is a euphemism? Before I can clarify, he says, "No, thanks." I am unsure what I was rejected for, but whether it was pie or cake, it stings!

We've entered meh territory after a surprisingly strong start to this date. It doesn't matter since David isn't a viable partner anyway. Our conversation returns to normal first-date chattiness. It's pleasant. We finish our meal and say our goodbyes when he surprises me by asking to meet again. "Oh, ummm."

David's awkwardness returns. "It's okay. I'm sorry, I thought we had a good time."

"No, David, I did have a good time. You seem like a nice person, but you live so far away. I don't have time to travel often, and I'm sure it's also a stretch for you."

He nods, eyes on his loafers. "I guess if anything ever changes, give me a call?"

"Sure, of course, and thanks for a nice night out."

I TEXT Emma the highlights from the driver's seat. What a strange date. Considering he did want to meet again, why didn't he want to swing by for a slice of whatever he thought I was offering? David had some good to him. Despite his annoyance at my baking, he was sweet and humble, but the attraction wasn't enough to consider a long-distance situation.

The engine turns over, and while I back the car up, I notice the red glow of neon in the strip mall. Noble Martial Arts. A collage of memories starts playing in my head at once: me as a girl and later as a teen begging my parents to let me learn karate. They would laugh me off or explain with slow, deliberate patience that karate wasn't ladylike.

My life has changed substantially over the last few years. I moved to Haven Cove, ditched my long hair in favor of a pixie cut, started wearing comfortable clothes that made me feel good, and even got a tattoo on my ankle. In short, I stopped listening to the messages I'd heard my whole life about being feminine and what a woman's place is. I started just being me and figuring out what I enjoyed. Call me rebellious. Perhaps it was time to explore karate, too.

4

TED

Teaching martial arts, or I imagine any skill, could be redundant and get boring after a while if you focus on the rote events. The actions of every class are the same. Start with a rallying creed and stretching, practice the quarterly moves, do weapons training, and finish with sparring, forms, or self-defense. Phil used to struggle with the grind of repetition. He'd marvel at what he called my "unyielding development mindset." Big words to say I keep my focus on the students. Seeing their individual growth, watching them struggle with a move and then mastering it, enthralls me. Knowing I had a small part in their progress (the most minor part, but even so) makes my pulse race to consider. I'm trying to hold onto that, now more than ever, while everything else about Noble is fading away.

Class time is the best. The sounds of shouting and exertion and getting to talk to my students, some of the advanced belts more colleagues than students, and the parents of the Tiny Tiger classes. Their connection keeps me present. My mind doesn't fret about attrition or increasing the cash flow to the school. The anger at Mark loosens its grip on me ever so slightly.

The last class of the night is almost done. It's 8:50 pm, and the Advanced Prep class will end in ten minutes; then, I'll clean and lock up by 9:30 pm. There's an odd number tonight, so when I call for sparring, I partner myself with Paige, the smallest and youngest student. I trust myself to adjust to her skill level, making the sparring practice challenging but not painful or intimidating. Adapting to meet a student where they're at is a skill developed with time and intention. I'm aware of who can do it and those who will go as hard as possible regardless of who they're up against… I guess there's an alternate school of thought that would have everyone suffer as they learn, but it doesn't belong at Noble, as far as I'm concerned.

"Bow to your partner." Everyone bows. "Touch gloves." There's padded pounding all around. Some older teens practically punch at each other instead of giving a friendly knuckle bump, but they're all smiles and challenge. "Go!" The room erupts in motion. I try to watch the partnerships while sparring with Paige, but it isn't easy. I block a round kick and counter with a cross, which she dodges with a quick back step and swivel. "Good dodge!" I barely get the praise out before she's at me with a jab. I duck to the right and put my weight into my right foot to aim a jump front kick at her. She jumps back and crosses her arms in front of her. A loud ding rings out. I look at the door as a woman I don't recognize walks in. My breath rushes out of me, not solely because I take a solid kick to the side of the head.

Paige is so surprised to have landed the kick that she stops fighting and leaps in the air, hands up triumphantly. "Thas free poins!" She cheers through her mouth guard. The black belts hear her proclamation of three points and laugh. Paige is correct about a kick to the head being worth three points, but she doesn't understand that some of our school use the battle cry for another reason.

"High five! Great round." We slap our gloved palms. "I've got to go help at the front. Can you take it in turns with Harrison and Adrian?" She nods yes, and I call for the end of the round. I quickly explain to the other two that Paige will join them and jog to the small front lobby area.

The woman is leaning against the front desk counter, observing the class through the window that separates the entrance from the studio. My skin prickles when she locks eyes with me. I don't need my glasses to tell she's stunning. There's urgency beneath my naval, telling me to get closer, pulling me to her.

"Hi, I'm Ted," I extend my hand, "How can I help you today?" Her handshake is firm, and her skin is calloused in some areas. Is she a martial artist already? Her reach would be a huge advantage for her.

"Hey, Thanks Ted, I'm Bet. I was wondering about taking classes."

"Wonderful! I can tell you about our membership options and schedules. Do you mind if I dismiss the class and come right back?" She agrees, and I hurry into the studio, praying the dismissal will be sufficiently impressive for Bet. "Back on your marks. Great class today." Everyone finds their starting positions in a neat grid. "Let's give a big shout when we bow out, okay? All together." I glance around the room. "Everyone set!" They snap up straighter. "Who are we?"

As a unit, the class bows, and as they rise, they shout, "We are Noble!"

"Class dismissed." The attentive energy dissipates instantly as everyone mills around and throws gear into their bags.

I return to Bet, but Paige passes me in the lobby, and I tap her shoulder. "Excellent job coming for me today."

"Yeah, that was a nice kick to the head." I turn around. Bet is right behind me, grinning at Paige.

Paige pushes her hair behind her ear and blushes. She murmurs, "Thanks," and trots off.

I turn back to Bet, "Saw that, huh?"

Her left brow arches in a delicate curve. "The impeccably aimed kick of a middle schooler, or you giving her full credit despite being distracted?"

"Oh. Uh. I…" I laugh, and heat rises up my cheeks, which is saying something because I'm still sweaty from class. I have no idea how to reply, so I move behind the counter to fetch the paperwork. "I've got flyers with all our information here. I imagine you want to see the schedule and understand the cost?"

The sly look on her face turns more serious. "Yes, I don't have much time or money, if I'm honest, but I've always been curious about learning. I thought it couldn't hurt to check." Her clavicle is more pronounced as she shrugs.

"Understandable. Why don't we talk about class times first to see if anything will fit your schedule? I'll mention here I do offer private lessons if it comes down to it, though there are many benefits of being in a class amongst peers." I turn the schedule around so it's facing her, and she places her hand next to the paper. Our hands are so close I feel the warmth from her fingers against mine. This closeness is a coincidence, yet something in me wonders, and now I don't know what to do with my own hand, so I keep it there.

Bet studies the schedule with a slight frown until she blows air out of her mouth in a defeated exhale. "I don't think it can work, at least not for the next few months. I'd only be able to get to Advanced Prep. Not a class for beginners. In the fall, work slows down for a little. I'll come back then." She pulls her hand from the counter, causing cold to invade my fingers.

"Wait, wait, that's not how this goes. Let's get creative. You're a beginner in martial arts. Have you done any other athletics?" I've got to figure this out. New students aren't easy to come by in a small town, and signing her up might prevent Mark from breathing down my neck. Plus, Bet truly wants to learn... This feels like it has to happen.

"I've done yoga for a few years." She offers the information meekly because she doesn't see the connection, but I do.

"Perfect! You've got bodily-kinesthetic intelligence, then. That's a big deal. You're still a beginner at our sport but know how to imitate movements; you can tell your body to do something and achieve it."

She's skeptical. "I don't know how that helps with the schedule."

"Sure," I nod, "My thought is that since it's temporary and you can change to another class in a few months, plus you've got the kinesthetic intelligence going for you, you *could* attend the Advanced Prep class to get started. It's the class you just saw the end of. If it turns out you're uncomfortable there, I could also start you on private lessons until you can join another class."

Bet chews her lip and then smiles in the same playful way from before. "I don't know. I don't think I'd want to fight Paige."

"You wouldn't have to spar until you're ready, or I'd spar with you."

"What about the tuition?" She's looking hopeful, but my stomach clenches. This is where it falls apart, and I've been forbidden to make concessions.

"Well, here are the options," I slide her the pricing sheet and see her brown eyes widen before I can continue, "This is the annual price. We can break it down to monthly, and, ah, I can comp you the first uniform and gear. If you don't mind some lightly used gear?"

Bet seems stunned for a moment, then takes a small step backward. "I... I'm sorry. Thank you for the offer. There's just no way I could... I work at a florist, and I barely make enough to..." She shakes her head. "I'm sorry, I can't afford that much."

Beneath the counter, my hands are in fists. Phil wouldn't have let someone who wanted to learn walk out the door. I bite my tongue, and Bet's hand is on the door, and I can't do it. "Wait." She stops but doesn't turn around. "Maybe we can get creative here, too." I'll deal with Mark later. "I'm supposed to start new students at these rates, but technically, they're next year's. I could get you in at this year's rate." I start fumbling through papers to find the old tuition sheet. A change in the light tells me Bet has returned to the counter. "Here it is!"

She looks at it as if it's not to be trusted. "Oh! That is a big change. It's still a lot, but I think it's doable. I'd need to pay monthly."

"Of course, monthly is fine."

"And, could you still let me have the used gear? I don't care if it's used." She's going to say yes!

"I'd be happy to. Dusty gear is sad gear."

She smiles at my quip, and her body relaxes. "I didn't expect to be able to sign up. I knew it was a long shot when I came. Thank you for working with me."

Bet slides her credit card to me, and I promise to bring a uniform for her on Thursday. Her absence is palpable when she leaves, and even the overhead lights seem to dim. I watch her through the glass until the door opens again and snaps me back to reality. Staring through the windows is becoming a hobby of mine, I guess.

"Shouldn't this be locked by now?" Abby looks at her watch and back up at me.

"Yeah, I just had a new student sign up."

Abby skips to the counter and smacks her hand on it, "That's great news!" I agree, but too slowly, and she detects the hesitation. Abby knows me better than anyone. After dating for years and then gradually transitioning to my best friend, she should. "It is, but?"

"But I gave her the old rate."

Abby recoils, shaking her head. "Something amazing, but Mark still won't be happy."

"I can't do it. I can't turn away people who want to learn. I can't let students quit because of an impossibly high rate increase. Not when we're okay, you know? The school isn't going under. There's enough to pay for all our operating costs, including me and what should be Mark's salary." I'm preaching to the choir. Abby has heard all about this.

"He's greedy. He thinks he can make a fortune and do nothing."

"If he runs off all our students, we'll be in real trouble. Can't make a fortune from a closed business."

Abby sighs. "I know. Let me help close up so we can get you outta here." We walk around the studio tidying and wiping down surfaces with disinfectant spray. Out of the blue, Abby asks, "It wasn't the girl with the short black 'do, was it?" Her eyes are narrowed at me.

"It was. Why are you looking at me like that?"

"I saw her in the parking lot. She's very pretty." I raise a brow and give her a slow blink. "You don't think she's pretty?! She's gorgeous! Ted. Ted! Tell me you think she's prettt-tyyyyyy!" Abby extends the last word in an over-the-top plea.

"She was pretty. Yes."

"So you're going to ask her out?" Abby abandons her roll of paper towels and spray to poke me.

"Ah! Stop that!" I grab her cleaning supplies and bring them to the back to put away. "I don't know anything about her. I'll be teaching her; it would be weird. Besides, she could be married." Wasn't wearing a ring, though.

"Or it could be awesome! Think about it."

"Sure."

"Sure?! You really will?!"

I won't tell Abby I've been thinking of nearly nothing else since I spotted Bet through the window. "If it will make you happy, I will *think* about it." Abby muffles a squeal behind her hands, and we head back to the front, turning lights off as we go.

I flip the lobby lights off, but Abby makes an "Oh," hops her belly onto the counter and reaches into a cubby by the computer to extract my glasses, "Don't forget these."

5

BET

Making class time work on Tuesday and Thursday would be a stretch, but it was a chance worth taking. It'd been two days since meeting Ted and signing up for the month, and I can't say my brain has rested since. Can I keep up with an advanced class at all? Would the other students dislike my being there? What if I slowed them down? Then there was Ted, or as Emma called him, "Man of the Year Ted." He had been so kind to me, but my mind kept returning to his interaction with Paige. He must be an outstanding teacher. Then there's the fact he's somehow so boy-next-door handsome he could model. Those are supposed to be a dichotomy, but I swear it's true. His heavy brows match his dark wavy hair, and his strong jawline, still visible beneath a scruffy beard, distracted me more than once Tuesday. I'll never tell Emma, but I may have dreamed about him giving me private lessons.

Now it was Thursday, and I was heading to my first class from Daisy's, praying I would hit all green lights on the way so I'd have time to change. Thankfully, luck is on my side, and I arrive an entire three minutes early. I speed walk into

PETALS & PUNCHES

Noble, ignoring my nerves and focusing on getting in uniform.

I see Ted first. He's talking to some of the other people in uniform wearing red and brown belts, who are tossing their shoes against the far wall. I follow their lead and hurriedly take my shoes off while imagining how I could snag Ted's attention to ask about the uniform.

"Bet! You made it!" Ted sidles up to me and smiles as I peel off my socks. My relief that I don't have to devise a way to interrupt his conversation is brief, followed immediately by fear that my gross socks, which I've been working in all day, are so rank he'll turn green and pass out à la the cartoons of my childhood.

"I did. Um, do you have the uniform?" I meet his gaze, hoping to distract him from the toxic sock situation. His eyes are dark brown like mine, except they have little golden flecks ringing around the outer part of his iris. I'm reminded that iris flowers bear their name because they come in a wide variety of colors, and the Greek Goddess Iris used rainbows to travel between heaven and earth.

"Of course," Ted snatches a neatly folded, shiny, black stack with a white belt on top from the counter, "Here you are. The bathrooms are just beyond the studio."

"Thanks!" I take the bundle and hasten through the studio, where still more students are lined up at the back. They seem to be in height order. Everyone is wearing the same black workout material I now hold, and I notice there are black belts here. You don't have to be an expert to know that's the highest level. Shit. I'm going to get my ass handed to me, aren't I? I change at lightning speed, leaving my work clothes wadded up outside the bathroom door, then join the line.

Except my place in line is ridiculous. By my calculations, it makes perfect sense that the older students would be taller and more likely to be black belts, leaving my tall frame smack amid three black belt students. My white belt is a shining beacon of discomfiture.

The men around me exchange glances; they obviously know each other. One of them, a muscular gentleman with a crew cut, gives me the impression he's going to say something to me, but at that moment, Ted addresses the class.

"Everyone! Set!" There's a sound of hands hitting legs as the group snaps to attention.

Ted shouts, "We are Noble," and the rest of the class recites, "We show honor. We live with integrity. We respect all people. In this way, we are strong!" I guess I'm supposed to learn by doing because I was not briefed on any of this. Noted.

From the far corner of the room, I see Ted point to star emblems on the padded floor before him and say, "Go." Each time he makes the command, a student bows and runs to the star he indicates. He quickly works his way across the room, and when he directs me to a star, the side of his mouth quirks up—a hint of a smile for me. Nobody else is smiling, though, so I try to maintain a serious composure.

We start out doing a punch and block combo. I struggle to keep track of which arm is supposed to be higher or lower, making my blocks come off more like a waving dance move, but the real problem is holding the middle stance. Middle stance is a form of torture where you take the position of a wide squat and hold it for eternity or until Ted says you're done. Not being able to maintain the position for long surprises me, but I suppose it uses different muscles than chair pose.

Side kicks are next. I feel better about these until Ted appears and asks if he can position me. This is exactly what yoga instructors do when you're fucking up. He demonstrates the circular motion I should make with my knee first, picking it up and toward my midline. Then, leaning over and thrusting my leg out "like a stomp." When I achieve my best kick, he asks me to pause, then gently grasps my leg and pivots it forward so my toes are more parallel to the ground and my hip feels too tight. My hip is uncomfortable, but my attention is drawn to the careful, supportive grip against my thigh.

I wobble when his hands drop from me, and he gives me a full smile. "Just like that." He turns away and instructs the class to line up at one of the seven bags at the front of the room. These are unlike punching bags I've seen on television. Instead of hanging from chains, they have a broad base on the floor, and the bag sticks up from it. I can tell they're heavy but movable as some students rush up to space them more evenly. Ted tells us to practice "any side kick we want" (whatever that means), and I join the end of a line with two black belts.

The first guy in my line does a step before he kicks the bag, then jumps and swivels his hips so his other foot also makes a hit. He runs to the end of the line behind me as if nothing had occurred. The second guy does a jump side kick like he's suspended on ropes or has a green screen behind him, except I literally saw him with my own eyes, and neither of those things is present. He turns to re-enter the line but stops to talk to me. It's the blonde crewcut man from before. "You're new, right?"

I gesture to my pristine belt. "Very."

His chuckle is raspy as he reaches out for a handshake. "I'm Cooper. You'll want to start with a number three side kick. It's the first part of what Roy did. Like this." Cooper demonstrates stepping behind my front leg to approach the bag before throwing the kick. "I always think the number three is easier than the number one by itself. Give it a try." He moves back, and I try but don't travel enough distance with my step and end up barely making contact with the bag. I jog to the back of the line, and Cooper winks at me. "You'll get it."

A few minutes pass, and Ted calls us to switch to warrior combos. He makes rounds of the room, inspecting people's forms, and giving personal instruction. I want him to come to my bag and tell me about warrior combos, and it looks like our timing is perfect. I approach the bag, and Ted walks up to my left. "Hi, Ted."

"How's it going, Bet?"

Cooper speaks from my right at the same time, "I can show you the warrior combos." I look between them, trying to figure out who to reply to first.

Ted says, "Thanks, Cooper. Let's get your gear before you go hard on the bag." I follow him to the side of the room, and as I turn, I swear Cooper scowls. Ted picks up a black duffel bag tucked under a chair and hands it to me by the strap. "Here you go. Go ahead and try everything on. We can make sure it all fits."

The bag is positively stuffed with items. Inside are gloves, shin pads, a helmet, a chest plate, nunchucks, and what looks like a foam baseball bat. "Wow, I didn't expect this much, Ted. Thank you."

He waves me off. "It's nothing. When you've been doing this, as long as I have, you end up with rooms full of spare gear. I made my best guess at your sizing; I probably have an alternative for you if anything is off."

Trying everything on reveals Ted was spot on about my sizes. Now that I think about it, the uniform itself fits perfectly. "Everything is great! Impressive eye."

"Well, you're easy to…" he trails off momentarily but then finishes, "easy to find the right size for, I mean."

We hold each other's stare until one of the younger students calls, "Mr. Ted, come see!" Ted rips his eyes toward the voice, breaking whatever spell we were under, and I run to rejoin my line.

Cooper is waiting. He teaches me combinations one through three before Ted moves us to the next activity. Sparring. I decide in an instant that I am most definitely not sparring today. I'm way out of depth. My muscles are already soup. I return to the chair my new bag is under and remove my gloves to discover bright red marks between my pinky and ring fingers. It doesn't hurt, though. Hmmm.

Ted successfully reads my sitting down as a pass on sparring and gives me a nod of acknowledgment before putting everyone else in pairs. There's a tiny squeeze of guilt when I realize there'd be an even number if I participate, but Ted partners up with the smallest kid. Today, it's a shaggy-headed boy no older than 13.

The difference between what is happening on either side of the room is staggering. My seat is on the lobby side of the class where the younger pupils are. This half of the room is full of happy faces, even some giggling. The kids dance around each other, dodge, and strike gently. Maybe I *could* spar one of them. The far side of the room is heavy. There's only one woman amongst five strapping men, all serious and competitive. They're also dancing around each other but not playfully. Everything they do is intense. Their punches are sharp and hard, and their kicks are fast. I can barely track what is happening except that they are all going at each other, not with abandon, but calculation. It's intimidating. It's also hot. I'm forcefully reminded of attending a Blue Grass concert with Emma years ago, where we both swooned over the deft playing of the stand-up bass player. We'd decided the stereotype about musicians getting as many women as they want might have some truth to it. Perhaps it applies to any talent that can be beheld.

After three rounds, Ted calls everyone back to their stars.

He cries, "At Noble!" And the class responds, "We live Noble!" The group bows in unison, and he dismisses us. I walk to the bathroom to retrieve my clothes and shove them into my bag when I detect a large figure looming over me.

"Hey." It's Cooper. I see Ted walking toward us behind him. His eyes register Cooper, and he abruptly changes direction.

"Hey." I stand and put the bag strap over my shoulder.

Cooper grabs the back of his neck. His arms are massive. "Uhh, I wanted to say it's cool you joined. It's tough starting in a class like this, but you, you know, hung in there." I huff a laugh, and he asks, "Bet, right?"

"Yeah, and thank you. For the help today. I've got a lot to learn."

The gap between the end of my sentence and his next one is minuscule as if he was holding back the question. "You want to get coffee sometime? Dinner?"

"Umm…" I'm completely caught off guard. In my silence, he dips his chin down and raises his brows, giving him a puppyish expression. I guess it can't hurt. He didn't even call it a date. "Sure."

Cooper's mouth splits into a satisfied grin. "I'll walk you to your car." He puts an arm around my shoulders, and I pull away. Before I can protest, he puts both hands in the air, exposing his palms, "So sorry, that was too fast. Won't happen again."

I instantly want to cancel whatever plans are not yet made, but I steady myself with closed eyes and a breath. I need time to process. "Way too fast, but… okay." He escorts me to my car, and I reluctantly exchange numbers. Mom will be happy, at least.

6

TED

My current struggle with Mark is not tuning him out. Every conversation is the same. What is our most recent profit? How many new students did I sign up? Why can't I make more money? Followed by complaining about something I've done. I know it's essential I pay attention, but I'm exhausted by trying to meet him half way.

"Ted? Hello?!" I must have missed a question. Mark's gruff voice is annoyed.

I pull my focus back to the call. "Sorry, you broke up. What were you saying?"

"You need a new cell service. I don't have time to repeat myself. I asked when the next demo team performance is."

The question pulls me into an upright position. He's never asked about the demo team, or any class, or any of our community involvement, for that matter. How does he even know about it? "Our next performance is the Independence Day parade."

"What about after that?"

"It'll be August. We offer to perform at schools when

they're in session and do all the Haven Cove parades and city events."

"So you're taking a vacation all summer, then?"

"No, there are no events for us to perform during the summer after the 4th, and with school out, there's…"

"Sounds like another excuse, Ted. No wonder we aren't seeing more new signups if we're not advertising. Is the team at least sharp? Ready when you find something?"

"I. Not really. So, the demo team is formed by interested students who audition to participate each year. The parade next month is the last performance of this team's year, and then I'll have open auditions at the beginning of August to form the new team. Mark, I can run it by everyone to gauge their availability if you have another venue in mind. I'm sure the current team would be agreeable."

"If *I* have another venue in mind? I hope you mean when you find more opportunities." I bite the inside of my cheeks and pray for patience. At least, this feels like the end of the conversation. "It's not just me who sees these opportunities, Ted. Some of our most dedicated students have confided in me that they fear you aren't capable of doing the job." The coppery taste in my mouth and Mark's final words are barely perceptible through the static in my brain.

"He's bluffing." Abby's tone is soothing. I'd messaged her asking if she could meet up a couple of hours after the call with Mark ended. I needed to talk to someone who would understand. Mom had already been nervous about the changes since Phil passed away. I didn't want to stress her out anymore.

That left Abby.

I have other friends, but when I think of talking to them

about something serious, I can't even imagine it. I love those goofballs, but they never take anything seriously.

"He's not, Abby. He knew about the demo team. I tried to tell him about our classes and the team in our first conversation months ago, and he interrupted me and told me he didn't need to know about the operations. Someone else told him."

Abby turns toward me on the park bench, propping a knee on the seat. Evening light filters through the tree leaves around us, dappling across her. "Maybe that's true, but it doesn't mean they complained." Panic flashes across her face.

"What are you thinking?"

"Nothing."

"I know that look. Come on."

She pushes a strand of long auburn hair behind her ear. "I don't think what Mark said means that someone actually complained even if he did talk to someone… but. I'm sorry, but it does seem like a bad sign he *listened* to this other person. Why would he listen long enough to someone else when he won't to you?" I lean over, resting my elbows on my knees, and Abby puts a warm hand on my shoulder. "It'll be okay. Maybe I can help you find an additional event nearby to demo at. I'll put the word out that Noble is available, okay?" Abby is an Emcee, the only Emcee in a 50-mile radius. Lucky for her. The lack of competition helps keep her busy in a small area.

"Yeah. Thanks. That would be great."

"Done. Hey, did you ever ask out that girl? You said you were going to."

A sigh escapes me, and I massage my temples. "I said I'd think about it."

Abby withdraws her hand. "So no, then?"

"No, but because she's with Cooper."

"Shut! Up!" Abby punches me hard in the arm. "Are you kidding?!"

"Ow!" I rub where she hit. "*You* should enroll at Noble, punch like that. And no. I'm not kidding. He walked her out after the first class she attended, and word is they're dating."

"Who is this girl? Who told you they were together? Ted, could he tell you like her?" Abby talks fast, hands gesturing wildly before her.

"Her name's Bet. It doesn't matter who told me; it's just kinda known, and I don't know, how could he tell I like someone?"

Abby stands at my question, takes my hand, and pulls me up. "We're walking. Bet has terrible tastes if this is true." We stroll along the sidewalk. A breeze rolls in from the bay, making the air cooler than usual for this time of year. Palm trees are gently swaying along the water's edge. The bay has a slight chop, sunlight sparkling along its surface. It's gorgeous. My mood doesn't fit the scene at all. "It's been one week. It's not like they could be serious. They've been on one date tops!"

I shoot a sidelong glance at Abby. "I'm not trying to agitate old grudges. Especially not now. Cooper could be who Mark talked to."

"He wouldn't. Okay, he might, he's an asshole, but I'm telling you, even Cooper wouldn't complain. Also, for the record, it's obvious when you're interested in someone."

"Oh really?"

"Definitely. You look at them differently. Smile more. Get real winky, which is so dorky."

"Winky?!" I pretend to swipe at her, and she hops off the sidewalk. "I think this is enough talking about me. Tell me about you. Something good."

She skips a few steps ahead, then turns and walks backward in front of me. "Something good. I got a new gig in

Franklin planning a Labor Day BBQ Event. Bad news, they want to call it a BBQ Blow Out." I laugh, and Abby pumps her arm in victory. "Good news, it's almost D&D Night. Are you ready to DM?"

"Oh, I'm ready. Planning this campaign has been a perfect escape from recent events. I think the better question is if everyone else is ready." Our Dungeons and Dragons group had been going on and off since high school. The members fluctuate occasionally, but the core group of Adventurers includes PJ, Melissa, Mitch, myself, and Abby as the newest member.

Abby smirks, "Something else good! Things are going well with Wes. I'm meeting his folks next weekend."

"Congratulations! Long time coming. I know you were nervous about not having met them yet."

Abby jokingly abuses Wes as we make it back to our cars. Her banter makes me feel lighter than I have in days. We'll find some more events for the demo team. I'm sure I can get enough volunteers to perform at them. That should please Mark, at least for now. There wasn't anything I could do about Bet, but maybe Abby was right about her, too. She and Cooper could be short-lived, and I'll just have to see. Bet seemed like the first potentially good thing to happen in a while. When she walked in, I can't recall ever feeling so drawn in so immediately. Like air returned to my lungs when I didn't know I was having trouble breathing. But what use is it if the feeling is one-sided?

7

BET

The delivery driver we rely on when we have a lot of deliveries or more complex ones called in sick this morning. I hope Robert feels better soon. His absence means I'm on delivery, and Lily runs the shop alone. Deliveries are enjoyable; I don't mind. Time driving is a quiet time to think, and seeing the expressions on the recipient's faces is a great bonus that can keep me going for days. Still, I need to be expedient and get back to Lily before the lunch rush.

My first stop is St. John's Hospital. Hospital orders stem from emotional experiences and can be the peaks of jubilation or utter despair. I've made arrangements for new mothers, people coming out of surgery, and people in remission after battling cancer. They're bright, colorful, and often even arranged in a sprawling or explosive way. Other events: accidents, illnesses, and deaths are nearly always demarcated by white subdued bouquets. Although mightily different, all life's moments get flowers. If they're done well, they mirror people's emotions.

I didn't take the order for this arrangement, nor did I do the work. I'll only take it as far as the front visitor check-in desk and then leave it with whoever is working at the time, but I can tell you it's a boy. Pale blue carnations, yellow daisies, and baby's breath erupt from a basket lined with a blue gingham cloth. A blue teddy bear is nestled against the basket handle. I arrange him just so and place the basket on the counter before Muriel spins her chair and rolls it over to me. "Oh, it's lovely! Great job!"

"Thanks, Muriel. This one is all Lily." I check my phone for the order info to mark it as delivered. "This is for the Pattons in 239B."

"You got it. I'll get it right up to Mama."

"Thanks, have a good one."

Next up is a wedding. This is the one that will take time. Weddings can be complicated for florists depending on their responsibilities. If the couple has an event planner, they usually take care of the on-site setup as part of their services. In this case, no event planner means I'm doing setup. The van crunches over the gravel of the First Baptist parking lot, but I don't get out immediately.

Weddings.

Time may heal all wounds, but I don't *prefer* the memories. I ponder how Aidan is doing. Ugh. It's better to think about tonight. It's my first date with Cooper. He'll pick me up and take me to Food Worx, our semi-permanent food truck rally. The trucks are open later than most restaurants, which suits me. Friday means I have more than usual baking to do.

I hop down from the driver's seat and start unloading heaps of pristine white calla lilies, sprigs of lavender, zip ties, and white satiny ribbon. These supplies go into the sanctuary. The table centerpieces and the bridal bouquet are already made. I collect them last and bring them to the social hall at the rear of the building. The room is buzzing with people, and the mother of the bride spots me immediately. "Flowers! Flowers are here! Thank goodness!"

In response, I raise one of the centerpieces, and she hurries over to me. "They're gorgeous! These will go right in the center." She sweeps the one I'm holding away from me and places it in the middle of a long row of tables. Her happiness is an instant relief.

"The smaller ones are in the van. I'll bring them in next." She's already talking to the caterer, who is arranging an end table of finger foods, but turns to give me a thumbs up. I make several trips to the van, ensuring the flowers are perfect before entering the room. The mother of the bride (Dottie, I learn) is thrilled each time and places them on the tables where she wants them. I hand her the bridal bouquet last and explain that I'll be setting up in the sanctuary when I notice she's crying. "Dottie, is everything okay?"

She takes several gulps of air. A strangled sort of sound comes out of her before she can talk. Dottie puts her free hand over her heart. "It's perfect." She gasps. Before I know it, she's wrapping me in her arms and pulling me close. I return the embrace, and she whispers an apology. "I'm so sorry. I don't know what's wrong with me."

"Nothing is wrong with you. Your daughter is getting married."

Dottie steps back, wiping her eyes. "Thank you."

I excuse myself to the sanctuary. It's much quieter in here. Since I'm alone, I snatch my phone out. It's been buzzing most of the morning, and I know it's Emma.

EMMA BEST BEST Bestie

> Looking forward to your night with Hiya?
> 7:35 AM

. . .

EMMA HAS CALLED COOPER 'HIYA' since I gave her the first class rundown. She'd been enthralled to learn that people in class do shout the sound the same way it's portrayed in movies. I told her, after googling, that the spelling might be 'kiai' or 'kihap' depending on the practice. She rejected this information, however, when I couldn't tell her what type of practice Noble was. She'd laughed and told me she'd be spelling it the way it sounds to her thank-you-very-much.

EMMA BEST BEST Bestie
> What do we know about him again? 7:35 AM

EMMA BEST BEST Bestie
> Nothing as I recall, Except that he touches too soon and is a black belt. 7:36 AM

EMMA BEST BEST Bestie
> Did you find out anything else? 7:40 AM

EMMA BEST BEST Bestie
> .... 7:40 AM

Emma Best Best Bestie

> Because I did! 7:41 AM

Emma Best Best Bestie

> I'm not good at cliffhangers, message me, I'm DYING! 9:03 AM

Bet Greene

> Hahaha! I'm here. Deliveries today, I'm setting up a wedding then one more office stop. 9:10 AM

Emma Best Best Bestie

> Wedding? You alright? 9:10 AM

Bet Greene

> Yeah. I'm good. 9:11 AM

EMMA BEST BEST Bestie

> GOOD! Okay, so I found him on Instagram. Cooper Hanson. Looks like he's been single a while. There's a picture of a blonde beauty queen he's tagged with a lot a year ago but nothing since then. He is ripped. Many thirst traps. In addition to the black belt, he also lifts weights, like a lot. Possible gym rat vibes. No parental pictures, but lots of bros. 9:11 AM

Bet Greene

> mmmm. How did you find him? 9:12 AM

EMMA BEST BEST Bestie

> Don't hum. I swear I can hear you grumble from here. Easy. Cooper black belt Haven Cove and voila. Not many to choose from. 9:12 AM

EMMA BEST BEST Bestie

> He's gorgeous, Bet. Yeah he's into himself but does that have to be a bad thing? He takes care of himself, maybe he'll take care of you too? 9:12 AM

> **Bet Greene**
> I don't need someone to take care of me. 9:13 AM

> **Emma Best Best Bestie**
> You don't. But sometimes it's NICE. 9:13 AM

> **Emma Best Best Bestie**
> You can be independent and take care of each other too. 9:14 AM

I'm not so sure. My parents' relationship isn't equal, and Emma's isn't. It doesn't feel right to point it out, though.

> **Bet Greene**
> Despite the popular theories otherwise, I do always give people a shot. 9:15 AM

> **Emma Best Best Bestie**
> Does your mom know you're going out with someone? 9:15 AM

> Bet Greene
>
> No. Don't tell her. She would disapprove of karate and I'd rather see how it goes first. 9:15 AM
>
> Bet Greene
>
> I gotta get decorating, Em! You know the drill. 9:15 AM

Emma Best Best Bestie

> Okay, GL tonight! Live stream me! 9:16 AM

PHONE AWAY, I start bundling calla lilies. The trick to making a bouquet of lilies is zip ties drawn snugly beneath the blooms. I'm using green ties today, the same color as the stems, in case any part becomes visible should a ribbon slip. Not likely for these, as they're being affixed along the aisle on the end of pews, but I want to be careful regardless.

After two hours, I stand at the back of the church, inspecting for any flaws for the third time. I keep making the second pew's arrangement hang either too high or too low, but thankfully, everything looks aligned now. I find Dottie, she approves, and I mark this job complete.

It's 11:30 am when I'm on the road, and I worry I might not make it back as soon as I'd prefer. I'm headed to The Law Offices of Parish & Parish. I've never heard of them, but my Maps App tells me I should have. They're located in the same strip mall as Noble. At least I know where they are; navigation should not be a hang-up. As I drive, my phone buzzes, and a glance at the screen reveals it's not Emma.

Cooper Karate

> I need to cancel tonight. 11:41 AM

Emma will be devastated. I guess I don't need to update his contact to Hanson.

I answer after parking in front of Parish & Parish. Turns out they're right next door to Noble. In my defense, I've never seen the door open before, and the windows are dark.

Bet Greene

> Okay. 11:47 AM

After dropping off the vase of wildflowers to the new secretary, a gift from her fiancé to congratulate her on the new role, I peek into Noble's window. What I see stops me mid-step. My right foot halts mid-air and then comes down, so I'm staring into a window like a child pining for a puppy in a pet store.

A Tiny Tigers class is in full swing. Ted is at the front, demonstrating a double punch and pulsing his middle stance, something he does when he wants students to get lower. Most of these pre-schoolers follow decently, but one is lying on the floor spinning in a circle, and another is standing there idly looking around. Ted walks around the class and first grabs the attention of the one watching imaginary butterflies. When he arrives at the floor spinner, the boy refuses to get up. I expect to see Ted's stern face (after my three classes, I've cottoned onto some of his expressions). Instead, he lays on the floor beside the kid and starts walking his feet, moving himself in a circle. He must ask the class to join because they all begin imitating the same move. I can't hear them through the glass, but they're all giggling, including Ted. His eyes are crinkled, nearly closed, and his smile is so broad it takes up his whole face. My heart feels like it will expand through my chest, and then Ted sees me and freezes. Through two windows, he somehow sees me.

I panic and run away, speeding back to Daisy's. It's 12:09 pm when I arrive, which is not too bad. My phone goes off again.

Cooper Karate

> Aren't you going to ask to reschedule?
> 12:10 PM

8

TED

We were in the middle when my friends and I started playing Dungeons and Dragons—the middle of high school, the middle of the social ladder, the middle performers. Things weren't bad for any of us, I don't think, but we all longed for something. To be popular or get the attention of the boy or girl we were into. Typical school-aged woes from the middle. None of that mattered when we were in another realm. I remember back then, I used to download pre-made campaigns when it was my turn to be the Dungeon Master. I'd review the rule books and stay true to every word. Comparing our measured beginnings to our current games is laughable. By the end of the last campaign, Melissa's character became a possessed half-loaf of manna that PJ's Barbarian character lovingly swaddled and carried in his "not-a-fanny-pack, pack."

Mitch's house is dimly lit and drab. He inherited it from his grandparents and, so far, has not bothered redecorating. The couch is a dark brown and green plaid with no spring. The furniture is all natural wood, but doesn't fit the current fashion and is also dark brown and covered with dust. I can't complain, however. Despite feeling like we're at your Grandma's house in the '70s, it's the perfect place to meet. Mitch is the only one of us who doesn't live in a smallish apartment, and his sizable oval dining table easily fits the five of us with room for snacks.

I scope the table from behind the safety of my screen, which keeps my campaign notes and dice rolls hidden from view of the party. Everyone has their tavern-style beer mug filled, and eyes are on me. I begin narrating, switching between my role as Dungeon Master and in-game characters, "You come to in a musty room. Your hands are bound behind your back, your mouth is gagged, and an itchy burlap sack is over your head. As you're trying to remember what happened, you hear the sound of heavy footsteps. At least one other person is in the room with you."

"An unrecognizable cutting voice addresses you. 'Finally waking up, I see. Don't do anything stupid. I assure you there is no escape until we are done talking. I am well-guarded. Plus… You're here for a reason. One that could make you wealthy beyond your wildest dreams, for my client is willing to be most generous in his desperation to right some wrongs."

"His boots thud closer. 'It is time for each of you to realize each other. Allow me to introduce you.' The man unmasks you," I point to Abby, "he takes out your gag but leaves your arms bound. You see he is alone and wearing an ornate black half mask over his eyes. 'Sasha Sleight. Widely regarded as a master of stealth and trickery. Long rumored to be the current holder of the kingdom's missing scepter, though it has never been proven. Tell us, Sasha, is it true?'

Abby sounds innocent, but her affect turns wicked as she replies, "Me? You really think I could get past the most heavily guarded treasures in the land and escape without getting caught? I'm flattered."

The party smirks at Sasha's cheeky reply.

"'Very well. I suppose we all will make our assumptions. We also have,'" I point to Melissa, "The man uncovers your eyes and removes your gag, 'Brandon Magewell. No assumptions here. Brandon is known to be the most powerful sorcerer in the Magewell line in 50 years.'"

Melissa straightens her back. "What of it? What makes you think I'll help in whatever scheme this is?"

I let out a low chuckle in reply, "'We'll see.' The masked man walks to the next person," I point to Mitch, "he removes the mask and gag."

Mitch yells, "I stand and tower over him; I try to headbutt him to knock him out!"

I reply, "He dodges, prepared for your actions. 'Settle, Brüt. Your strength, weapons knowledge, and fighting prowess will undoubtedly be needed on your journey. Yes, we have Brüt, of local fighting fame. Too bad about that loss in Weston…'" My lip curls up on one side.

Mitch groans, then shouts, "That was rigged, you bastard. I can prove it!"

I make a tisking sound, "The man ignores you and moves to the last captive," I point to PJ, "he removes your mask and gag, 'Finally, we have Yarx of Pthil, notorious Barbarian…'"

PJ interrupts, "Um, I'm not… whoever you just said."

"The man inspects you closely. A frown forms on his face. 'Who are you?'"

PJ's brows raise high. "I'm Lore Singer, traveling bard."

"'This is… not as planned. Mistaken identity or not, you are now part of this group, bard.'"

PJ's mouth falls open. "Mistaken identity? You mistook *me* for a *barbarian*? Your people must be idiots. I'm out of here."

"A door slams down the singular hallway you can see. The

man may not be so alone after all. 'You will stay, or you will die. I have no qualms about killing an extra.'"

Abby narrows her eyes. "Strange how your men managed to get me, Brandon, and Brüt here but made such an obvious error with Lore."

Mitch agrees, "Yes. Extremely strange. I'm afraid a bard will get in the way of whatever the task is."

Melissa nods in agreement and adds, "Which you still haven't explained. Let's hear it. Then we'll decide what to do with the bard."

PJ raises his middle fingers at Mitch and Melissa. "Stop calling me 'the bard.' I'm Lore Singer. There are songs *about* me! You don't know me!"

PJ looks like he's gearing up to start a ballad about his plight when the doorbell rings, breaking the immersion. Mitch sings, "Pizza's here."

"Thank, God! I'm starving!" Abby gets up and returns to the table with a roll of paper towels. Mitch follows soon and places two boxes in the center of the table. All of us stand to reach for a slice.

Abby swallows her first bite and asks how everyone is doing.

Mitch answers first, "Same old, same old. Delivering boxes for the man."

Melissa looks at Mitch with doe eyes. Abby and I have suspected she's interested in him for years, but she's also an apprehensive person. Even when we started playing, she found it difficult to make her character speak. She's come a long way from there. She quips, "How is Jeff Bezos anyway?"

Not missing a beat, Mitch replies, "Just had a beer with him yesterday. Said he's going to give me a promotion to co-pilot on his next space visit." He winks at Melissa, and her pale complexion turns bright pink as she looks down at her lap.

PJ chuckles. "You? Piloting a rocket ship? Sounds like a great way to die. No thanks." Mitch tosses a bit of crust across the table at PJ, but he catches it, and everyone reacts, "Ohhhh!" After the laughter dies down, PJ offers his updates, "School starts back next month, and I'm glad because delivering food to my student's homes is pretty demoralizing."

"Don't enjoy driving for a living?" Mitch questions.

PJ sighs. "The driving isn't the problem. I mean, it's honestly not usually too bad. I'm just salty from yesterday. One of my kids from last year answered the door and couldn't believe I was delivering their egg rolls. They were totally aghast. Asked if I was still teaching. Makes me rethink my entire life."

I jump in, "Sounds like jobs are sucking for most of us. Nothing much has changed for me, with the glaring exception of Mark talking to other established students and *listening* to them. Says someone complained about me."

Sympathetic faces look up from their pizza. PJ verbalizes the vibe, "Sorry, man." I shrug.

"How about you, Melissa?" Abby directs the question to her personally to help her find an opening. I know it's purposeful. She's a gracious conversationalist, which is part of what makes her a great Emcee.

Melissa's coloring is back to her normal alabaster. "Things are good. It's wedding season, so business is steady."

"Any fun assignments recently?"

"I had one with a real ice sculpture at the reception, a giant heart with an arrow. That was a first. I tried to get some shots with it in the foreground and dancing behind it. I haven't edited those yet. Hopefully, they turn out."

"How much you reckon they spent on ice?" Mitch asks.

Abby answers, "You don't want to know. The figure would blow your mind."

"How about you, Abs- what's up with you?"

I interrupt her response with a sing-taunt, "She's meeting Wes's family tomorrow." The announcement perks everyone up and earns me a glare from Abby.

"I was going to tell them!"

"Sorry, I'm excited for you. It slipped out."

Abby turns from me to face the group, who stop their celebration to listen. "Ted has a crush on a girl named Bet but won't ask her out because he *thinks* she might have gone on a date with Cooper." I slowly widen my eyes at her in what I hope is a look that asks where she found the audacity. She meets it with a sly smile and says, "It slipped out."

PJ high-fives Abby. "When do we get to meet the lovely Bet?"

I turn my indignant eyes to PJ. "Did you not hear the part about Cooper?"

Mitch leans his elbows on the table. "You aren't seeing this right, man. Their dating is even more reason to ask her out."

Melissa agrees, adding, "It would be so romantic. You rescue her from the frat boy experience and show her how she deserves to be treated. If you're interested, she'd probably like being asked out. It's a nice compliment," her eyes flick to Mitch, "when a man asks out a woman."

The fact Melissa weighs in has me doubting my position. Maybe expressing my interest innocently, in whatever this early stage of their dating is, gives Bet an option? My heart leaps at the thought, but all the complications make the feeling catch and suspend in my chest unnaturally. "I can't. It's too risky. Cooper could even be the person complaining."

Mitch shakes his head. "You're still walking on eggshells about ancient history. Who cares if he is the one complaining? Nothing you can do will change it. You may as well lean in, and if he loses a hottie, then good for you, Ted. You win."

PJ tosses down his napkin. "He's got a point."

Abby gently pushes my shoulder. "I told you… Let's play. Fascinating start to the campaign so far."

PJ snarks, "Yeah, for *you!*"

Everyone laughs, including PJ. My tension eases as I get us back into the story.

9

BET

When Cooper asked if I would request to reschedule our date, I was convinced he was playing some game. If he wanted to reschedule, why hadn't he suggested it when he canceled in the first place? Was he craving attention? Looking for some sort of ego boost?

It didn't make sense, so I asked.

Bet Greene

> I figured if you wanted to reschedule you would have asked to do so. You're the one who canceled. 6:23 PM

Bet Greene

> If you changed your mind about going out with me, that's fine. It doesn't hurt my feelings. People change their minds about things all the time. 6:23 PM

MY VALUE IS NOT dependent upon your wanting me. I thought it but didn't type it. I could tell Cooper was typing and erasing on the other end as the indicator ellipses kept going on and off. He committed after a few minutes.

COOPER Karate

> I'm sorry. I should have asked you for another time, I was in a hurry. Are you free Saturday or Sunday? 6:25 PM

SO HERE I AM, ready for another Sunday date. A knock sounds from my door at precisely 7 o'clock. Nice. Right on time. I open the door to greet Cooper and immediately hope my face doesn't betray that I am positively gawking at him.

Cooper, outside of his Noble uniform, hits differently. Instead of the black one-size-fits-most athletic gear, he's wearing jeans that hug his muscular thighs along with a tank top that fully displays his shapely (and enormous) arms. His body is not my type, but my first thoughts are strictly about what nibbling his traps might be like, and oh my god, I'm objectifying this man. I demand my mouth start making words, and my brain grinds into gear. "Um, hey." It was the best I could do.

He smiles at me with unnaturally white teeth. His face is perfectly smooth, not even a hint of facial hair. "Hey. You ready?"

"Yeah, let me just," I use my thumb to point inside and jog to fetch my purse from the couch, "Okay, ready."

He turns to walk toward his truck, and I internally die as I realize I would pay anything to have jeans that fit my ass as perfectly. Maybe he is my type. Maybe this is what it feels like to be converted.

The ride to Food Worx is filled with polite conversation. Cooper tells me he likes my outfit; he asks about my job and hobbies. I learn he's a certified personal trainer and aspiring fitness influencer. He describes his workout and diet schedule in detail. As Cooper tells me about his protein intake, my confidence starts to flounder. I don't think I'm an obvious fit for his lifestyle or even his style in general. Why did he want to ask me out? Surely, we've outgrown the *She's All That* I-dare-you-to-date-this-person time of our lives.

Cooper finishes up, sharing that Sunday is his rest day as we exit the truck. "It sounds like you won't eat any of my baking."

"Depends on what you bake and if it's a Sunday." He laughs.

"I make some protein-y peanut butter coconut balls sometimes."

Cooper's voice takes on genuine excitement as he suggests I replace the peanut butter with something called PB Fit. "It's so much better than peanut butter! Tastes exactly the same, but it's low fat."

His enthusiasm is contagious. "Sure, I'll try it out! Where can I get it?"

"You will?" He seems surprised.

"Yeah, I love experimenting. Most of my baking is vegan; a lot of experimentation has gone into vegan baking, and it's positively delicious because of it. If this stuff is as good as peanut butter but has other advantages, I'm about it."

Food Worx parking is in a field. A fact I'd forgotten when I strapped on my shortest black stilettos. I try to keep my weight forward, in the balls of my feet, but my sharp heels keep sinking into the soft earth, resulting in many muttered swears. Cooper strolls by my side without complaint until I nearly fall and growl at the ground in frustration. "Want some help? I could…" He mimes a piggyback ride.

"No, no, I'm okay. Should have worn flats. I'll stop snarling, I promise."

He cocks his head to the side. "Snarl all you want if it helps."

When we arrive at the truck area and the promised solid ground, I wonder if his offer will stand on the way back.

The food trucks are arranged in a large circle on one side of an abandoned parking lot. Trucks serving beverages are on the left, while food is on the right. Beyond the circle are picnic tables and a poorly lit stage with a local country band playing. We walk around the trucks investigating our options, stepping around the queues of people waiting for the more popular choices (Korean BBQ and California Taco). After we complete the loop, Cooper says, "California Taco probably has some vegan options. I can grab some beers, so we have them while waiting in line."

"Well," I measure my words carefully, "I'm impressed at your consideration, but I'm not vegan for the record. I just prefer vegan baking. That said, my vote is still California Taco, and a beer sounds great."

Cooper chuckles and mumbles what might have been 'thank God' before we part ways, him heading to the Brewski truck and me in the opposite direction to join the line for tacos. I have not progressed at all when he returns. "I got you an IPA." I accept the golden beverage with thanks before he asks what made me want to learn martial arts.

"Probably Karate Kid." Cooper guffaws but stops when I continue, and he realizes I'm not kidding, "It is a little funny, I guess. I remember watching that movie over and over. I used to try to imitate the moves in my living room."

"Why didn't you take lessons as a kid?"

I sigh. "I did want to. My parents are real traditionally minded. I was only allowed to wear frilly dresses, and they spent a lot of time teaching me proper etiquette. Karate didn't fit their vision of what a lady should do."

He hesitates before replying, "So, you're saying you can teach me what the tiny little fork is for?" One of his brows arches high in question.

I can't help but laugh and give his shoulder a playful nudge. The man is solid muscle beneath the shirt. "It depends on the tinyness of the fork. If it's the smaller of the standard two sizes, it's the salad fork. If it's smaller than that or has less than four tines, it could be a dessert fork or used for oysters."

"Damn. You learn something new every day."

Without me realizing it, we've made it to the front of the line. Cooper asks what I want, and I'm not prepared. "I haven't looked at the menu. Um, whatever, standard chicken taco." He gives me a thumbs up and orders for both of us. The tacos are handed to us nearly as soon as they're ordered, and we balance our plates and beer over to the table area.

The ambiance is nice for a crowded parking lot filled with old tables. We're near the back, far enough away from the stage that the music isn't too loud and it's less crowded. The night air is soft, and the aromas from the truck kitchens are wafting in on it. Strands of lights pulled over the tables emit a glow instead of the harsh spotlights around the trucks.

I bite into my first taco, and it is delectable. "This is an excellent taco. What'd you get?" Glancing over at Cooper's plate gives me the impression...

"Just chicken." Yep. That was the impression.

"You got plain chicken? No cheese or veggies or anything?"

"It's great lean protein."

"Isn't today your rest day?"

Cooper raises his beer. "Yuh! Couldn't have this otherwise." I get caught up looking at Cooper again. He is impeccably put together. Absolutely jacked. But at what cost? "So, what do you think about Noble so far?"

His question breaks me from my thoughts. "I'm enjoying it a lot. I'm sure I'm an embarrassment to the class since you're all much more advanced, but everyone has been supportive and kind, and I feel like I'm learning."

"You're doing great. I don't think anyone would mind you being in class. Out of curiosity, why are you in the advanced class?"

I nod my head as I swallow a bite. "Fair question. I told you I work at Daisy's Daisies. It's a lot of hours in the floristry business. Plus, I bake for Gerard's Cafe, next door to Daisy's. There wasn't another class I could make it to for now. I might be able to change to a more appropriate class in a few months, though. Ted was exceedingly nice to work things out so I can attend."

Cooper huffs and shakes his head at the table. "Ted." He rolls his eyes.

"What?"

"It's nothing. Ted is just... We go way back. It's weird he's teaching when everyone knows he's a coward." My appetite is gone, and I set down the last few bites of taco. "Watch him in class. He won't spar me. Guarantee." I scan my memory and can't recall Ted ever sparring with Cooper. He has sparred other black belts, but not Cooper. Huh.

The conversation isn't sitting well. I'm feeling defensive, and I'm not totally sure why. Time to change the subject. "So. Important question. How long does it take you to get ready for a date?"

Cooper's eyes glint. "What sort of date?"

"We'll start easy and say this one."

"30 minutes."

"30 minutes! You aren't wearing makeup. What takes 30 minutes?"

"I have to shave. And moisturize! And the hair!"

I give him a questioning stare. "What could you possibly do to your hair?! It's a buzz cut!"

We have fun banter. Cooper grabs us another beer. We stay until the lights are turned off, and it's a good time.

On our walk back to his truck, my heels are sinking into the damned quicksand with every step. I'm a cheap date, and the couple of IPAs I downed make the strange ball-of-foot walk required to reach the truck much harder. This time, I'm laughing as I wobble. Cooper gives me a peculiar appraising look, and when I nearly topple over on the next step, he says, "That's it," and scoops me into his arms.

I weigh nothing to him. I'm confident he could toss me into the air if he wanted. Being tall all my life, this is a novel feeling for me, and I don't dislike it. We arrive at the truck too soon, and Cooper gently places me next to the passenger side door.

Back at my place, he walks me to the door. His expression is burning and sultry. "Thanks for tonight. I had a great time."

Cooper leans against the doorframe. "Me too."

"We could go out again. If you want."

He pushes off the frame and comes close to me. "I'd like that." He sweeps further in and kisses me. Too deeply. Too hungrily.

I pull back, away from his eagerness. "Message me, and we'll set up something."

Cooper nods and wishes me a good night. It was a good night.

There is just one problem. I can't stop thinking about Ted.

10

TED

A fucking "Get Well" plan. Are. You. Fucking. Kidding me?! I am fully stewing after the surprise morning phone call with Mark. I know it, but I can't let it go. I don't *want* to let it go. I'm so angry that reveling in it feels good. Taking it out on the bag feels good.

I was at the school early this morning for inventory when he called. Turns out inventory will need to be completed at a later time. Tomorrow. All I can do now is hit the bag. I pound it until it slides to the wall, then push it back onto the floor and do it again. When I'm making contact with it, my brain turns off. Between the kicks and punches, flashes of conversation play and feed my rage.

"I'm emailing you a Get Well plan to turn the school around. You can't ignore the goals I've set." He's never even been inside the studio! I do a switch kick.

"What's the plan for retention when tuition increases?" I've told him we'll lose people. They won't be able to afford it. He hasn't bothered to meet any of our students. He hasn't bothered to meet me in person! I do warrior combinations on the right side, then switch and do the left.

"If we can't reach our goals, things will change." A barely veiled threat, and that word- "Our." I run at the bag and do a number two jumping roundhouse. The bag falls over. When I reach down to turn it upright, I notice my knuckles are bloodied. Tiny Tigers are starting soon. Recognition works itself through me. The kids can't see me like this. I need to disinfect the bag.

When I hear the word "our" in reference to Noble, I think of Phil. Me and Phil. It's our school. Except that's not true. It's the worst part, but now "our" means me and Mark. My heart crumples in on itself at the thought. The squeezing intensifies as I ponder what exactly he plans on changing. Maybe it won't be ours for much longer.

Hands and classroom clean once more; I do breathing exercises before the Tigers come in. I usually enjoy my youngest students, but today I'm worried. I can't match their energy.

However, my doubts don't stop them from coming, and in a few minutes, the first students rush in. "Mr. Ted! Mr. Ted!" Two small collisions meet my legs as Colleen and Rys hug me on either side. "You have a bandaid." Colleen grabs my hand to inspect.

"Hey, you two. Yep, I'm okay. Just a little booboo."

"Hi, Ted." I direct my attention to Anne, their mom. She's batting her eyes at me.

"Hi, Anne," I smile briefly and walk into the studio with the other kids streaming in. The other thing about Tiny Tigers is the Moms. The flirting started a couple of years ago. When I'd boggled about it, my mom advised that I'd reached a certain age, placing me firmly at the intersection of hot and accessible. There are three who flirt with me overtly. At first, it was a challenge to manage. I admit there was initial temptation, though Phil wouldn't condone dating a parent, so it was reasonably easy to look the other way. The challenge remains in managing the relationship. I don't want to lead them on, but I do need to have polite, professional interactions. Hopefully, Anne's batting is the worst of it today.

I must be exuding the edge I feel because the kids are subdued, which makes me feel worse. I'm squashing their joy. They don't deserve to be affected by my foul mood. I don't deserve them right now.

The day drags on and on. I snapped at a boy demanding that I watch him in the white belt class, then later at a young woman in our family class who was distracted and didn't follow directions. Minor things. It's my fault each time, and my disposition sinks lower and lower.

11

BET

I should get a cat. I like cats. They're great partners, independent but cuddly, and so much simpler than figuring out dating. The more I go out with Cooper, the more I think cat-lady might be a calling for me.

It's been a few weeks, three dates, and a fourth this weekend, and it's… I don't want to complain, but as I stir in the PB Fit to the third attempt using it in Coconut Peanut Butter Balls, I have to admit I have formed something of a mental list. Emma was not pleased when I tried to discuss some of my concerns, but maybe over the phone would be better? I scroll back through our message history, not for the first time, to revisit what might be our first-ever argument.

EMMA BEST BEST Bestie

> How was mini golfing? 10:02 PM

Bet Greene

> I don't know Em. I think we're running out of things to talk about. 10:02 PM

EMMA BEST BEST Bestie

> How? You could literally talk about anything. 10:02 PM

Bet Greene

> His interests are limited to working out and dieting. 10:03 PM

EMMA BEST BEST Bestie

> No offense, but your interests are pretty limited to baking and flower peddling. 10:03 PM

Bet Greene

> Ouch! Okay, I'm not sure that's fair. Listen, he got upset when my score was lower than his. Not outright or anything but I could tell. He sulked. 10:05 PM

. . .

Emma Best Best Bestie

> It's not possible you're reading into things is it? 10:05 PM

Bet Greene

> He won't let me call him Coop, even though it's obviously his nickname! Why are you defending him? You've never met him. 10:06 PM

It takes her a long time to reply here. Not normal Emma behavior. However, none of this conversation is normal Emma behavior.

Emma Best Best Bestie

> It might look like I'm defending him, but I'm trying to protect you. I know you, and you do this. Serial-dumper style. You need the experience of pushing through. When you fight for a relationship and overcome little things. That's how love grows. 10:11 PM

> Bet Greene

I don't think love should be hard. Not this early. Not ever, really. I know the whole work to keep your relationship alive, but if it's dying after a month and you aren't in love... And let's pretend we are in love and we've been together for years. The work should be something we want to do, it shouldn't feel like work. 10:13 PM

> Bet Greene

And you're right, you do know me. So can't you believe me over someone you've only seen on Instagram? 10:13 PM

> Bet Greene

I didn't even say I was going to break up with him, I'm rating the golfing as a 'meh' is all. 10:14 PM

Emma Best Best Bestie

I'm sorry. I hope you find the type of relationship you're looking for if it's not Cooper. I have to go for now. 10:20 PM

This interaction was hands down the weirdest I've ever had with Emma. It's haunted me for days. Did I do something wrong? Was she okay? Were we okay? All our messages since then have been normal, and she even admitted that being unable to call him Coop is a non-starter.

These PB Fit balls are not working. All the would-be-balls have tasted great, but the lack of oil makes them fall apart, which is a problem. I'm trying to make these "clean" enough for Cooper to enjoy them, so I'm resisting doing what I know will work and adding oil. So far, everything I've tried ended in a mound of crumbs. I pop the latest iteration in the oven, wish them luck, and decide to FaceTime Emma. I'm itching to share my list, and the conversation will be better this way.

Except when Emma answers, she's been crying. The skin under her eyes is pink and splotchy, and her mascara (she's wearing mascara!) has smeared. I'm used to seeing her makeup-free with her hair up in a messy bun, but today, it looks like she's ready to go out on a date. Or *was* ready. "Emma, what's wrong?"

She sniffles into the mic. "Nothing."

"Are you kidding me right now? You've been crying." Chad walks across the house in the background. I lower my voice, "Did he do something to upset you?"

Her eyes are pleading. "I can talk in a few. How. How are you?"

Before I answer, Chad booms from another room. "I thought you put him to sleep?!"

Emma turns away, sniffling. "I did. He must have gotten up. I've got him." She exits the room, and it occurs to me that I'm the asshole. Our argument wasn't entirely about me. Hot shame prickles my chest. Why haven't I asked her how things have been since he came home?

Chad's voice sounds again, "I'll be back later." A door closes.

I hear Charlie's small sounds and movement, and then Emma returns. "I had to put Charlie back down."

"Tell me what's going on."

Her tears renew. I wish I were there to wipe them. "Chad is home, but," she gasps between sobs, "but things aren't better. He. He doesn't help, and he doesn't…" Emma's voice is so puny at the end I can't make out what she says.

I'm unsure if I should ask, but I gently probe, "He doesn't what?"

"He doesn't appreciate… anything." Emma shakes her head, but her words are more assertive when she continues, "It's like, I do all the cleaning and cooking and everything with Charlie, but it's never good enough. He asked me to put makeup on in the morning. I thought maybe he would take me out, but he's going out with the boys. He doesn't think I'm pretty anymore. Maybe he doesn't love me anymore either."

The discussion is similar to ones we've had before. When Emma and Chad were dating, I pointed out his habits. How if she didn't have dinner ready by 6, he'd make a comment but never offer to help. How he seemed to want to parade her around like a trophy. It's worsened over the years, but I stopped bringing it up when they got engaged. She chose him. I had to respect her decision. Now, hearing it from her. This was new territory.

"Have you talked to him about how you're feeling?"

Emma shakes her head again. "No. I've tried other things. I put little love notes for him to find around in the morning and make his favorite dishes. I started a diet. I even bought some things for the bedroom. Chad doesn't seem to care."

Fucking Chad. "Okay. That's a lot of kind things to try to

reach him, I hear you. Do you know what it is exactly you want him to do?"

She bites her lip. I'm relieved to see her eyes are dry now. "I want to feel like I used to. Like he sees me."

"Great. You deserve to feel seen. It might be a good start if you tell him what he might do to give you that feeling."

Emma purses her lips to the left side. "Didn't know you became a marriage counselor."

"There's my Emma with the snark!" I shoot finger guns at her.

"I thought you'd tell me to divorce him." She laughs, but my heart drops.

"I try to consider what you want. You know? Thanks for sharing with me. I should have asked how things were when he came home."

She smiles weakly. "I shouldn't have sat on it for so long. I can't imagine how, but I'll try to talk to him. You're right. I'm sorry about getting onto you about Cooper the other day. I think… I think I was a little jealous. That you have the freedom to leave, and I have to believe things won't be this way forever. If we put in the work, things will get better."

"I believe that, and please," I pause dramatically, "call him Coop."

Emma throws her head back, laughing. "Wait, why did you call?"

I grimace before quietly admitting, "I… developed a list of problems with Coupé de Ville, but we don't have to talk about them."

"Oh my God, yes, we do. Please, enlighten me!"

I share how restrictive his diet is, "It's like restricting joy as much as it is food," he can't go to the store without spending half an hour on getting ready, how he's started to make comments about my fitness routines, and he's been progressively more possessive and pressuring me for more physically.

"Wait, you haven't slept with him, why not?"

"You'd know if I had." My shoulders slump. "I don't know, I *am* intrigued by all those muscles," Emma closes her eyes and nods in agreement, "but it doesn't feel right when I keep wondering about Ted."

Her mouth falls into a perfect O. "Man of the Year, Ted?!"

"I'm afraid so. It's almost like they have some history. It's Coop's fault! He brought Ted up, and what he said doesn't make sense!"

"No, no. It's not Coop's fault. You're crushing on Ted. What a creative excuse to carry around with you, though. Congrats on your artistic interpretation. Sooooo… What are you going to do?"

"Go on a date with Coop tomorrow. Stop thinking about how patient Ted is with the kids in his classes and how his hair is always a little bit messy. I bet he doesn't take half an hour to get ready to go to Walmart."

"Oh, girl. You have got it bad for Ted. Why didn't you tell me?! This is juicy! You know I need juice."

"I… I honestly didn't realize until talking with you. It's just been bouncing around my head. Saying it is different. When he's instructing, he asks if he can touch me before doing it. I have never had a yoga instructor ask permission. He's so considerate."

"Didn't you say he was cute, too, or am I making that up?"

"He is. He's adorable."

Emma aims a glare at me. "You aren't exclusive. You could date them both."

"Oof, I don't think so. Sounds exhausting. Not to mention that Coop, on our first date, said Ted was weak and that he shouldn't be teaching. I have to be fair and say I don't know Ted well, but I'm pretty sure they grew up together."

Emma spends the rest of the conversation devoted to finding out everything she can about Ted. Unfortunately, all his social media profiles are set to private. The only thing she turns up is an obituary, which she reads aloud, "'Ted Dawson Sr. leaves behind his loving wife Sadie, and his son Ted.' It's dated 21 years ago. How old is Ted?"

"Geez. I don't know, I think our age. Around 30ish?"

"He was so young."

"Yeah," I let out a whoosh of air, "it's so sad. I can't imagine."

12

TED

"You printed it out? You could have emailed me. Kinda old school, don't you think?" My mom gives me a hard time while flagging down our waitress for a coffee refill. A true marvel at multitasking. She catches the waitress's eyes and lifts her empty mug. The woman hastens over to our table, swiveling her hips around other patrons, chairs, and tables with a carafe. A renewed smell of fresh coffee wafts around as she pours, and Mom smiles, closing her eyes to savor the scent. She thanks the waitress and turns her attention back to me. "So things are not improving at all?"

"No! They're worse than ever. Just look at this!" I smack the sheets of paper on the table and push them toward her. She picks them up and reads, forehead furrowing as she reaches the end.

"I see why you're upset. Reading this," her eyes flick back to the heading, "Get Well Plan is like reading a list of the concerns you've shared with me." She pauses to sip from her topped-off mug. I'm unsure how she drinks it so hot; I swear she could drink it straight from the percolator. "I have some advice, but you might not like it."

Here it is. Mom knows I love her advice, even if it can be something I don't want to hear and occasionally delivered bluntly. The thing about Mom is she's taken the same tactics with me my whole life. When I have a problem, she listens first and gives empathy. She's excellent at it, and I know because she's told me she hopes I can resolve the issue myself and purposely holds out on advice unless necessary. She adjusts in her chair, face furtive. "Hit me with it."

Mom clinks down her cup onto the tiny plate it came with. "I know you think these demands Mark is making are impossible. You might be right, but you haven't tried to think of ways to achieve them outside what you're already used to, which are the most obvious."

I let her words settle before laughing at my own lack of originality. "I hear you're saying I need to think outside the box, invent some new way of doing things. Recruiting people or making money to reach these new goals. I have no idea how to even start."

"You need to *crowdsource* the *community at large*," She emphasizes the words.

"We're already out in the community, though. We've even done additional demos to attract people. I can't force people to join." Mom sighs heavily. "You have an idea already, don't you?"

She grins wickedly. "Matter of fact, I do. Remember the Fall Festival? We used to have so much fun."

"Yeah, vaguely. We haven't had one since I was in high school."

"Bring it back. Noble can host it."

"What?" I'm laughing again. "How would that even help?"

Mom picks at the remnants of her cinnamon roll. "Take it or leave it, but I think it could help quite a lot." She starts ticking off points on her fingers, "If Noble sponsors it, that's your name on all the advertisements around town, social media, and the news. You'd build connections with other local businesses, which you may be able to leverage. Of course, you'd charge an entry fee, too. It'll take a lot of planning and coordination, but you could bring everyone out, give our town a fun outlet, and help other businesses, including making some money for Noble."

"I didn't realize there was a cost to enter."

"Because you were a kid! But yes, there was a small cost of entry."

My brain somersaults at the thought. "Geez, this is brilliant! Except I don't know how to put together something this big, I…"

Mom is exasperated. "Your best friend does it for a living. *Crowdsource.* You know it's problematic how you try to do everything independently. You should work on that next." She makes a satisfied smile before it disappears behind her cup.

"Thanks, Mom. I guess I have a lot of work to do." I plant a kiss on the side of her head and offer her some cash for my part of brunch. "I'm going to call Abby."

"Good luck. Same time next week?" Mom and I have been brunching on Tuesdays for years now. We have our rotation of favorite places down to a science.

"Of course. Can't miss Gerard's!"

13

BET

*D*on't cancel. You can do it. There's no reason to cancel; you *do* like him. The mantra repeats in my head as it has all day long. Cooper and I are slated to go out after class tonight. I'm meeting his friends for the first time. Hooray. Right?

Except for some reason, I'm dreading it and apparently broadcasting the feeling despite myself. Lily asked if I was okay three times at the shop. When I'd admitted feeling apprehensive about meeting Cooper's friends, she'd been full of platitudes only a spicy woman of a certain age could give.

"If you have to ask 'should I' about anything, staying, going, you already know the answer."

"When a guy likes you, you know it; when they don't, you feel confused."

"Never date a show off unless you're ready to hear about how great they are all the time." Lily knows a lot about my dating life, but I didn't expect her to root for me to dump Coop. I asked her where all this was coming from, and she replied flatly, "He doesn't make you happy." A punch to the gut prior to Advanced Class.

As class begins, Cooper plops beside me on the ground to get our gear on. "Hey."

"Hey… You all right?"

Awesome. "Yeah, I'm good. Just tired."

"Maybe class will help wake you up. You're gonna love the boys tonight, plus here's a little surprise. You kinda know some of 'em already." Cooper looks highly pleased with his announcement, and his eyes pulse toward some of the other black belts. I think their names are Brian and Ron.

"Oh. Um. Wow, okay."

"Right? We're like a whole Noble crew!" He winks at me and jogs out to the line. "See you in a few."

Maybe I could fake being sick. I already told him I was tired and class would totally make that worse. All gear affixed to my body, I run to join the line, begging my brain to think positively. Tonight would be fine. Fine. Fine.

The clock is savage. Class flies by except for one shining moment when Ted witnesses me execute the best side kick of my life, and I can tell he's impressed. The perplexing gloom I've noticed hanging around him the past week lifts, and we hold each other's gaze. It feels like a spotlight illuminates us, and the rest of the class fades to black. Then it's over. Ted turns away. Color and sound return to normal. An absurd fear wriggles under my skin that Coop noticed whatever had transpired. Time picks up the pace again, and before I know it, we're dismissed.

We take off our gear and stuff it into our bags. Cooper squeezes my shoulder; it's intended to be friendly, but he rubs over my clavicle the wrong way, and I wince. "See you in 30?"

"Yeah, I'm just going to wash up and get changed. I'll head right over." We're driving separately tonight. Since his friends will be there, I advised him we should. I'll have to exit earlier than he wants to for some midnight baking. It's

Chocolate Chip Zucchini Bread tonight. It's easy to make in large batches. In the past month, I've improved at selecting easy and scalable recipes for date nights.

IN THE YEARS I've worked with Lily, she has never texted me, nor have I seen her text anyone. Yet here I am, sitting on the toilet seat in the tiny Noble bathroom, dressed and makeup applied, hyping myself up to go when I notice I have a message from her.

LILY LYONS

> Youve got a good gut Trust it 7:06 PM

I WONDER if it's the first text she's ever sent. I make a note to ask and maybe point out how to use punctuation on her phone.

 The feeling of being trapped is building, and I want to be out of this stall. It's hard to admit to myself, but Emma isn't wrong about my proclivity to break things off early with people. This time, I'm committed to giving Cooper a real chance. I should meet his friends. The orange flags on my radar need to be set aside because the problem is my radar gives false positives. If I trust my gut, I'll be alone forever. Alone is nice. I haven't minded. Except recently... Well, forever is a long time.

 Getting lost in my thoughts has led to more progression of the dastardly clock, and if I'm going, which I am, I need to do it. With one last glance in the mirror, I quietly close the door and walk into the studio.

One person is left, and he's wailing on a bag. It's Ted, although it doesn't look like him. Sweat is flying from his body with every move, and it feels like I shouldn't be here. I've never seen anyone hit anything with such abandon. This is private. A little scary. Impressive. Ted isn't shouting, and I kind of wish he was because the grunts and huffs of exertion may not cover up my steps and the close of the door, and I do not want him to know I'm here, that I saw.

Three easy steps from the lobby, and I'm convinced I'll make it unnoticed. I peek back at Ted one final time as I step through the doorway, but my gear bag collides with the side of the door frame, making a loud thwack. Ted yells in surprise. We lock eyes again. The spotlight returns, but this is a spotlight of heat and embarrassment. I'm mortified. "I, I'm sorry." I back out of the room, longing for the exit.

Ted's voice sounds from the studio door, "Wait. Please?"

He's out of breath, and the words are raspy, but the need in his question weighs heavy, and my feet stop moving. I repeat my apology, "I'm so sorry. I went to the bathroom to change. I didn't mean to intrude. I'll go."

Ted reaches a hand out to me from across the room and steps forward. "Don't. I mean." His chest heaves from the effort. "I mean, if you need to go, then of course, but I should apologize. I didn't know anyone was still here." I can tell he wants to say more; my brain snags on his reply- 'Don't.' He wipes at the sheen of perspiration on his forehead.

"Your hand!" I drop my bag and step toward him. "You're bleeding. Are you okay?" He laughs, and the sound matches his hair and reminds me of dark walnut wood. This may be an awkward situation, but my chest is instantly lighter. "Laughing at an injury is a strange response?"

"Oh, this is only a knuckle scrape. I'm laughing because, well, obviously, I'm not fine, and it's all catching up with me." He shakes his head as if in disbelief.

"We should wash this up. Give me one second." Ted watches me fish my phone out of my purse. I quickly text Cooper that I'm not going to make it. The lie comes too easily. Too guiltlessly. I'm too relieved. Before he can reply, I stuff the phone away and take Ted's hand in mine to see it closer. His knuckles are rough with callouses, and the first two slowly ooze blood. "You were really pounding that bag. Why don't you wear the gloves?" We start the trek back to the bathroom. "I assume you have a first aid kit."

Ted shrugs. "When you've been doing this as long as I have the gloves feel like they're in the way. My hands are used to the abuse, I guess. I don't usually get bloody knuckles."

"I get weird redness even with the gloves. My hands must be babies. Look!" I turn my hands over so Ted can see as he rinses off in the sink.

"Petechia! Good for you. It means you're a beginner who's hitting hard enough. You'll stop getting it after a while." He turns the faucet off and dries his hands with paper towels.

I'm suddenly aware we're standing inches apart in the small space. It should be uncomfortable, but it isn't. I back out the door quickly to give him more room. "That's what it's called. Alright then." We're both silent for what feels like a long time, and for some reason, I can't look at him, though I'd swear he's looking at me. "So, and you don't have to answer, but you said you weren't okay. What's up?"

Ted sighs, and I note that I was right. He is looking at me. His eyes shift from softness to pointedness as he answers, "The short story is I'm afraid I'm going to lose the school. Or else it will shut down."

I nod. "You've been here forever. I imagine that would be extremely stressful and scary." I want to know everything but resist prying. Ted and I aren't close. Feeling like I've known him forever is yet another part of the faulty radar. What is wrong with me?

He grabs an extra chair for me, and I listen to whatever he is willing to tell. Ted talks about the tuition increases, which seem to be the root of his fears. He speaks to the accounting implications as an expert, which confuses me. Why are they increasing? It's probably some corporate strategy, then. What touches me is when he speaks of his love for teaching. His sincerity breaks open something in my chest, and the memory of him spinning on the ground in the children's class plays in my head.

"Now I understand why you've seemed so down lately. This is a lot to be going through. You are," I check myself before continuing but decide it's safe to say, "a great teacher."

His throat bobs before he thanks me, and I excuse myself lamely. I *do* need to get to the zucchini bread.

14

TED

*O*rganizing... Scratch that... *Attempting* to organize a huge event is hell. Even with Abby's guidance, my early mornings are like being in a bubbling vat of information and barely keeping my nose above water. So many things need doing.

We immediately decided to hold the Fall Festival in the strip mall parking lot right in front of Noble. It's convenient, sure, but it's also where the festival was held previously, and Abby was excited about the consistency. "It'll be that much easier to attend for people familiar with the event, and we have an angle with nostalgia!" I need to get a permit from the city to hold it, but they won't grant it until all the other businesses in the strip mall agree to endorse the event. To entice my neighboring shops, I need to show them how it will benefit them. That leaves me in a situation where I need to recruit other businesses from around town to participate in what is a hypothetical festival. My mornings are filled with calls to confused business owners who don't know who I am. I'm exhausted from trying to gain purchase and being left to flail.

Not helping is my preoccupation with Bet. Since the night we talked, the thought of her could be my shadow for as much I can shake it. Classes since then have caused me to amass questions for her. Where'd she go to school? Not around here, or I'd know her. What is her ankle tattoo? I can't catch a full glimpse of it in her uniform. She's obviously busy, but what does she do for fun? What music does she like? How does she take her coffee? Or does she drink coffee at all? How are she and Cooper doing?

I squeeze my eyes shut. When I arrive at that inevitable question, I push down the tiny kernel of hope that maybe things aren't perfect. She had canceled on him the other night. I know it. She'd gone to the bathroom and came out in a black skirt and white crop top. Breathtaking. Then she'd texted someone and stowed her phone away and stayed. With me. I hadn't told her the whole story… but how she'd listened. She said I was a good teacher.

It's been a couple of classes since then, and I can tell they're still together, yet there are also moments of tension between us. Bet must feel them, too. Or I could be crazy. Maybe I am! The Fall Festival would get me there if nothing else has already. There are some facts, however, and I'm finding they're impossible not to dwell on.

Fact. In the last two classes, Bet has said hello and goodbye to me. Purposefully seeking me out.

Fact. Yesterday, she'd walked straight past Cooper without so much as a nod in his direction to greet me. A fact she doesn't know but which I caught was his stern frown.

Fact. I am in *so much trouble*. Bet couldn't be dating a worse person for me to be hung up on.

Fact. I've never felt like this about anyone before, even Abby, when we first started dating. The magnetism between Bet and I is sizzling, irresistible, and comfortable—everything all at once. I think this is why I ache to ask her so many questions. It feels like I know her already; it's unnatural not to, and I need those knowledge gaps filled.

But maybe it is only me. Any of these could be coincidence, simple friendliness, or pity. The idea knots my throat. Worse still, there's nothing I can do about these feelings.

My phone buzzes. The distraction is welcome. I have to stop this line of thought.

ABBY Taylor

> Have you called the list I gave you from the Pecan Street area? 8:02 AM

Ted Dawson

> I started on it. I'm not explaining it well. They don't want to commit unless it's a sure thing. 8:02 AM

ABBY Taylor

> Wait. What are you telling them? 8:03 AM

> I'm saying we're trying to bring back the Fall Festival, and we'd love for them to come and participate. Then they ask when and I explain we aren't sure but are aiming for October 15th. Then they ask when we'll know for sure and I tell them I wish I knew but would let them know right away when it's locked in. 8:04 AM

ABBY Taylor

> No! Oh, bud. 8:04 AM

ABBY Taylor

> I'm swinging by. Don't call anyone else. 8:05 AM

ABBY Taylor

> Would it help if I gave you a script? 8:05 AM

SHIT. I knew I was doing it wrong. Maybe not in-need-of-a-script wrong, but I'll take whatever help I can get.

15

BET

For the most part, Cooper had taken my cancelation last week in stride. He was less upset about my absence than he was about my not replying to his texts promptly. I told him I fell asleep right away—another lie.

I still feel guilty for lying. It's not a habit I've been in, and after some inner turmoil, I think I understand they came from trying to protect his feelings. I sense it would be particularly hurtful if he knew I stayed to talk to Ted. However, I still have to maintain my integrity in my mission not to be a serial-dumper. Going forward, the lying is over, no matter where it leads. Ted is another issue. Since seeing him and having an actual conversation with him (although short), he's even harder to keep out of my thoughts. There will be no room for lies or Ted tonight because I am finally meeting Cooper's friends.

Am I excited about the prospect? I'm trying to be. Maybe seeing Cooper amongst his long-time friends will show me another dimension of his person. That would be refreshing.

An accident on the highway delays me, and I arrive at the

bowling alley ten minutes late. The volume level moving from outside the building to inside is a zero to one hundred experience. The sound of balls striking pins is muted against blaring music and the crowd. Cooper is standing over the kiosk at Lane 15. Other men around him peer over his shoulder at the screen and up to the connected scoreboard above.

I score some vaguely patriotic red, white, and blue bowling shoes at the counter, then head to the lane. "Hey, Cooper, everyone!" Nobody hears me. It'll be a bar-style shouting conversation tonight. I clear my throat and try again, this time earning head turns and greetings.

Cooper abandons the kiosk and surprises me with an uncomfortably deep kiss before making introductions. "Guys, this is Bet. Bet, you know Roy and Brian," He indicates the two black belts from Noble. I guess I was wrong about Roy's name. "And this is Chuck."

I shake each of their hands and try to set their names to memory. "Nice to meet you, ah, or at least be formally introduced."

Chuck leans into the circle to talk and asks, "You drink beer, Bet? I'm getting a pitcher."

"I do, thanks!"

"Great. Be right back." He shuffles around groups of people and joins a queue in front of a dark window, which I'm assuming is the bar. I immediately like Chuck. I never discovered why Cooper wanted to ask me out, but the unbelievability of it has lessened with time. Meeting Chuck reminds me of the question and the feeling of not fitting in. Cooper, Brian, and Roy are an obvious match. They're all sleek, put together, and wearing clothes to showcase their- *ahem*- assets. Chuck is wearing a graphic t-shirt and jeans that could be from anywhere. He's a little chubby, and a wedding ring is on his finger. He looks fine. Cute even, but like me, he is an odd member of this crew.

"So, how do you all know each other?" I start the conversation while changing shoes.

Cooper thumps Brian and Roy on the back. "These guys? Known them since 1st grade. We all had Mrs. Daniel's class."

Brian corrects him, "It was 2nd grade, but yeah, we've been friends forever. Started at Noble that year, too."

"That's a long time to do the same sort of extracurricular. I've never done anything for so long."

Roy moves his hand in a dismissive wave and says, "It's different when you're young, more casual, and it hasn't been the entire time since then. For example, we'd pause karate whenever baseball season started."

"Still, you always came back to it. It's rare to have such dedication and lifelong friendships."

Chuck returns to the lane and sets down an icy pitcher of beer and five mugs. "Help yourself, everyone." We all grab a glass except Cooper, who hangs back. Chuck rolls his eyes and exhales dramatically. "Come on, Cooper, I know it's not Sunday, but surely you can have a beer with us."

Cooper's mouth is a flat line, and he shakes his head. "Discipline. You could use a little."

Chuck laughs. "No thanks. I'll have a brew and a dad bod and be happy instead." I pour myself a beer, and Chuck adds, "See, your girlfriend gets it."

Cooper scowls, but for a mere flash as I change the subject. Maybe I imagined it. "What about you, Chuck? How did you meet everyone?"

"I'm a few years wiser than this lot."

"You mean older." Brian pushes Chuck's shoulder.

"Is that what I mean? Hmm… My family moved here when I was a senior in high school. They were sophomores, but we all played soccer together. I know you got sucked into the web through Noble, but tell us about you. Why do you put up with this lug?" Chuck nods his head toward Cooper and winks at me. Yeah. Chuck is cool.

"In my defense, I didn't know any better at the time." I tease.

"Let's get the game started." Cooper's tone is serious. He's first to bowl, so he picks up the heaviest ball on the rack and positions himself before the lane.

I'm not feeling his attitude, but I am enjoying his friends, so I continue chatting, "You all seem really into sports. Karate has been my first foray into a sport. I've done yoga for a couple of years now, but it was more about art when I was in school. I took a watercolor class, clay sculpting, and photography. My parents wanted me to do ballet, but I hated it and begged them to stop." Cooper returns from the lane, and Roy takes his place. "What do you all do for work?"

Brian tips his beer to me and replies, "Produce Manager at Freshies."

"Oh, I love Freshies! It always has the hard-to-find ingredients."

Chuck asks, "You like to cook?"

"I do, but I do a lot of baking, mostly."

"She does *vegan* baking." Cooper clarifies.

"Fascinating," Chuck is rapt, "I'm the Head Baker at Casa de Pan. We should talk shop."

"Seriously? The expensive bread place?" Chuck erupts in laughter as my face heats. "I mean, not like an insult. Casa de Pan is amazing. I just can't afford it."

Recovering, Chuck tells me not to worry. "I take it as a compliment. We are priced at a gourmet end, we'll say. So, what sort of vegan baking do you do?"

What I do is barely worth mentioning compared to being a Head Baker. "It's nothing. I work at the flower shop next to

Gerard's Cafe, and he stocks whatever I bring him each morning for some extra income."

"Gerard's, huh? I'm going to check that out. What sort of things do you make for him?"

"It's your turn." Cooper looks at me with an intensity I can't place. He's acting touchy; I'm not imagining it.

"Ah, well, I'll go roll some balls, then tell you all about my cheesecake." I walk to the ball return, but not before hearing Chuck say I'm a keeper.

Halfway through the game, attention has turned to the scoreboard. We're all still talking, but it turns out everyone is an evenly matched bowler. Which is to say, we're all decidedly mediocre, but the closeness of our scores makes the game competitive and fun. On the 6th frame, I bowl a 5-7 split. I pout, but when I turn around, everyone has their hands in the air, cheering things like, "Easy spare!" It's ridiculous.

"Next pitchers on me if you can pick it up!" Roy shouts. I point at my eyes and back at him to make sure he knows I hear him and turn toward the lane with renewed determination. The ball leaves my hand, and it feels right. It looks right. I can't stop watching as it careens toward the right side of the 5-pin. The 5 spins and takes out the 7. I leap into the air, tucking my knees like a cheerleader. The men behind me yell like I've won the Super Bowl. Even the lanes around us look over, perplexed by the celebration.

Cooper swings his heavy arm over my shoulder and says into my ear, "You aren't having another beer, are you?"

He's probably worried because I drove here, but I'm okay. The game is progressing slowly, and these aren't full pours. "Yeah, I was going to. Don't worry though, I won't drink too much to drive safely."

His brow furrows as if my response doesn't make sense,

but then something clicks into place. "Oh no, not that. It's just, you know, don't drink your calories."

I twist out from under his arm, at a loss for words. I'm sure my expression is doing some talking. Before I can form words, Roy has returned. "Here we go!" He starts pouring into each of our mugs on the table.

Without discussing it, we have paused bowling in lieu of renewed conversation, but I barely hear it. This is the second time Cooper has tried to put his lifestyle choices on me, and suddenly, all his strange behavior from tonight makes sense. He's possessive. The too-aggressive greeting kiss, the public displays of affection that don't fit the atmosphere, interrupting me when I'm getting on with other people... He's trying to mark me as his territory or demand my attention remain on him. Other instances where his behavior rubbed me the wrong way begin floating up in my memory.

Then, like a pendulum, I start doubting myself. This may be how Cooper shows affection. Could I be misreading his intentions? If he believes in operating at a calorie deficit in the evenings, perhaps he's legitimately concerned for my health and good habits. Still, if that's the case, he needs to learn how to present his concerns better.

I'm jolted back to reality at the mention of Ted's name.

Brian tenses his shoulders. "You think he won't be around much longer, like he'll be fired?"

Cooper shrugs, and the muscles in his neck flex. "I don't know. I'm not in charge, but it didn't sound promising." I'm trying to understand what they're discussing. Cooper looks pleased. Brian and Roy are uneasy. Chuck is idly looking around the alley, clearly disinterested. "Anyway, it might do us some good. Ol' Three Points has had his turn."

Roy starts to say something and stops. I get the feeling he's choosing what he says carefully. He swigs from his mug and says, "We do need another teacher. An additional one, I mean, but who would do it?"

"I don't think Mark is looking to add headcount. I don't know. A black belt. Could be any of us if we're interested, I'd wager." Cooper is interested. I know it. He knows it. The people two lanes over know it.

"Did you call Ted 'Three Points?'" I pick the most innocuous-sounding part of the discussion to get more context.

Roy quickly answers, "Let's leave it to an event occurring long, long ago."

Cooper shakes his head. "Remember, I told you he won't spar me? You've seen it yourself by now, I'm sure." This is true. There have even been times when Ted has seemed to avoid the pairing purposefully. "Because he did fight me once. Not in class."

"Wait, he fought you?"

"Oh yeah. Like a little bitch, too. Snuck up on me from behind when we were in 5th grade."

I internally bristle but carefully control my expression. "And he, he hasn't sparred you since then?"

Cooper laughs. It is not kind. "He has, plenty of times. We call him Three Points because I've scored so many on him it's an embarrassment. I guess at some point, he decided it was best not to even try. I told you! Weak!"

I glance at Brian and Roy for any clues that Cooper may be exaggerating, but they give me nothing. They're both stiff and quiet. The story doesn't make sense with the Ted I know. 5th grade was so long ago, too; maybe it doesn't even matter... Except he still won't spar. I've seen it. Does that mean there's truth to the rest of the story?

Chuck pipes up with a completely different topic. Fair, he likely doesn't even know Ted, not having any involvement with the school. "Bet, I'm sure you get asked this all the time, so I apologize in advance, but how tall are you?"

The question wakes up the rest of the group. Smirks and exchanged glances take the place of the preternatural still. "5'10"," I try to complete the sentence with a dig on insecure men, but the rest of my words are drowned out by the 'Oohs' and chuckles.

Chuck, Roy, and Brian give wide-eyed attention to Cooper, who crosses his arms. "What's your point?"

Chuck explains as if he's talking to a 5-year-old. "See, Cooper, if Bet is 5'10", there's simply no way you're 6'2"." He looks at me and explains, "We've been having this debate for a while now amongst ourselves. We all know our heights, naturally, but Cooper insists he's 6'2"."

"Because I am! Come on." His friends smirk and shake their heads, but I'm annoyed. It could be good-natured, but in the context of everything else… I leave the alley, having enjoyed Cooper's friends more than his own company. I'm torn about how I feel about him and what to do, and I'm worried about Ted.

16

TED

For the first time in my life, I wake up dreading work. I feel as dispirited as when I came home and crashed into my comforter. Physically gross, too. By the time I got back from class, I was so depleted I didn't eat, shower, or read. The only thing I took time for was scooping some kibble into Hitch's bowl and giving him a short skritch between the ears.

It happened after the beginner class. Two parents hailed me once I dismissed the group. Parents and students alike come to chat after classes, usually about life in general. These two looked uncomfortable, though, and I had an ominous feeling. They told me they'd been talking and wanted to know if the tuition costs were really going up in January or if Noble would reconsider. They said it wouldn't be something they could afford at the new rate and didn't see any reason to continue now if they could get a pro-rated refund.

As much as I've anticipated losing people in January, I never thought they would leave now. I wasn't ready for it. Of course, I've had these conversations before. A family pays for several months in advance and then decides martial arts isn't a good fit, or they don't have enough time, or a young child loses interest. The policies for refunds are easy to explain. This wasn't the same. These families wanted to continue. Saw the value in class. Gabby and Thomas were great students who gave their all.

I asked what I could do to retain them, and they explained how they loved the school and wanted to stay but knew they wouldn't be able to. "We may as well get our refunds now and put the money toward another program. No offense to you." I could taste the bile in my mouth and worried I would vomit right there at the front desk. I'd told them how I love having them as part of the Noble Family, inquired again if I could do anything to make them stay, and explained that they would qualify for a refund for the remaining months paid if they decided that was best. Neither had initiated the refunds, but they could. If they do, the chances are high that other families will follow suit.

I strip my bed to wash it, brush my teeth, and shower. Feeling clean gives me the tiniest bit of relief. Hitch weaves through my legs, demanding attention. "Hey, bud. I think I'm going to go visit Phil." He makes a trilling meow and rubs his head into my hand. It's early, and I should be spending what energy I have whittling down the long list of to-do's for the Fall Festival, but instead, I grab a protein bar and head to Phil. I'd give anything to talk to him. His headstone is the best I can do.

This isn't my first time visiting Phil's grave, but I'm still unsure what to do here. I've tried talking, sitting in silence, even having a picnic. Keeping the site clean is the one thing that's felt natural to me. It's strange. I'm drawn here when I need Phil the most, even though I can't figure out how to make these visits anything more than depressing. I miss him more after. Yet here I am again. This time, I don't bring anything for the site in my rush out the door.

No matter the time of year, the grass is a lush carpet of green. I dust off Phil's headstone and lower myself onto the ground before it. The dew soaks my jeans, but I don't care. It feels unnatural to speak aloud to nobody, so instead, I imagine the conversation with Phil in my head.

Phil and I always greet each other with a hug. I remember the day I realized I was as tall as him. "Hey, Phil."

"Hey, Ted." He mirrors back at me, even imitating my voice. He'd wobble his head a little as he did it. "What's up, son?"

"I'm stressing."

Phil would cackle, definitely. But whatever I said would be met with a kind smile. "You're always stressing. What is it this time?"

"Noble. We're losing our families because the classes cost too much. I'm trying to enroll more people and retain the ones we have, but nobody will listen to me. It honestly seems like I'll be fired, or the school will close. This would have never happened if you were still here."

I try to imagine how Phil would react, what he would say. He was known to give the most sensical advice in life but now remains unmoving with his reassuring smile. I plead, "Tell me what to do. Please!"

Silence from the Phil in my mind. A loneliness so intense takes hold of me that I feel separated from the very air. Some people find peace in visiting the cemetery. Am I doing it wrong? I lay back on the ground, my shirt now soaking up dewdrops, too. The sun is creeping up slowly. If I go back home now, I could make some headway on the festival. It's all I know to do, but I can barely bring myself to sit up. I breathe in the earthy smells for a few deep breaths instead. Just as unmoving as the imaginary Phil.

I put a hand on my chest to feel the up-down of my lungs and turn my head to the right. I may be the only person here so early, but a bird hops around in the distance. Another deep inhale, and I turn my head to the left. I sit up so fast I'm lightheaded.

There is someone else here.

Across the lawn, a long, thin form is stretched into an elegant arch. Bet's short dark hair and body shape are instantly recognizable even from a distance. She's moving from one yoga position to another, and her body is like a song. Slow and smooth. Strong and deliberate. Pushing, then pulling. Why is she practicing yoga at the cemetery?

For one second, I debate leaving. It could be rude to interrupt; perhaps she's even visiting some loved one. The thought is gone as fast as it comes, and I'm already walking toward her. She's doing a complicated something when I reach her. Her knees balance on her elbows, her hands the only part of her on the ground. Blades of grass stand upright between her fingers. She hasn't noticed me, so I clear my throat.

Bet exclaims, loses balance, and tips forward.

"Oh no, I'm so sorry! Are you okay?" She rolls on her side, and I extend my hand to help her up.

Several things happen at once. Her face sparks with recognition; she grabs my hand, and our connection fires through my whole body. She exclaims, "Ted! You wear glasses?"

I subconsciously reach up to adjust them. "Yes, usually. I take them off for class, or they go flying across the room. You've got some grass…" I pick a blade from her forehead. "What were you doing just now? The pose, I mean."

"The one you scared me out of? Crow pose."

"I've never seen anyone do yoga in a graveyard before."

"Ah, yes. I haven't either, besides me. Though I do recommend it, look at all this shade! It's quiet. Peaceful. The grass is springy." She cuts her eyes at me, "Thank goodness."

The side of my mouth quirks up to match her teasing grin. "Do you, umm, are you here to visit anyone?"

"Oh. No. I usually find older portions of the grounds and visit there. Are you here for someone?"

"Yeah. Phil. My... He was Noble's proprietor and my mentor. Kind of like a father to me, actually. He died a few months ago."

Bet lowered her head. "I'm sorry for your loss." A beat of silence passes before she raises her eyes back to mine. "I have flowers. If you want to take them to him, I mean."

I agree. Bet gathers her things into a small canvas bag, and I lead her to Phil's resting place. It's hard not to hold her hand on the way. She's walking close to me, and my hand yearns to renew mingling with hers. When we arrive, Bet kneels before the headstone and places a small bouquet in front. "Hi, Phil. I'm sorry I never met you while you were here."

"He would have enjoyed you." A thrill courses through me as she offers me her hand. I think she wants help standing up, but she tugs me down, so I'm sitting with her. "Thank you for the bouquet. Weird question: why did you have them if you weren't here for someone?"

"Weird answer. I always have flowers close to expiring from the shop, and it feels like the least I can do. If I hang around some long-forgotten grave, they deserve a little liveliness."

"That's so nice of you."

Bet nods. Her eyes are soft and search mine. I wonder what for. "Tell me about Phil."

17

BET

I was startled and fell flat on my face, literally eating cemetery dirt in front of Ted. Still, my pulse stays elevated for far longer than the fall justifies and even picks up the pace when he gently plucks the grass from my hair. He's wearing glasses, and he looks like the most handsome version of Clark Kent imaginable. The square black frames compliment his jawline and those heavy brows. His appearance distracts me so I temporarily forget where we are. Grant Memorial. Not a place to check someone out, even stealthily. Why is he here so early? I start to ask, but he beats me to it, and oof, I'm here for yoga, and he's here to visit a beloved person in his life, and I hope he doesn't think I'm a disrespectful asshole.

The best thing I can do is treat his experience, his reason for being here at 6 am, with reverence. So I ask if I can put flowers on Phil's grave and then to hear about him.

Ted opens up slowly at first. He tells me about Phil and him in the context of Noble. Phil was his teacher as a child, and as he grew up and found he was interested in teaching martial arts, Phil mentored him again. Let him teach some classes and help even when he was in high school. Phil encouraged Ted to take an Entrepreneurship Program at the local community college when he graduated. Ted did so and only found out about Phil helping pay his tuition after getting the certification. Ted became a lead teacher, and Phil taught him the ins and outs of managing the business. He implemented some of Ted's ideas to improve Noble's operations, including starting an exclusive class of adults and changing uniform suppliers.

At some point, as Ted speaks, his words start to flow easily, as if a dam has broken. The stories he shares become more personal. The sun is getting higher in the sky, but Ted would be glowing even if it was 3 am. "I remember once in high school, I'd had a crush on this girl, Wendy, for years, and I finally decided to ask her to prom. It was nothing so dramatic as in movies, but she declined, and I was heartbroken."

"She must have been crazy." It slips out. Shit.

Ted stares at me with a fierceness that I have no idea how to comprehend before resuming the story, "Well, Phil saw me later and knew something was wrong. When I told him, he said something similar. She was crazy not to see my value, but I'd be crazy to stay pining away for someone so blind. He always had advice like that. Simple but not obvious. At least not to me, until he came out with it." Ted's beautiful, warm baritone laugh sounds again. If I could drink it, the sound would sustain me.

"He was a rock and a guide for you. I can't imagine losing someone so close. It must be tough with the stress of Noble right now, not having him around." Somehow, we've gotten closer, and our knees are touching. Ted doesn't move back, so I don't either.

"Phil never gave me any business-related advice about this situation because it was unfathomable. The school is fine, you know? We're making budget fine. I could see an incremental bump for tuition next year due to inflation, but not this. As much as I try to imagine what he would say, it won't come." He's playing with the grass around him, eyes on it. "Mark is… It almost feels like he's trying to sink the school sometimes."

Bells ring at the mention of the name Mark. Cooper had used that name, but I didn't know who he was or his relationship with the school. It's easier to ask Ted. "Who's Mark?"

Ted's body language is unmistakably depressed, yet somehow, his shoulders slump inward more. "Phil's brother. It's so strange—Phil and I. My dad died when I was in the 5th grade. It was the worst part of my life, and I was struggling. Phil helped me through it. He, you know, he could never replace my dad, but he became a father figure. I know he felt the same bond. He even told me he would…" Ted's sentence trails off. He shakes his head, then picks back up, "The weird thing is, all those years, I never met Mark. Still haven't. He exclusively calls me and emails. I knew Phil had an older brother, but it was a fact about him and nothing more. They weren't close. He's never been inside Noble, as far as I know. I honestly don't know where he lives. I don't think he came to the funeral. If he did, he never identified himself."

Ted sighs heavily. I know there's more he wants to say, but the weight of it seems to have made talking difficult again. "I'm sorry about your dad and Phil." I subconsciously put my hand on Ted's knee and squeeze, raising Ted's gaze back to me. "This Mark fellow, are we sure he actually exists?"

The question earns a laugh, but this time, it's bitter. "Sadly, yes."

"So, what are you going to do?" I regret the question as soon as it leaves my mouth. What is wrong with me?

Fortunately, Ted doesn't seem to take it negatively. "I'm trying to execute an idea my mom had. Haven Cove used to have this annual Fall Festival. It was wildly popular. The whole town would come out."

"You're going to bring it back?"

"I'm going to try. If Noble can sponsor it, I guess there's an admittance fee, and we'd split the income from the event amongst the sponsors. Other businesses can rent a space for a little money to have a booth to sell from. I hope to make the budgetary goals he set for me this year and maybe… Maybe enough over that to convince him to lower the tuition?" Another sigh. "If I can pull it off, he'd have to be happy, and we wouldn't have so much attrition for the new year."

I assert, "It could save the school." The conversation I witnessed at the bowling alley echoes in my memory, but I don't dare bring it up. It's all hearsay, and I… I'm realizing now that I don't entirely trust the source.

A nod from Ted. "Yeah, but it's hard. I've never tried to organize anything like this, and it's not going great."

"I'll help!" I don't know how I can help, and it's a wild commitment I don't have enough time for, but a sincere one.

Ted whips his eyes back to mine. "You will? You don't have to. I shouldn't have told you all this. You're… too easy to talk to."

I can't stop my smile, but I indulge in it briefly before coughing and assuring him I want to help. "It's too late! I'm on your side now, and there's nothing you can do about it! Bwahahaha!" I proclaim, pointing my finger in the air for emphasis. "Come over tonight. I have to bake, but I don't mind company. You can tell me where you're at so far, and I'll see how I can jump in."

His eyes widen, but Ted agrees and thanks me profusely as we leave for our respective jobs.

18

TED

*N*ervous? Me? Yes. A thousand times, yes. But why? I ask myself the question several times. There's no need for this feeling at the moment. I'm going over to Bet's apartment, but it's because she wants to help with the Fall Festival. She's still with Cooper; there's no chance of anything else. This isn't some first date. Platonic is what it is. Utterly platonic.

Yet I flew home after my last class to wash up and checked my reflection in the mirror enough times to annoy myself. On the way over, I review the talking points in my head. I've brought over all my notes and the timeline Abby made. The timeline will be the linchpin. If I explain it first, I can travel back to the waypoints and unpack them in more detail. I'd take Bet's help wherever she wants to, wherever she can. When she'd offered the generosity, the sincerity in her voice, it shook me. I could barely believe it. Then she followed it up with the invitation to her house. Even she seemed surprised at the offer, but I'm grateful. Curious, too. Why does she need to bake?

I knock on the door and hear Bet sing the words, "Be right there!" The door opens, and Bet is wearing black stretchy pants and a tank top that could be a solid orange, but I can't tell because a flowery apron obscures it. "Here you go." She tosses an apron with a chicken print to me.

I guess stressing about what I wore was more futile than I thought. "Ah, I'm not a great baker."

"All you have to do is follow my instructions. I follow yours all the time."

"Touché." I tie the apron around my waist and follow her into the kitchen.

Bet's iPad is propped up on the counter. She scrolls to the top of a tab she's opened. "We're making two things tonight. This one is new: Banana Bread with Chocolate and Miso. Fingers crossed." She opens another recipe page beside it, "This one is a classic. Vegan Peanut Butter Chocolate Chip Cookie Bars."

I recognize the picture as something I've eaten countless times. "You know who has a great bar like this? Gerard's. My mom and I brunch once a week, and Gerard's is on rotation for us." For some reason, Bet's cheeks go bright pink. "Who are you baking for, anyway? You work at a florist, right?"

She clears her throat. "I do. I'm a florist at Daisy's Daisies and Other Flowers."

"Oh, I know that place. It's right… next to Gerard's. No." Bet nods her head yes. "You're the one making all of Gerard's case?"

"No, I mean, not all of it. I do contribute at least one or two vegan confections most days. So, thank you! I'm glad you like my bars."

I look at her with all the seriousness I can muster. "I do not *like* the bars. I'm obsessed with them. When they're available, I have one every time and then take one home for later.

Oh my God, I have to know what other things you make for him!"

"Pretty much all the vegan stuff. Vegan baking is a passion of mine."

"Not the cheesecake, though." Blush climbs her face again, so pretty against the darkness of her hair. She presses her lips together. "You're kidding me! It's the best cheesecake I've ever had in my entire life. How do you make it without dairy?"

"Cashews."

"Cashews?!"

Bet giggles at my disbelief, and my heart is suddenly in my throat. "I know it sounds weird, but really and truly, it's cashews. I can teach you how to make it if you want?"

I do want. I'd listen to her teach me how to make boxed macaroni and cheese if it meant we were standing side by side. I struggle to answer neutrally and land on, "Yes, but another day. I'm sure this chocolate miso business is worth exploring. Plus, I brought all the festival plans to show you afterward."

"Sounds like a plan."

Bet is making a double batch of these recipes, so my job is to mirror what she does in my bowl. I can tell she's been doing this for a while. How she measures perfectly and deftly moves around the kitchen as if following a choreography is entrancing. I carefully try to replicate her motions but am slower and accidentally overfill my tablespoon of vanilla. Bet reassures me that you measure vanilla with your heart, and my bread will probably be better than hers, but I think she's just being nice.

I can't resist asking her questions as we stir, taste, and tweak. Her apartment is modest and simply decorated, but it still intrigues me. "How did you end up in Haven Cove?"

She shrugs as she whisks. "It's a long story."

"I love a long story."

Something sad crosses her, but it's gone as quickly as it comes, replaced by a lopsided grin. "Alright then. I'm not sure where to start." She laughs, and it sounds a bit nervous. My nerves, however, have left the building. "You said you and your mom have brunch every week. I wish I had a relationship like that with my folks. I think I ended up here for a couple reasons. It was convenient. I've been working with Lily at the shop for years, but I was commuting from Marysville every day. It's a two-hour drive, and it was… ridiculously taxing. I also came to realize I needed space from my family, which sounds horrible. They are wonderful people, but they didn't like some of my decisions as I grew up and evolved. There was a lot of pressure to act differently than I feel."

"I understand." I glance at her without turning and quietly correct myself, "Actually, I don't. We're mostly new to each other, but you're such a hard worker. You put in hours at your job and have been there for years. You support yourself by doing something you love with baking. You pursue your interests and are a dedicated student. Even with such a full plate, you offer to help a… a friend - me."

Bet looks at me with a pained expression. "Thank you. For saying all that. You're kind." There's a pause, but she continues, "I think with my parents… It's like they live in another time or another world sometimes. To them, they're looking out for me. But, like, something happened, and I started finding myself. I stopped dying my hair blonde and cut it short, which devastated my dad. I'll never forget he told me, 'It's a young woman's responsibility to have long, beautiful hair when she can.'" She scoffs at the memory. "My style changed. I used to wear dresses and heels daily but was more comfortable in jeans and a shirt. My mom told me every chance she got, "You'll never find a man looking slovenly." My expression must give my repulsion away because Bet laughs and points a fork in my direction. "You should have heard our fight when I got a tattoo."

"The one on your ankle?"

"The very same." Her eyes flick to mine. "It's pretty unoriginal, but it suited me at the time. Still does." Bet raises her pant leg to reveal a small phoenix.

"Transformation. It's cute, too."

"Thanks! I think these are ready to go in. Do you want to dig into the festival stuff or start the bars?"

Changing tasks seems likely to end our conversation. "Let's do the bars. I gotta take secret notes, so I have this recipe."

"I'll give it to you! No need for clandestine jottings."

We start mixing ingredients again. "So, you aren't close with your parents?"

"It's not that. I mean, it's not the closeness I wish we had, but I talk to my mom every week, and we visit each other and everything. Since the incident, it feels like everything I do disappoints and worries them despite my being happier than ever. They can't see it. Starting at Noble is another example. They're going to be disappointed when they find out I'm studying martial arts. It's not 'behavior befitting a lady,' but I love it so much and knew I would! Even when I was little, I wanted to."

I'm elated to hear she's enjoying her time at Noble but more perplexed by another comment. "Wait, what incident?" Bet halts halfway through pulling a drawer open. It's like I've pressed pause on her for a moment. Maybe I shouldn't have asked. "I'm sorry. I didn't mean to pry."

"No," she resumes searching for a half cup, "I didn't even realize I'd said it. There's no reason I can't talk about it… I just haven't with anyone who wasn't there. My parents call it the incident." I have the impression she's convincing herself it's not a big deal to share this information. Then she bluntly states, "I was engaged once when I was 18, and my fiancé left me the day before the wedding."

"Oh!"

I want to empathize with her, but she continues before I can do anything more than exclaim. "It was a long time ago, and I'm so glad he called it off. Looking back on it, we were way too young. We didn't know ourselves, and I think he saw that. I didn't, not at the time. I was shocked, and it was painful, but I grew to understand. Then, when I had all this space away from a relationship, I got to experiment and find out what I value. He moved to California and started working at a vineyard." She laughs at the memory. "When we were together, we weren't of legal age, but he was committed to never drink. Anyway, I'm so grateful we didn't go through with it, but my parents… They were embarrassed, I think. Everyone in Marysville was invited, and we had to tell them not to come. The peace I eventually got after the initial shock never reached my parents. They aren't wrong when they track back all the changes they see in me to that event. The incident."

"They see all you've been through as negative instead of positive?"

Bet nods sadly. "One day, I hope they can see how happy I am, and maybe they won't care as much about what they believe are mistakes."

Every molecule in my body is aching to wrap Bet up in a firm hug. Instead, I tell her a truth. "I'm sorry they can't see your growth as a success. I lo- Everything you mentioned; your hair and casual comfort, your phoenix, and coming to Noble are all wonderful."

She's not crying but sniffs before saying, "Look who is easy to talk to now! Thank you for making it easy."

"It's my pleasure."

We had stopped progressing on the recipe, but after a few silent seconds tick by, Bet jumps us back into action. She passes me a second mixing bowl to make the cookie part of the bars, and I catch her squinting at me. "What is it? Gonna double dog dare me to do something?"

"No, it's nothing."

"Oho! Now I know it's something. Spill it!"

Bet sighs as if in defeat. "I don't know if I should ask. You don't have to answer. I, uh, heard a rumor."

My heart races. Bet doesn't have to tell me what she heard. "It's probably true."

"It… it is?"

I bite my lip until it hurts. "That I'm a coward and won't spar Cooper?" The words taste bitter in my mouth. "Yeah, I see why they think so."

Bet looks at me with concern. "Why?"

"How to explain? When my dad died. I didn't know how to deal with it. I felt like I was dead, too. There was this huge part of me suddenly missing. Nothing mattered to me anymore. I stopped caring about anything because all my attention was on my pain. I stopped doing homework. I stopped going to Noble. Then, one day, it was a particularly terrible day because I had a note in my backpack from my teacher requesting a conference with my mom. I was walking home from school, and I heard Cooper talking to some of his friends ahead of me, and he said something. I can't remember what, but it was some smart-ass remark, and all his friends laughed, and I just. I ran up to him, tapped him on the shoulder, and punched him in the mouth. It felt good to beat on him. Like I was siphoning off some of the pressure. Then the mortification set in a minute later."

Silver lines the bottom of Bet's eyes. "You were a kid in pain, Ted. Kids… People deal with pain in all kinds of ways they wouldn't normally."

I nod and give a half-hearted smile. "I know. I've forgiven my younger self, mostly. I saw someone having fun; the existence of fun was unfathomable to me. I admit, in the moment, those punches were gratifying, but immediately after… I've never felt worse in my life. My mom and Phil made me start going back to classes, and Phil," A sigh crosses my lips, "he believed if I sparred with Cooper fairly in class, I'd feel better or learn something, but I couldn't do it. He'd partner us up, and I'd block his moves, but I could never bring myself to hit him. Not after what I'd done." A tear tracks down my cheek, and a slender finger swipes it away. Bet is standing in front of me, so close.

"Even now?"

I nod. "I stopped trying a long time ago. I don't need to spar with him. However, this did result in my nickname. Three Points. Despite my blocking, when we did spar way back then, he earned quite a lot of points. He's always been a talented martial artist."

"You're a talented martial artist!"

I chuckle. "I do okay."

"I'm serious." Bet insists, "I'm imagining it now… You were only blocking, and he kept coming at you?" She takes a step back, looking appalled, and the oven timer sounds. As Bet retrieves the bread, she says, "I can't believe they're still on about all this. Fifth grade? Plus, the circumstances are… I'm sorry, but so obvious."

"It comes up less than it once did. At this point, it's more of a feeling than a topic of discussion. Could he be, you know, trying to impress you?" I say it casually, meekly. Her disgust makes me turn my head to hide the smile I can't entirely suppress.

Once the Peanut Butter Chocolate Chip Cookie Bars are setting, we sit at her small round table, and I show her Abby's timelines.

"Who's Abby?" I store the question away to inspect later.

"My friend. If I can pull this off, it'll be because of her."

We brainstorm ideas for the festival and how to get there until 2 am when delirium set in and we say our goodbyes. I'm happier than I've felt in months.

19

BET

I'm not sure I can honestly report this as an "awake" state, but I'm moving at 5:30 am. If anything else had kept me up until 2, I'd have regrets, but talking with Ted? It was like how talking to Emma is. Comfortable and, engaging, and fun. So, while I may be a walking zombie today, it's worth it to feel natural in someone's company.

My hair is still wet from my morning shower as I grab my largest coffee travel mug and head to Daisy's. Even after reviewing all of Ted's plans for the Fall Festival, I'm unsure how to help *except* by asking Lily to sign on as a vendor. We could sell flower crowns or autumn bouquets and hand out business cards to everyone. There has to be another way I can assist; I just haven't put my finger on it yet. It's frustrating. If we were in Marysville, I'd be able to rally the whole town. Small-town life has some advantages; everyone knowing everyone can be a blessing or a curse. For things like this, it's a blessing. If I only had a bigger network here!

Lily is bent over a flower cart beside the work table when I arrive. "Good morning!" My voice is croaky, though Lily is usually the first person I speak to in the morning, so she's used to my frog impression.

However, her voice is always crystalline because the first person she speaks to is herself. "Good morning, dear. We've got quite the list today." Her knobbly hand sweeps toward the stack of orders on the far side of the table.

I leaf through them. "Looks like you've started the Bryant funeral. I'll start the big one for Whitcomb." Lily's lip curls up like she knows something I don't, but I figure it out when I walk into the cooler, and she's already loaded the cart for the Whitcomb order. "Witchcraft!" I shout at her. She cackles in reply. "I wonder what this is for." The order hadn't specified an event. Unusual for one this large.

Lily cuts her eyes at me. "I know what it is. He promised to take her out on their anniversary every year, and he did. Or so he thought. He was a week early, so when he wished her happy anniversary, all hell broke loose."

"Could be. I have another theory." Lily and I always play this game when we have a mysterious order.

Lily trims the stem of a white alstroemeria. "Let's hear it, then."

"All I'm saying is this is a lot of flowers for one person. I think he's living a double life—two whole families and the wives have discovered each other. Now he's apologizing to both."

Lily's laugh is raspy but full of life. "And he put in a single order?!"

I shrug and start de-thorning roses. "He's efficient. Gotta be when living a double life."

We trade more theories, each one becoming progressively more ridiculous. After exhausting such possibilities as faked death, stalker, and creepy first date overcompensation, it feels like a good time to ask. "Um, Lily, do you remember Haven Cove having a Fall Festival?"

"Yes, of course. We haven't had one in years, though. Why do you ask?"

"My Ted. I mean, my friend, Ted, is trying to revive it. It's important to him, and I wondered if we could do a booth for Daisy's Daisies? We could sell seasonal flower crowns for the kids. I'd totally work it."

"Well, if it means this much to you, you can *Bet* on it. When is it?"

This was the part Ted was having trouble with. Getting enough interest to convince the other businesses in his strip mall to agree to host so he could seek a permit from the city. "We... don't know yet, but are hoping for mid-October."

"Hmm. Right around the corner not to know more. Has *your Ted* spoken to the Chamber of Commerce yet?"

I narrow my eyes at the stressed words, but Lily is right. It's already August, and we need things to start happening yesterday. "I don't think so. Is that something he should do?"

Lily nods as she arranges. "Definitely. We have a meeting coming up next week. He could talk to a lot of the local entrepreneurs all at once, but he'll need a more definitive plan for them to commit."

"I'll tell him we have some figuring out to do. I don't know all the details, but I do know one of the neighboring businesses is holding out, and they all have to agree." My voice shrinks as I add, "It's horrible. Noble depends on this working out."

Lily's hands drop from their work, but what gets my full attention is the quaver in her words as she asks, "Noble? Phil's karate school?"

I push aside my stack of newly harmless flowers. "Yes! Ted was something like his assistant. They were really close. You know it?"

She uses the back of her hand to wipe at her eyes. "I

know- knew Phil quite intimately. He was a wonderful man."

Over the years, Lily has shared many things with me. She's freely recounted her childhood and business knowledge and given me sage advice on life generally, but I realize now we've never broached her romantic relationships. I'm not sure how much I should press, but my intrigue demands that I ask, "Lily... Were you two together?"

The tears that lined her eyes were already dry, and she seemed just as surprised by them as I was. She pauses, gathering her response. "In the ways that matter, yes."

A smirk warms my cheeks. "Ted loves Phil, too. But his brother inherited Noble, and the school is in trouble."

"Mark? Phil would have never intended for Mark to get the school. Never, I'm certain." Her expression darkened. "You've got to be ready for the Chamber. I'll try to support him in the meeting.

"Thanks, Lily. I'll let him know."

I take out my phone at least six times before lunch. I want to tell Ted about attending the Chamber of Commerce meeting, but I hesitate to text him such big news. Plus, it would be nice to see him. At 12:30 pm, I decide I can't wait to tell him the good news and I'll swing by Noble when I clock out if he's still there.

Bet Greene

> Hey, hope you're having a good morning. I have some good news and ideas for the festival. Will you be at Noble at 7ish?
> 12:31 PM

Ted responds immediately, and something flutters around my stomach. He will be there.

As soon as we close up shop, I drive to Ted. When I arrive, he's in front of a family class, but another student is helping him lead. He must be watching for me because he sees me immediately. Ted taps the gentleman helping and points in my direction before jogging out. "Hey."

His hair is mussed from sweating, and I resist combing it with my fingers. My greeting comes out breathless, "Hey."

Ted smiles broadly, flashing his white teeth. "You have some good news?"

"Oh yeah! I was talking to Lily about the festival. First, she agreed Daisy's Daisies could take out a booth. Then we talked more, and she recommended you attend a Chamber of Commerce meeting next week. You can talk to a lot of business owners all at once. She showed me the website."

Ted steps behind the front desk to the computer and gestures for me to follow. "Can you show me?"

I join him at the computer and type in the address. "The calendar is here. Next Wednesday at 8 pm. She did say she'd back you up in the meeting, but we'd need to have a solid plan for people to sign up."

He chews his lip, looking at the calendar. "I've never talked to a big group of people like this before."

"You'll do great. I'll help you practice. We just need to get the agreement of the last business owner here. Everything else hinges on it."

Ted's expression hardens with resolve. "Thank Lily for me, this is a great idea, and thank you." His voice is close to a whisper as he says it. He clears his throat and says, "I need to put this on the calendar." He reaches for a pen on the desk, but it falls, bouncing on the carpet. We both reach down for it blindly in the tiny desk area, and our fingers intertwine. Neither of us pulls away. A suspended feeling takes hold of me, and I'm unsure how long we've been crouched down, my fingers between his.

It will be essential to end things with Cooper.

20

TED

"Wait, who's idea was this?" Even over the phone, I could detect the suspicious squint in Abby's eye.

"Bet's. Well, her boss recommended it, actually."

"Hmm, and Bet knows all of everything going on since when, exactly? Listen, Ted, you can't drop information like this without the backstory. I didn't know you finally started talking!" She's right. I usually tell Abby everything, but these last few days with Bet feel like something I'm not done treasuring on my own. That aside, I knew I had to tell Abby about the Chamber immediately.

I lift my shoulder to balance the phone between it and my ear while I unlock my door. "We ran into each other, and I ended up telling her. She wanted to help and invited me over. Your timeline was dead helpful explaining it all."

"BORING! Fine, keep your secrets. The Chamber meeting is an excellent idea, though. Here's another. I've been thinking we should mobilize the gang, and now is the time to do it. If Bet wants to help, could she come to D&D on Friday?" I'm instantly at odds with myself. Yes, I want her there. Introducing her to my friends is like a dream. But now? And Abby… I adore her, but she wants to meet Bet as much as I want to invite her, which scares me a little.

Hitch wraps himself around my legs in greeting. "I'll ask her if she's free. We need all the help we can get."

"Yesssss!"

"Everyone better behave," I warn.

"We won't scare her away, don't worry." A fine sentiment, except I did worry. I was already worried right now. I want to text her and tell her Abby agrees about the Chamber and invites her to D&D, but we exchanged numbers so recently, and I'm just home from seeing her. Bet had come to Noble to tell me about the Chamber of Commerce meeting. Made a special trip, and there was a moment when we both reached for a fallen pen. I know she felt it, too, like our blood flowed through each other.

It was too soon to text her. I'll see her at class tomorrow and catch up with her then.

DESPITE MYSELF, I'm always searching for Bet. It's silly. I know when she's likely to be around and the exact classes she attends, but I look for her all day despite the knowledge. I'm primed to spot her immediately when Advanced students begin arriving. Like clockwork, she parks her car five minutes before class starts, grabs her gear bag, which she keeps in the back seat instead of the trunk, and rushes through the door. It's barely enough time to get her gear on before class. Of course, she's coming directly from work and isn't the only student who does. I'm grateful they make it at all, even when they're late.

Today, as I'm watching her ritual and chatting with other students who've already arrived, I (unfortunately) notice Cooper, too. He must have been waiting in his truck because he appeared out of nowhere, almost like he was sneaking up on her. As they make their way to the studio, I can't help but notice how Bet is walking faster than him, staying ahead, and Cooper looks displeased. He's talking to Bet hurriedly, forehead lined.

Their dynamic changes as soon as Bet opens the door. She sees me right away, our eyes meet, and she beams. The light of her smile finds a home in my chest, and I could be floating an inch above the floor. Cooper is his usual self, a muscled golden boy exuding confidence. I can't talk to Bet now because class is starting in T minus one minute, but I jog to her as they're putting on gear. "Can I grab you a quick moment after class today?"

"Of course." She nods and reaches a hand to me. I grab it and help her up to stand. As I'm walking to the head of the class, I hear Cooper ask, "What's that about?"

Bet keeps up admirably for a relatively new student who jumped right into our Advanced Class. Maybe it's because she sees the senior students and imitates them. Still, she successfully added a forward thrust to her side kick in this class. Some of our high-ranked students can't do that! I have to monitor myself to ensure I spend my time evenly among the class. There are other students besides Bet, even if she is the nicest to observe.

In the last ten minutes, I tell everyone to get their full gear on for sparring, and to my surprise, Bet approaches and sheepishly asks if she can try. It's her first attempt. "Yes, definitely. Gotta have your headgear, though." She smirks and runs off to her bag, and I quickly evaluate who to partner her with. Brian is here; he's good at adjusting to match his partner's skill level. He'd be my first choice of the options available, but how will Cooper react? The decision is easy to make. Even if he has something to say about it, I've observed Cooper wailing on beginners before. I am not in the practice of partnering him with anyone who can't keep up. It's easy enough to explain if he'd like a little chat.

As students return in gear, I pair them up. When I partner Bet with Brian, I see her expression falter through the face shield, but she obediently bumps gloves with him and gets into fighting stance. She's probably nervous. Sparring nerves are common. Even black belts get them sometimes. I try to give her a reassuring nod and count them in, "Three. Two. One."

The room fills with action as opponents circle each other, bouncing from one foot to another. The movement is limited to that for a few seconds, but jabs and round kicks quickly start being thrown. Blocks and dodges occur in response, growing the motion to a chaotic pace. Not for the individuals focusing on their one partner, but for me taking in the whole room? Yes, chaos covers it.

I allow myself a moment to enjoy the mad bustle before focusing on the pairs to give feedback. My attention, of course, strays to Bet most of all. I want this to be a good experience for her. I want her to keep sparring in class. I compliment cleanly scored points as my feet take me nearer to her.

When I'm within eyeshot, I feel a surge of pride in Brian. He's slowed his pace and is encouraging Bet to come at him. Bet is trying, too! Her forms are on point, but she executes them slowly so Brian can block and dodge easily. Drawing nearer, I hear their muffled exchanges. They're trying to talk through their mouthguards. I can't make out the intended communications, but they're clearly having a good time. Excellent. "Good partnership, Brian! Good form, Bet! Try to make your strikes as quick as you can."

Ten minutes fly by, and I dismiss the class. The usual friendly chatter begins as everyone strips off their sweaty gear. Bet runs over to me immediately before making the trip to her bag. "Hey! You had something you wanted to talk about?"

Cooper is visible over Bet's shoulder. He's straining to hear us, and his mouth is turned down in a frown. "Yeah, thanks. I talked to Abby about the Chamber of Commerce meeting, and she agrees it's a great idea, so thanks again to you and Lily. She also thought,... do you know what Dungeons and Dragons is?"

Bet's eyes flash in surprise. "I know of it, but I've never played or anything." About what I expected.

"Some of my friends and I have been playing since high school. Our next meeting is this Friday, and Abby thought it would be a good time to see if any of them could help. She thought I should invite you." I add clumsily, "Only if you want to; you've already been a huge help."

"No, I'd love to. Keep helping- I'd love to help more." Bet shakes her head. "I'll need to get home before too late so I can bake."

"Oh, yeah, no problem."

"Is having someone who doesn't know how to play going to be a drag to your friends? I don't want to mess up the game."

I laugh, picturing it. "No, no, no. Don't worry. They'll be so excited to have someone new. We may not even get to play much, to be honest; we'll have to build your character first." Bet narrows her eyes. I wish I knew what she was thinking, but she doesn't say. "I'll text you the details. If you need a ride or anything, we could go together."

"Okay, we'll figure something out." I start walking toward the door, but Bet says, "I wanted to spar with you, by the way. Next time." She skips ahead of me and starts putting her gear away. Cooper asks her questions and gestures sharply as he speaks, but I'm floating again. Hovering myself to the front desk to start closing up.

21

BET

I'm annoyed. I don't want to break up with him while I'm annoyed. The problem is every time Cooper texts, it sets me off, and wowie, has Cooper been texting. After class on Tuesday, he'd demanded to know what Ted and I had talked about. When I wasn't immediately forthcoming, he'd slammed his palm into my car door over my shoulder. I couldn't tell if he was frustrated or trying to intimidate me, but I wasn't having any of it either way. I told him I'd be leaving, and he could calm down before reaching out. Then I got in my car, watched him walk to his truck, locked my door, and shook. Cooper is a big dude, and while I didn't want him to know it, his aggression scared me. Since then, he's texted 57 times. They started late Tuesday night, came in through Wednesday, and today began with an additional three before I woke up.

Sixty texts isn't always a lot for a little over a day; the thing is, I'm not responding to many. Which is bitchy, maybe, but I don't want to end things over the phone. He deserves an in-person conversation. I scroll to the beginning. Up, up, up the conversation until I find the first ones from Tuesday night.

Coupé de Ville

> I'm sorry, you don't have to tell me what you and Three Point were talking about. I get it. None of my business. Doesn't have to be. 10:02 PM

Bet Greene

> Thanks for saying so. 10:05 PM

Several selfies of him flexing in a mirror follow here. I was already asleep and didn't reply.

Coupé de Ville

> All out of Powerlyte. So sad :(6:59 AM

Coupé de Ville

> I've been thinking we should meet our families. 7:10 AM

Coupé de Ville

> At the gym now 7:15 AM

A delightful 3-hour break here. Even when distressed, Cooper takes gym time seriously.

Coupé de Ville

> What are you doing? 11:21 AM

Coupé de Ville

> Can I come get you? 11:23 AM

Coupé de Ville

> Come on, reply! 11:26 AM

Bet Greene

> You know I'm at work. 11:30 AM

LORI THORN

Coupé de Ville

> I miss you <3 11:31 AM

Coupé de Ville

> Want to go to the gym this weekend? I think you'll like some of the new core regimens I can teach you. 12:02 PM

THEY CONTINUE like this until the tone takes a decided change late Wednesday.

Coupé de Ville

> I just don't understand why you wouldn't want to tell me is all you know? It's a trust thing. 11:07 PM

Coupé de Ville

> You don't want to get involved with whatever he has going on. He's not the right type of person 11:10 PM

Coupé de Ville

> He won't even be around long anyway. Don't board a sinking ship. 11:15 PM

Here's where I silenced my phone.

Coupé de Ville

> Are we okay? 5:55 AM

I stare at the most recent text. Can I make it through another day of incessant messages?

Bet Greene

> Can we talk after class tonight? 6:00 AM

I'd give about anything to message Emma about this, but she's not up yet, and I don't want to risk waking her. She knows about helping Ted and D&D (she even helped me do a little research last night), but I haven't told her about deciding to end things with Cooper yet. Even though we got to a good place, her accusation of being a serial dumper echoes in my head sometimes. We're scheduled for a FaceTime call tonight when everything is settled. I'll catch her up then.

. . .

Cooper never replies to my question. Doesn't message me at all during the day. I'm annoyed again, this time at the abrupt change in strategy. When I arrive at Noble, things get downright disturbing.

Cooper isn't here.

His truck isn't in the lot, and I start to worry. As usual, Brian and Roy are lined up at the far end of the room. I swiftly put my gear on and take my place beside Roy. "Hey, do you know where Cooper is?" There are mere seconds before class begins.

Roy shakes his head slightly and shrugs. He turns to Brian and asks him, but Brian gives the same response. "Haven't seen him since Tuesday. Why don't you know where he is?"

My turn to shrug. "He's supposed to be here."

Ted starts instruction, and the time for conversation closes. I barely keep up with the class. My thoughts are completely wound up in Cooper. I hope he's okay and begin imagining where I might search for him until my brain takes a dark turn, remembering him hitting my car. Would I be okay? Surely, yes. I beg my brain to stop thinking terrible things, but it does not yield. Goddamned tenacious, these intrusive thoughts.

When class ends, I rush to my bag to get my phone. No messages. No calls.

I press my favorite contacts and call Emma. To my relief, she picks up. "Hey."

"Hey, isn't our call a little later?"

The sun sets earlier this time of year, and the parking lot is dimly lit. "Yeah, it is. I just have a weird feeling. I'm, um, well, I'm supposed to be breaking it off with Cooper tonight, but he didn't come to karate class, and I don't know, it's all…

I'm a little freaked out. I'm being stupid; it's probably nothing."

"Girlfriend code. I got you, Bet. Safer to be on the phone, and it's never stupid."

"Oh no. He's here. I see his truck, I'm sure of it." I spot his truck idling at the back of the lot on the way to my car. The headlights turn off, and Cooper steps out. Emma is talking fast, but I can't hear her. "I'm putting you in my pocket, Em. Wish me luck."

I slip the phone into my pants pocket, hoping the screen's light doesn't shine through the fabric. "Cooper, I was worried about you. You didn't respond, and then you weren't in class. Are you okay?" As he comes nearer, I note his walking is off-kilter.

"Course I'm not okay!" He leans against my car roughly, and the whole vehicle rocks slightly under his weight. He reeks of alcohol.

"Cooper, you're drunk. Did you drive here?"

"None of your concern, izzit? You wanted to "talk," well here. I. Am."

I step toward my driver's side door and shake my head. "I don't think we should talk with you in this state. Can I call you an Uber? Or if you have Roy or…"

"I know you're leaving me. I know why, too, but I wanna hear you say it."

"Fine." This is happening. He already knows. "You're right. I don't want to go out anymore. It's nothing in particular, Cooper. We're just into different things."

"Bullshit." His eyes flash, and I back up again. The cool metal of the car presses into my back. "Nobody leaves for that shit. Tell me the truth!"

Something steels in my gut, and I stand at my full height. "The way you're behaving makes me think you don't want the truth."

"You're a slut." He spits on the pavement. "You're fucking Three Points. How you can give up this for him…"

"Don't be disgusting. I'm not fucking anyone, but if I were, I'd hope it would be someone kind-hearted and not a middle school bully." Cooper sneers. The contortion destroys everything handsome about his face. He steps toward me, and my arm goes up like a barrier between us. "No!"

To my relief, he stumbles back. "You were *lucky* to have me. Looking the way you do. This was your one chance, and you *blew it!*"

"Real classy, Cooper." He starts walking toward his truck. My heart is pounding, but I call after him, "You can't drive like this. Let me call your friends or something."

"Fuck you, slut."

"BET! BET!" I hear Emma faintly from my pocket.

"Hey, I'm okay. He's leaving."

"Thank God, are you really alright? What an asshole!"

I sigh as I drop into my car. "Yeah. I still need to process it for sure. It was scary to see him drunk, but breakups are always emotional, right? I… I don't know how to feel, but I am going to follow him and make sure he gets home alright."

"Let him crash."

"Emma!"

"He said horrible things to you!"

"Yeah, he did."

I hear her exhale. "Keep me on the line until you're home. I need a little break before we FaceTime, but I've got everything ready to go if you're still up for it?"

"Thank you. Yeah, it's now or never; the game is tomorrow. I hope he doesn't live too far away." I've never been to Cooper's house.

As I attempt to follow Cooper's truck stealthily, I fill in Emma on the last couple of days of his text behavior and how he'd reacted so poorly to Ted talking with me.

22

TED

"She's on the way." I lay my phone face down on the table.

The energy in the room tightens. PJ says what everyone is thinking, "I can't believe we get to meet this girl. Ted, bringing a girl to D&D." He leans back and crosses his arms over his chest.

"Not sure why you're saying that in such disbelief. I've brought a girl before." I gesture toward Abby. "I'm the *only* person to have invited someone else to join us."

Everyone looks around, doing the math. Mitch admits, "He's got a point. Though it has been a long time, Abby is old news."

Abby cries, "Hey!"

Mellisa clears her throat with a gentle *ahem*. "How was meeting Wes's family, Abby?"

I've heard this story already, and as Abby grimaces, I egg her on, "Now here's a story worth hearing."

Abby cuts me a glare but answers. "It was, ah, interesting. I guess his parents are kind of like hippies? They were welcoming but also awkwardly open about some things."

"About what things, Abby?" She purses her lips and blinks at me slowly.

"Sexual things."

At this, Mitch and PJ sit up straighter, leaning in toward the table. Melissa softly exclaims, "Oh my!"

"Wait, wait, I need to get this straight," PJ is all grins, "You meet his parents for the first time, and *they* initiate a conversation about sex?"

"More or less, yeah," Abby moves her head side to side, "I could tell they were a little... free-spirited right away; they were wearing flowy sort of tunics and no shoes. They were super polite, you know. They had dinner ready, a raw food lasagna."

"Ugh, gross. Raw lasagna?" Mitch's face is pure disgust.

Abby laughs. "No, not raw lasagna. That would be gross. They're on a raw foods diet, which has particular heating restrictions. I don't know too much about it, to be honest. Only that it was yummy."

Mitch frowns. "Still sounds nasty."

"I mean, I don't think *you* would like it," Abby retorts, "Anyway, it was all pretty normal until we got to talking about jobs. They shared this weird look; Wes was mortified, so I had a split-second heads-up that something was off. Then they told me they're Sex Coaches."

Mitch interrupts again, "Wild because I've been meaning to tell y'all. I'm a Sex Coach."

PJ rolls his eyes. Melissa goes bright pink and starts inspecting her hands.

"Har, har, Mitch," Abby continues, "They're licensed through a national organization. I'd never heard of such a thing, but it requires education, I guess."

"Bummer."

"I mean, if you're interested in a career change, I know

some people you can ask about the path to Sex Coach." Abby teases.

"Okay, it's an unusual profession, but this doesn't seem so bad?" PJ asks with anticipation.

"You know there's more!" Everyone chuckles, and Abby continues, "Basically, after they told me about being Sex Coaches and what they do, they immediately started asking me questions about me and Wes. They asked if we felt fulfilled with each other and if we felt secure enough to share our fantasies. Wes had a hand over his face the whole time, and I was so embarrassed. Then they asked how often we're intimate, and Wes finally told them it was none of their business."

Melissa shakes her head. "So awkward! I can't imagine."

Abby nods. "I can't deny that. They seemed a little judgmental after he told them to stop, but they did respect his boundaries. Things went back to pretty normal after. Wes apologized to me the whole way home. I guess this is why he didn't introduce them sooner. He was even worried I'd end things. Ridiculous. There is one part I'm grateful for. We're more solid than ever. It's like he had this concern weighing over him, and now it's alleviated."

Mellisa swoons. "Oh, that's nice."

"Yeah, when's the wedding scheduled?" PJ quips. Abby's silence is an answer. His eyes widen, "Oh really?!"

"I mean, he hasn't asked yet, but… I do kinda think he will soon."

A flurry of responses happens at once, but the doorbell rings, hushing everyone.

"I'll get it. You all… behave!" I warn as I walk to the front door.

Bet's black jeans hug her long legs, and her white sleeveless T-shirt accentuates her lithe frame. Nobody has any business looking so perfect in such a simple outfit. "Hey Bet, come on in. Everyone's at the table."

She nods and follows me, but as soon as she's inside, Abby jumps up from her chair. "Help her carry things, you rube!" She sweeps past me and grabs the square tin from Bet's hands.

"Oh, it's okay, it's just a little…"

"Nonsense. I'm Abby, by the way. It's great to meet you."

Bet smiles. "Nice to meet you."

Everyone introduces themselves. If I could reach their legs beneath the table, I'd kick all of them in the shins for their shit-eating grins and exchanged glances.

Bet slides the tin toward the middle of the table. "I brought some goodies." Mitch and PJ both reach for the package eagerly. "I made some extra since I know Ted likes them."

PJ opens the box first and extracts what I recognize as Peanut Butter Chocolate Chip Cookie Bars. "You didn't tell us she was a baker, Ted!"

Mitch adds, "Yeah, holding out, dude. Not cool." He takes a bite and offers a muffled thanks to Bet.

Abby, forever the organizer, asks, "Should we talk business, or should we play first?" Then to Bet, "I think Ted said we need to help build a character profile for you, right?"

Bet raises a finger, "Actually…" She reaches into her purse and brings out some papers in a trifold. "I didn't want to hold you up, so I did a little something. Mind you, I'm not sure it's right." She pushes the papers to Abby, who unfolds them, eyes wide.

"You made your character?! A cleric! Perfect starting character, plus we could use one." Abby continues to scan the character sheets, making commentary here and there. "Girl, you crushed it. I can't believe you've never played before and were able to put such a solid character together."

"I can't take all the credit. Emma helped me. She's my bestie. She even looked into some rules and beginner guides while I was at work."

Abby passes the build around the table so everyone can get to know the new player. "Only one thing missing. You need a name."

Bet blows air through her lips and rolls her head back. "Ugh, I know. I've been thinking about it for days, but I can't come up with anything good."

Mitch offers, "We all have terrible names, don't worry. The more over-the-top absurd, the better. I'm a fighter with a first name only, Brut. Abby is a rogue named Sasha Sleight. Don't even ask about PJ's name."

"It's because I have the best name, and you're all jealous." PJ turns to Bet, "Lore Singer, bard of legend at your service." Everyone rolls their eyes, and Bet laughs.

"Okay, okay, I get it. How about Claire Ic-arus?" Everyone erupts in laughter, and I catch a pleased expression from Bet.

PJ slaps his leg and says, "You're going to do just fine in this game."

The doorbell rings again, and this time, Mitch gets up to answer and returns, carrying four boxes of pizza. Melissa, Abby, and I scoot to the kitchen and return with napkins, beer mugs, and a bottle for everyone. Abby begins passing beers out, "You drink, Bet?"

"Heck, yes. Thank you so much. And you all eat pizza! What a relief."

Mitch mumbles through a cheese pull, "You know someone who doesn't?"

Abby interjects, "Dear Mitch, you see, some of us eat more than *exclusively* pizza."

"I eat other things, too! Cheeseburgers and Tacos, duh."

Bet helps herself to a pepperoni slice. "The guy I was dating had a super strict diet. It was a lot."

I'm holding my slice, about to bite into it, mouth agape, when I freeze. Abby registers the past tense as well. She slowly sets down her mug, which she failed to sip from. I shake my head at her slightly, which I'm certain she sees, but she ignores me. "Did you say you were dating someone? Cooper, right?"

Bet doesn't realize that everyone is holding their breath. "Oh, you know him, too. I was, yeah. Um, but we broke up last night."

"Oh!" Abby exclaims, her face lights in a smile. "I… am so sorry to hear that."

Mitch swallows his bite of pizza. "I'm not. Dude's a dick."

PJ and even Melissa nod their heads.

I don't know what to say, and most of my focus is working full-time to keep from smiling, which I'm doing a horrible job at. To my relief, Bet is also smiling, and I swear she even steals glances in my direction. She raises her glass toward Mitch, "Kind of a dick, yeah. There's no love loss. He's… you know, he's not *all* bad, but definitely not for me. Little controlling. Little bullying sometimes." Abby is boring holes in my direction, and I stop policing my lips, letting a foolishly large smile occupy my face.

"Cheers to your freedom, then." Abby raises her beer, and everyone follows suit to clink rims.

As we eat, the conversation naturally travels to the Fall Festival. Abby enters what must be project management mode and practically starts assigning tasks. She asks Melissa to design advertisements for the event so we can plaster them around town and to be the official festival photographer; PJ can make sure the local schools know about the event, and Mitch and PJ will organize the site and set up vendor maps.

"Abby, this is all great, but we still haven't even been to the Chamber of Commerce or have the permit." I protest hesitantly. Things still seem backward to me.

"Yes, speaking of the Chamber," she unzips a small computer bag and hands me a manila envelope. "Your job, immediately, is to get the last business owner to sign the agreement in here. I also took the liberty to take a stab at some of the math. You'll find a sheet showing my suggested vendor fees and ticket costs. Once you have the signature you need, turn those forms in for the permit immediately. It shouldn't take long to process, but we have to get it in by next Wednesday if you're going to give a solid presentation to the Chamber. Which…" She eyes Bet and me, "I thought you two could work on this part. I'll help, too, but since this great idea came from you…"

Bet accepts. It's hard to tell because we're sitting alongside each other, but I swear she's looking at me instead of Abby when she answers, "Of course. Any way I can help, I want to."

I am thoroughly humbled by my friends' willingness to assist. Everyone discusses the details of their role, even adding responsibilities to their plates. After we understand what's ahead, I'm more energized than ever. Things are finally organized in my mind. I know how this is going to work.

PJ changes the direction, "So, should we play?" I'm wired with the energy of having a plan, but I know time is zooming by, and Bet may need to leave. Starting the game now would take us into the wee hours, but I don't want it to fall on her.

"Sorry everyone, I'm not sure I can." I'm still searching for an excuse and lamely finish, "Early morning. I have to meet Connie, after all. The hold out from Super Pets."

Mitch, despite a severe stare aimed at him from Abby, says, "Bullshit. You're our most prepared DM, and I know you're not headed there too early. Do they even open before noon?"

I hesitate to reply, hands up in the air, but Bet must have caught our looks at Mitch because she says, "It'll be my fault. I have to leave soon so I can get my baking in. I have space to fill at Gerard's Cafe."

Melissa's small voice chimes, "You bake and work at the florist?"

Bet nods. "Yeah. It's a lot, but I feel lucky. It's not like I hate either job, and I can keep afloat between the two. It could be worse."

"Why don't you bake over here?" Bet's head swings to face Mitch. "I mean, not this time, obviously, but you could bake here and play. You'd have to bring everything you need, but I never use the kitchen. Shoot, Gran would probably be happy thinking someone was baking in her oven again."

"For real? Are you sure? It can take anywhere between two and five hours, depending on what I'm making."

"Ah, you definitely haven't played D&D before. So can a game." Mitch puts his hand over his mouth to hide his words from me but then clearly announces, "Especially with this guy DMing." He points a thumb in my direction.

Bet makes one of her crystalline singing laughs. "Deal. Thank you."

Melissa smiles sweetly at Mitch.

Abby asks, "Do you have enough time for us to catch you up with the story so far? It's a doozy."

The following 30 minutes are spent in character. Sasha, Brandon, and Brut recount their experience. Lore sings his.

23

BET

"Good morning, beautiful!" My mom sings through the phone.

"Good morning, Mom. How are you?"

"I'm great! I wanted to ask about your birthday plans. What will you be up to?" My birthday is tomorrow, and I know she's got something up her sleeve from her cheery energy. She may as well be jumping up and down.

"Not too much. I took the day off work. I've got karate in the evening, but mostly just relaxing."

"Fabulous because I'll be there by 4. We're going to have so much fun!"

"Mom, wait. What? Like today?"

"Yes, today! I haven't seen you in so long. I thought I'd come right over and help celebrate your day," A hint of sadness entered her voice, "You said you aren't doing much."

"No. I'm excited to see you. I do have some obligations, though. Okay? I won't be out of work at 4, but you can let yourself into the apartment."

"Of course."

A hope and a dream occur to me, and I can't help but ask.

"Oh! Could you bring Emma and Charlie? I haven't seen them in ages either." Silence. "Mom?"

"I'm here. I was planning on staying for a couple of days. I don't think they'd be able to swing more than an afternoon, do you? Your apartment is small, so…"

"Yeah. You're probably right." My heart drops a little.

"I can't wait to see you!" She's back to singing.

"See you soon, Mom. Love you."

I pocket my phone. Lily's gaze is a physical sensation against me. "That sounded interesting."

"I guess my mom is visiting for a couple of days."

Lily nods and doesn't break her heavy stare. "Wish I could see my mom. She's coming at 4?"

"Aw, Lily. I'm sorry. You're right. It's a blessing to see my mom." I mean it. Sometimes, Lily knows exactly what I need to hear to shift my perspective. "And yeah, sounds like 4 pm, but don't worry. She has a key to my place."

"You should leave early," Lily finally breaks eye contact and turns toward the order log, "We aren't too bad. Finally getting a little slower now."

I join her at the log so I can see for myself. "Why don't we agree on a we'll-see approach?" I counter. "I'm not going to leave you hanging; if we get a big order in, you'll need me."

Lily smiles. "Fair enough."

We don't take another large order before 4 pm. I'm looking forward to seeing Mom; however, realizing we *are* slowing down at Daisy's makes my mind stray to Noble and my agreement with Ted. Should I start trying to attend the beginner class? I don't want to. I'm certainly still a beginner and not on the same level as the rest of the class, but I know them now. I have a sense of belonging there despite my experience level.

I build a case for myself to stay in the Advanced Class on the drive home. It's not very strong. Aside from my feelings, all I have is the likely need to rejoin them when business increases again in November, December, and February. If the school is still open, then… If I can afford the tuition, come January… If Ted is still there. Or does his presence matter? I'm learning for me, but could I continue at the school if the worst happened? What would Ted do if he were let go?

All my musings halt as I pull into my place. Mom is already here; I park next to her sparkling white Cadillac. The juxtaposition between it and my barely functional turquoise Toyota is amusing.

I unlock the door and drop my bag, but the lights are off, and Mom isn't in sight. Highly unusual. Maybe she's in the bathroom. I flip on the light, and a giggle sounds behind the couch. I know exactly what's happening, and as Charlie comes toddling from the couch crying, "Aunt Bethy!" Tears streak down my cheeks as I snatch him into a hug and spin around.

Emma appears immediately after Charlie, Mom behind her. We take turns embracing and exchanging greetings. "Mom!"

"Yessss?" A sly simper.

"You lied to me!"

"I had no choice. I couldn't ruin the surprise."

"It is an amazing surprise. I'm so glad you're here!" Charlie is weaving in and out of Emma's legs, and I kneel to get on his level. "Charlie, if I remember right, sugar cookies are your favorite?"

Charlie claps, and I notice his hands are losing the roundness of babyhood. "Cookies!"

"You got it, kiddo." I stand up and say, "I was going to make some berry crumbles, but we can add some brown butter cookies."

Mom frowns slightly. "You're still doing this baking all the time?"

I chuckle, "Yeah, you knew that." I fetch ingredients for the two recipes from the cabinets.

Mom sits at the kitchen table. "You got back from work moments ago, and now you're working again, is all. It feels like one job or the other should be enough. You're doing too much."

"I'm barely breaking even. Besides, it's okay. I don't mind."

"You *should* mind." Mom looks around as if searching for something. Her eyes land on Emma, standing beside me, measuring flour into a yellow mixing bowl. "Emma doesn't work herself to death."

"Don't discount the work Emma does, Mom. She's working just as hard as me running her house and being a good mom herself." Emma smiles meekly at me and whispers a thanks.

"She's not worrying about money, though. Most young ladies your age are figuring this stuff out. Are you at least dating someone?" I knew this conversation was coming but didn't guess it would be so immediate.

Emma sidles so close to me as I brown vegan butter that our arms brush. "Not right now."

"Thank goodness she dumped that loser, Cooper. He didn't deserve her." My gratitude for Emma soars.

"Well, let me ask you this. Would you rather bake or do floristry?" Unlike the questions about my dating status and what I'm sure will come about martial arts and my apartment, this one catches me off guard. I have thought about it —a lot. I don't know the answer, though, and I didn't expect Mom to ask. Sometimes, when I dream of the future, I take over Lily's business when she retires. Other times, I work as a baker full-time. Occasionally, it's something completely different altogether.

"I don't know. I enjoy them both. I admit there would be

advantages to focusing on one instead of splitting my efforts. Doing that isn't an option right now."

Mom coughs. "It might be attainable if you set a goal. Just think about it."

"How's Dad doing?" A change of topic strikes me as refreshing.

We chit-chat through baking, then play dominos while Charlie munches on too many cookies. When he starts acting cranky, it's my cue to figure out sleeping arrangements. Mom will get my bed, and I take extra comforters and couch cushions to form a makeshift pallet on the ground for Emma, Charlie, and I. Charlie falls asleep immediately.

Mom excuses herself to my bedroom at 10 pm, leaving Emma and me to whisper across Charlie early into the morning.

I'M LATE DELIVERING the crumbles and cookies to Gerard's in the morning, but hey, it's my birthday. The cafe opened a short 30 minutes ago, so patrons are still sparse. Emma and Charlie open the door for me as I balance the two confections; Mom is on my heels. I tempted them all to rise with the promise of breakfast and fresh coffee.

"Gerard! Sorry, I'm running behind." I clink the plates onto the glass counter. "Good news: My mom and best friend are visiting, and we get to slow down and grab a bite to eat this morning."

Gerard is the sort of person you can spot across the room and pick up on his charisma. He swats my apology away and, at the end of the gesture, continues sweeping his hand toward my mom. She lays a delicate hand in his, and he kisses her fingers. "Enchanté."

Mom smiles approvingly. "Nice to meet you."

After a quick handshake with Emma and a wave for

Charlie, Gerard tells us to pick a seat anywhere. "I'm so glad you're taking a day off. Enjoy yourself." He directs the next part to Mom, "Your daughter is one of the hardest working people I know. Excellent baker, too."

Sitting down and sipping fresh coffee is an entirely different experience from taking it on the go in a travel mug. Everyone is enjoying themselves and their food, and Gerard comes to our table to join in the conversation here and there since it's a slow morning. When he finds out it's my birthday, he threatens to comp our meal. I don't get to put up a decent fight because the front door rings in a customer, and he hustles to position behind the counter.

"Bet?" The mellow baritone makes my stomach swoop up.

"Ted?" I stand to greet him. As I turn, Emma mouths, "Oh my God!" With a silent, excited scream. Mom, who never misses anything, sees her reaction and narrows her eyes in interest.

Ted isn't alone. He looks like a buffer, male version of his mother. Their hair, eyes, and nose are the same. Ted's defined square jaw is different from her heart-shaped face, but they could never deny each other. "Hi, what a surprise." Ted opens his arms as if to hug me as I stick my hand out for a handshake. There's a fraction of a second where I hate myself for it. A handshake?! What am I doing?! I retract it and hug him back; oh, and he smells like a forest, but the friendly embrace is over as soon as it starts, and now we're both standing around with our families, looking at each other. "This is my mom. Mom, this is Bet." My mom cuts her eyes at my name as I shake her hand.

"Bet. You're the one helping with the Fall Festival?" Her expression is open and warm.

I smile. Ted told his mom about me. "Yes, that's me. It's nice to meet you." I get out of the way of the table to introduce everyone. "This is my mom, my friend Emma, and her son Charlie."

Ted kneels down so he's at eye level with Charlie and tries to shake his hand, but Charlie doesn't know how. "That's okay, little man, better pound it then. Do you know how to pound?"

Ted makes his hand into a fist, and Charlie squeals with delight as he says, "Poun' it! Poun' it!" and bumps Ted's calloused knuckles with his own.

As Ted stands, I explain, "We were getting ready to head out, but I'll see you tonight at class."

Gerard emerges from behind the counter with our bill and sets it on the table. "No arguments from the birthday girl." He winks at me and spins on his heel.

"Wait. It's your birthday?" Ted is standing at a perfectly normal distance from me, but he feels close.

"Yeah."

"I didn't know." He sounds almost confused.

"It's okay. You have no reason to know." I don't know his birthday, either. It's never come up in conversation.

"I wish I did." Our feet haven't moved yet, but I swear we're nearly touching.

It feels like no one else is in the room for a breath, then Charlie asks, "We're gonna go?" Emma whispers a response to him.

"Are we still on for Thursday?"

"Yes. Did you get the signature?" Ted wilts.

"I tried everything. I think Connie is avoiding me. She's not there when I go in and never returns my calls. I've left five messages and emailed. I'm not giving up; it's just… discouraging."

Mom pipes in, "I don't know what you're talking about, but if you need something from someone giving you the cold shoulder, maybe someone else should make the appeal. Who *does* know this Connie?" Ted's mom nods in agreement from her seat at the table across from ours.

Ted chews his lip. "That's a good idea, but I don't know who would."

"Could Lily? She knew Phil. They are both longtime entrepreneurs." Daisy's Daisies and Other Flowers is right next door, and I stare in its direction, thinking. "I'll ask her." I start to walk over without thinking about the rest of the group.

Emma asks, "Where are you going?"

Ted understands but asks, "You're asking now?"

"Why not? No time like the present." I briefly explain to Mom and Emma to catch them up on the idea of the Fall Festival and let them know I'll be right back. This time, Ted follows me.

"Connie Compton, that old bag?" Lily cackles. "I know her. Should have figured she was the holdout."

"Could you… help convince her?" Ted asks sheepishly.

Lily laughs again, and her eyes track Ted head to toe. I'd say she was checking him out if I didn't know her. Actually, she is checking him out, but it's for me, not her. My theory is confirmed when she winks at me. "Write down all the details you're planning and your contact information." She passes him one of our order forms to use. "I can't promise she'll agree, but I can be pretty persuasive." She steeples her fingers together and strums them against each other like a movie villain.

"Thank you. Thank you so much!"

Lily practically kicks me out then, exclaiming about me being at work on my day off.

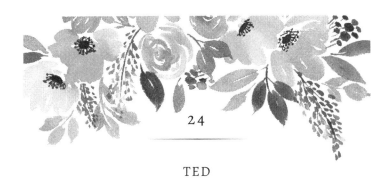

24

TED

The day was going differently than expected. I planned to catch Mom at breakfast and maybe peek into Daisy's next door to wave at Bet before hunting down Connie (again), then the usual classes. Instead, the morning is riddled with major events, both professional and personal.

I had hoped to pluck up the courage to say hi to Bet on the way out of Gerard's. Maybe even buy one of her delicacies and bring it to her. Anything I can do to see her. Then she was there, sitting at a table with her mom and best friend, and my mom was there, and this is how our parents met. Oh- and it's Bet's birthday. Surprise! It feels so wrong that I didn't know, as if it was something I forgot instead of recently learned. Then, before I can even start imagining what I can do to help her celebrate, she gives me the gift of Lily. I'm unsure if she'll be able to help sway Connie or even when she'll try, but I am beyond grateful for the attempt.

When Bet and I return, we walk in on my mom talking with Emma and Charlie. The conversation drops as soon as they see us. As Bet and her posse leave, my mom taps her nails against either side of her coffee cup with a look so wry, so maddeningly knowing, I'm forced to ask, "What?"

She sets her cup down, now completely serious. "I think you know what. I can't believe you've been keeping me in touch with all the festival developments and never mentioned once that you and Bet have… Whatever it is you have. Are you dating?"

"Mom! You'd know if I was dating anyone. Bet is helping me. She's a student at the school."

Mom rolls her eyes. "You *obviously* like each other. In case you were wondering."

I was wondering. Am wondering. I hesitate, gauging if I want to share the other part with Mom before saying, "She, uh, just broke up with Cooper."

I laugh as Mom struggles to snatch a napkin from the table to spit the sip of coffee she's taken. Her mirth crinkles the lines around her eyes. "You've got to be kidding. Of all people?" We swab up the spew she didn't quite contain with more napkins.

"Yeah." I couldn't bring myself to confess my feelings for her, so I changed the subject. "Remember when you accused me of not trying to save Noble?"

Another cut of her eyes. "I have never and would never. If you're referring to when I challenged you to think outside the box, you needed a push."

"Mmmm… Is it different," I tease. "Anyway, I woke up this morning with another idea. In case the Fall Festival doesn't work. It's not as big, but what do you think about Noble hosting a monthly Parents' Night Out? I could stay late one Friday a month for a few hours and do an easy kids program, an hour of karate, pizza, and a movie or something. It'd be cheaper than hiring a babysitter for the parents. I was thinking $25 per family."

"What a great idea! I'm sure you'll have plenty of interest."

"Thanks, I…" My phone ringing distracts me, and I snatch it from my back pocket. "It's, I think it's Connie!" I press the button to answer and twist to standing so I can take the call outside. "Hello?"

"This is Connie Compton from Super Pets, calling for Ted Dawson." She sounds annoyed.

"Yes, this is Ted. Thank you so much for calling me Connie, uh, Mrs. Compton. I was trying to reach you to discuss…"

"*Trying to reach me* is an understatement. I heard a noise outside last night and wondered if you'd shown up on my doorstep at 3 am."

"Um, yes, I admit I've been persistent. It's just…"

"You want me to reconsider support of the renewed Fall Festival, which I've already told you is more trouble than it's worth, and I'm not interested."

I sit on the corner sidewalk around Gerard's and try to melt into the earth. It's over. "I… It's important, and I wanted to see if I could do anything to make it less troublesome. If I understood how I could help, I'd do anything."

It's silent on the other end for so long that I check the screen, wondering if Connie hung up. We are still connected, though, and I jam the phone back against my ear as I hear her reply, "Unfortunately, there isn't anything you can do about the noise level disturbing the animals." Her words carried the weight of a final statement. I needed time to think about a reply, to come up with a solution.

My mind's frantic reeling stops completely when Connie hisses, "But…" I don't dare move. But what? "I was recently reminded of what it was like to start as a young business owner. How it felt when Super Pets was struggling." She pauses, then says rapid-fire, "If you bring me the paperwork by eleven, I'll sign it."

"Thank you! Mrs. Compton, thank you so..." The call disconnects, but I don't care. I have to go!

I rush back inside to kiss Mom on the head and tell her I have to get to Connie before she can change her mind, but I'm moving so quickly I stub my toe hard against the table. "Oof!" I swallow the swear threatening to escape, and fall into my chair. My toenail is split, it'll need some tape before classes start.

"Are you okay?" Mom asks. "Who was on the phone?"

I force my watering eyes up from my foot. "It was Connie. She's not happy about it but agreed to permit the festival. I have to go. Sorry to cut our breakfast short, but she gave me a time limit to get to Super Pets."

Mom's face lights up, and she gives my arm a playful slap. "You'd better hop on your good foot and get on outta here!"

Hitch greets me at the door, and I apologize as I grab the papers and dash back to the car, "Sorry, bud, only here for a second." In response, he jumps onto the couch and curls into an orange tabby ball.

My phone rings again as I pull into a spot at the back of the parking lot. Who else could possibly be calling now?

Mark. Of course.

It's 10:30, and unfortunately, I have time to answer. "Hello, Mark. How are you?"

"I was better before I opened your monthly report. How do you think I'm doing?" The school didn't meet Mark's monthly goals.

"You must have seen my note about the Fall Festival then. I'm getting the last business's agreement to host it right now, so the event is a go."

"A waste of time. We're not aiming for a one-time event; we need a consistent influx of cash through new paying members."

"An event will help us both have a financial boost, which we can allocate across the year and recruit more people to join. This could be huge for us."

"I think it's time I come to the school and see for myself how things are being run. I'll be there next week. Get things in order."

My face is hot with anger. He's like talking to a brick wall. "I agree. You should have come to the school months ago. And there's nothing to get in order because it's already there. I'll see you next week." I hang up and lean my head against the window. I shouldn't have snapped at him. Maybe I won't wait to organize the Parents' Night Out.

A few deep breaths later, I'm opening the door to Super Pets, contract in hand. The mixed smell of animal, feed, and cleaner invades my nostrils. The sole person in sight is a younger lady with dark hair down to her waist. She's leaning against a register, absently gazing into the nearby aisles.

"Um, hey," I grab her attention. She turns toward me. "Hi, I'm here to see Connie. Is she available?"

"You sure?" She wrinkles her nose. "Just kidding. She's in the office; I'll get her."

I station myself next to the second unmanned register and wait. It doesn't take long until I see the dark-haired employee walking beside Connie. They wear the same red polo and khaki uniform but couldn't look any different. The dark red of the shirt compliments the young lady's olive skin and dark hair. Connie's pink complexion and severe blonde bob can't stand up against the hue, and I'm forcefully reminded of an unhappy Humpty Dumpty as she limps toward me.

"Good Morning, Connie. Thank you again for agreeing to sign on for the Fall Festival." I extend my hand to her as she approaches and receive a wary eye before she shakes it.

"Hmph. Let's see the papers."

"Of course." I hand over the five stapled pages, but she doesn't read them.

"Where do I sign?"

"The last page, and there's a place to initial on the third page."

Connie sucks at her teeth while she flips directly to those places, scribbles her signature, and hands the packet back to me.

I thank her, but she's already stumping back toward the office.

"She's a real peach." The cashier says under her breath.

"Ha, yeah. Thanks to you as well."

"No prob."

If I go right now, I'll have just enough time to turn in the entire event application to the city and make it back for Tiny Tigers. I allow myself a celebratory yell from the driver's seat and shoot off messages to Abby and Bet.

Ted Dawson

> I got it! Connie signed! Lily is a miracle worker! 11:04 AM

Bet Greene

> Yessss!! I knew you'd get it! :) 11:04 AM

Bet's near-immediate response sends me soaring.

I'm so thrilled and relieved to have everything submitted for the Fall Festival; not even the pangs when I remember Mark will be coming to the school next week get me down. I even cobbled together a signup sheet for Parents' Night Out next Friday before Tigers class. There are already ten signups when I'm down to the last class of the day.

The final class is Advanced. Which means Bet will be here. Despite running into her at breakfast and texting her about Connie, I've been looking forward to seeing her all day.

She arrives 15 minutes early, unusual since she's typically rushing to get here from work, and she has her mom in tow. I recall something she said once: Her parents disapproved of her learning a martial art. Bet is an adult and doesn't need anyone's approval, yet I am considering if there's anything I can do in this class to help all the same. If her mom sees the value, would it make things easier for Bet?

I'm talking to Kenzie, an eager brown belt, when they walk through the door, but I wave as they enter and mark their interaction. Bet is giving her mom the tour and explaining class; her mom looks uncomfortable, and a stern frown is etched on her face. I can't hear exactly what they're saying, but I see her mom point to the school's placard with distaste. Phil had the sign engraved when he opened Noble, and it's been hanging there ever since, framed by two criss-crossing katanas. I know exactly what it says without having to read it. It's the words I've opened every class with for years. "We are Noble. We show honor. We live with integrity. We respect all people. In this way, we are strong." How many times have I repeated those words?

I excuse myself from Kenzie to properly greet Bet and her mom. Even I can't deny that Bet has a glow to her when I approach. Her smile is like the moon coming out from a cloud, transforming her face. Mrs. Greene sees it, too, and lets out a small harrumph. "Bet. Mrs. Greene. I'm glad to see you, welcome in. Can I get you some water?"

Mrs. Greene politely declines, but at the same time, Bet steps in front of her and hugs me. "You did it! I'm so excited. This is all really happening!"

Mrs. Greene isn't the only one making faces. Cooper narrows his eyes into slits and licks his teeth as he walks past us into the classroom. It strikes me as an unspoken threat, and I hope he doesn't act out in front of Mrs. Greene in this class. Bet pulls back, and the air between us is charged. "I know, I can barely believe it. I've been on cloud nine all day."

"We'll get so many interested businesses. I can imagine the parking lot and all the vendors!" Bet and I talk as we enter the classroom. They take a seat so Bet can get her gear on. I'd like to stay with them, but other students want to chat, too, so I make the rounds before heading to the front and starting.

Mrs. Greene is an open book. She nods approval at our opening mantra but pulls her head back as if catching an unpleasant smell when we move to our Fighter Combinations. I'm also keeping an eye on Cooper. When he catches me he sneers, but nothing more, which is normal. It may not have anything to do with Bet at all.

"Line one, face line two." The front line does an about-face. "Line two, get shields." The back line bows and scurries to the side of the room to fetch the rectangular red padded shields. "Who can demonstrate a tornado kick?" Everyone's hand hits the air except Bet's. I call up Paige and she runs to the front, ponytail bouncing behind her. "I'll demonstrate how to hold the shield first. If you're holding for a tornado kick, you want a wide base, so step a foot back as if you're lunging. Hold the shield with one arm through the back straps and secure the top strap with the other hand. Position yourself as you would with a round kick, facing your opponent at an angle toward the kicking leg. Everyone got that?"

"Yes, sir." The class replies. Mrs. Greene likes the formal reply.

"Alright then. Paige, don't hurt me." She snorts, but her reaction doesn't slow her down. She twists around toward her back leg, lifts her front knee, jumps, and strikes with her back leg. Everyone applauds. "Well done! Alright, get to it."

I hand the shield back and head to Bet out of habit. Tornado kicks are advanced. She will benefit from having the movements broken down. I take her through one part at a time. Turning by itself. Then we turn and add the knee lift, then include the jump, all until we get to the full kick. Her long legs reach so far that I have to move to the side, and though she struggles with the jump and switching her active leg, her motions are graceful. She makes it look more like ballet than combat. For the first time, I can't tell what her mom is thinking. She's watching Bet, but her expression is… pensive.

We move to less flashy combinations on the bag before I call everyone back to their original positions on the floor. "We're getting closer to belt testing, and many of you will be expected to know your forms. If I can have brown and black belts on the left side of the room and everyone else on the right, please." There's a flurry of motion as they find new positions. "Black Belts, can I get a leader?" Cooper doesn't volunteer—definite aberrant behavior. Okay, maybe he is pissed, then. "Thanks, Roy. If you take them through our form, I'll help the others." Roy bows, "Yes, Sir."

I head across to the lower belt ranks. "Most of you will be tested on The Lion Form." I catch Bet's eye and can't resist winking, "White belts won't be tested on any form, but it won't hurt to study it now." The corners of her mouth turn up.

She's a natural. Most students here have already put The Lion to memory at some point, but even so, Bet is shaming them. It's as if having a sequence has unlocked something for her. She flows from one move to the next as expertly as anyone, and when we get to the 15th step, a hook kick, her foot arcs high above her head and lands behind her in a perfect back stance. She's intuited the next move will use the left side. Watching her pick this up effortlessly is *hot*. So distractingly hot that my pants snug, and I panic that someone might see.

I purposefully rip my eyes from her and think about anything else. Her mom is sitting in this room! Mark. Mark is coming here next week. These do the trick, and I notice Mrs. Greene is enjoying the forms and definitely not noticing my intrusive boner. Thank God.

Class dismisses and I bid everyone farewell in the lobby. Bet skips up to me and asks, "Is your toe okay?"

I have to glance down to remember I wrapped it earlier, "Oh, yeah. I forgot about it. Cracked my nail this morning trying to move fast to take Connie's call."

She nods. I have the feeling she doesn't want to leave. "We're on for Thursday? With Connie's signature, our planning session will be a piece of cake. Which is good because that's what I'm baking."

"Yes! Absolutely. What kind of cake?"

"Traditional Vegan Chocolate Cupcakes. They are everything." She walks backward to stay next to her mom. An idea strikes me.

"Happy Birthday, Bet, and thanks for coming, Mrs. Greene. Have a great night, both of you." My last word extends because Cooper shoulders me hard as he passes. The women are oblivious to this aggression.

"Excuse me, Cooper." Even though this was purposeful. Cooper doesn't turn around, but he mumbles something under his breath that sounds like *fuck you, Ted.*

25

BET

My stomach clenches with nerves getting into the car. This ended up being the perfect class for Mom to observe, thanks to us not sparring, but even so, I brace myself for her review. I'm thankful Emma and Charlie are at home. Their presence will help curtail some of Mom's scathing. The passenger side door shut, and as expected, Mom's tone is all business. "There's something important we need to address."

I train my eyes ahead, resisting the urge to roll them, and put the car in reverse. "I know you don't approve, you don't…"

"We can talk about that later. I want to talk about Emma." I see her shift uncomfortably back and forth in my periphery. "She seems stressed."

"Well, yeah." I nearly laugh. This is so unexpected from Mom, which makes it all the more alarming. "Chad is a total Chad, as ever. He doesn't help and belittles her all the time. It's disgusting."

Everything is quiet except for the click of the blinker. The tension is palpable. "I don't know them closely enough to comment on their relationship, but a marriage is a partnership, and they should be able to make it work."

I steal a glance at her before the light turns. Mom is nodding as if affirming her statement. "I think Emma's put in enough work for several people. If one half of a marriage isn't willing to *make it work*, what then?"

"It hasn't always been rainbows and butterflies for your father and I, but we made it through."

"No," I shake my head, "It's different for you and Dad. Even during your struggles, you helped each other. She doesn't seem to get any support at all... If I'm being honest, the comparing and the virtue signaling about marriages requiring hard work is why she's still with him. She'd feel guilty for leaving. Is guilt a reason to stay when you're drowning? It's fucked up."

"Language, Bethany."

"Bet." I correct her.

Her only response is a sharp little exhalation through her nose. She doesn't speak again until I pull into my apartment complex. Before I open my door, Mom breathes, "I don't want to fight. I just thought you should know... She draws a lot of influence from you."

"Is that a bad thing?" I'm unsure what she's getting at, and I can't keep the challenge out of my reply. Knowing her values, I'd usually suspect she was about to lean into me about the sanctity of their union and how I wouldn't want to contribute to a broken home, yet something about her tone was off.

Now that I can see her, Mom looks like she's struggling. "No. I don't think your influence is a bad thing. What she does needs to be the right thing for her is all."

"I don't control her, you know?" She looks at me, "I *do* know it's a big deal. Her situation is sad. It's a horrible decision to be considering. If she is considering, she hasn't brought separation up to me."

Mom smiles. Her eyes are sad, but there's a glint of pride in them, too, which takes me off guard. She unclasps her seatbelt and changes the subject as if nothing special occurred. "Ted seems mighty interesting. You want to tell me about him?"

Emma picks up on our conversation in milliseconds when we enter the door.

No, nanoseconds.

Actually, It's as if she's time-traveled and is pre-aware. "We're talking about Ted? Finally!" Charlie is wrapped in a blanket, snoozing beside her on the couch. His cherubic face is entirely at peace, and I am jealous. Emma carefully dislodges herself from his side and joins us as we sit in the kitchen.

"The first thing you need to know about Ted is you won't like him very much. He's the lead teacher, practically runs Noble, and is passionate about it."

"Why wouldn't I like him?" I hear my own challenging tone in Mom's voice as she asks.

I cock my head to the side. "Come on, you've never liked karate."

She shakes her head. "I never approved of you learning it; it's not a woman's place to be aggressive. Ted *seems* to be a man. Being able to protect is a good thing for him."

I would have rolled my eyes if I wasn't so thunderstruck. I shouldn't have been; of course, it would be fine for a man to take up something she perceives as manly. On the other hand, could Mom approve of Ted? Emma interjects, "We need to dial it back to this morning. When you and he were talking. I knew…" She quickly glances at Mom. "You didn't tell me he's into you."

"What else do I not know?" Mom asks.

"I don't know if he is. How can I be sure? I'm helping him save his school. We're kinda focused on the mission."

Emma and Mom answer at once, "He is." Mom furrows her brow, trying to put everything together. "Is that why you're meeting him?"

Emma says, "You're so into each other I felt like I was intruding on something personal sitting at the table next to you. Plus, what he said about your birthday!" I know exactly what he said about my birthday. He wasn't aware it was today. I replied he had no reason to know, and then he said, *I wish I did.* Did he mean he wished he knew or that he had a reason to know?

"It is why we're meeting," I tell Mom about the situation with Mark coming in as the new owner and our plan to revive the Fall Festival to help appease his monetary goals while retaining students and securing Ted's position. "He's a wonderful teacher. I don't know what he would do if something happened to Noble."

Mom huffs a laugh. When I arch a brow, she says, "He *is* a good teacher."

"I'm surprised you're being so positive about all this."

"While I don't condone barbaric fighting, I am a realist. Besides, even if the subject matter is unrefined, it doesn't influence his teaching. What I want to know is why you aren't dating already?"

"You both seem confident he's into me, but we aren't dating because he hasn't asked me out. Soooo?"

They answer simultaneously again, but their replies aren't in unison this time.

"Why don't you ask him out?" Emma asks.

"That is a problem." Mom asserts. They look at each other, and to my disbelief, Mom amends, "Yeah, why don't you ask him out?"

My jaw drops in Mom's direction. I mouth wordlessly

like a fish out of water trying to breathe, which is precisely how I feel internally, too. I clamp my mouth and eyes shut to collect myself, then manage to ask, "This is your advice?!"

Mom puts her hand to her heart. "Why not?"

I can't help but glare. "When I was in high school and mustered up the courage to ask out a boy I liked, your response was to say he would think I was desperate." It was a particularly painful interaction because the boy said yes, and I was so excited and proud. Mom's reaction cut straight through those happy feelings, leaving them shredded at my feet.

"Of all the advice I've given you, this is the one that stuck?" Mom laughs so hard she snorts. "I'm sorry, oh, Bethany - Bet. *I* would never ask out a guy, but you're not me."

I shoot a wide-eyed look at Emma and tip my head slightly toward Mom. She's being weird. She called me Bet! Emma shrugs almost imperceptibly, then says, "You could, you know, ask him. He would definitely say yes."

"Thank you both for taking me out today. Mini golf and birthday lunch were the best. I think Charlie might be a shark at golf. Watch out, PGA!" It's a sincere thanks, but I'm happy to avert the topic of conversation away from Ted.

Emma's eyes crinkle at the corners. "You like how he swung the putter from between his legs and chased after the ball in an impossible way to count swings?"

"All I'm saying is he won, and at such a tender age. We could all learn from his methods."

"One method being declaring yourself the winner regardless of what has occurred," Mom smirks.

I reply, "See. You're getting it. What a positive mindset!"

Thankfully, the conversation remains light until Mom excuses herself. I wait for 30 minutes after I see the light turn off from beneath the bedroom door before I steer Emma and me into the quagmire. "I'm so happy you and Charlie came to visit. I needed this carefree time."

Emma smiles but sighs heavily. "Me. Too."

"Have things gotten any better with Chad?" I ask as gently as possible.

Emma stares at the warm bundle on the couch, his chest rising and falling beneath the blankets. She answers after a long while in a whisper, "No matter how hard I try, I keep imagining what life would be like if… If things were different."

"Different, how?"

She drags her eyes back to me, and I'm surprised there's no hint of tearfulness. Something else is present, a hardness to Emma I can't remember seeing before. "It's not right to think about it, but if we were separated."

"Thinking about things isn't a crime. Don't be so hard…"

Emma cuts me off, "It is when you're thinking about it the way I am."

I'm bewildered. My eyes focus on different things around the room. "What do you mean? Like murder?"

"No! No! Bet, Geez!"

"You said it was criminal! I was trying to remember the best way to hide a body! Jesus, Emma!"

"No. I mean, they should be criminal because it's like," She pauses a long moment, and her voice is weaker. This is hard for her to talk about, even with me. "It's like a fantasy. It's like I'm fantasizing about leaving him. It's stupid." She shakes her head and looks down at her hands in her lap.

"It's not stupid. You're not stupid, and I'll thank you to stop talking about my friend that way." She gives a weak laugh. "I knew having him back home wasn't going as you wanted. When did you start having these fantasies?"

"Ugh. I don't know. Over time, I guess? Months ago, they were these tiny intrusive thoughts. Like, I could get a job. Or, my parents and friends would help with Charlie. But I snuffed them out easily. Now, it's like a whole narrative. Like watching a movie of how life would be if we weren't, you know, together."

My heart is pounding away in my chest. Emma has always been too good for Chad. She deserves so much more: to be honored for who she is, not molded into some dude's idea of a trophy wife. At the same time, Mom's voice echoes in my mind. I'm always hesitant about this topic. It's her decision. I don't want to misstep. "Did you ever get to talk to him about all this?"

She sighs. "I try. He avoids talking about the things I'm unhappy or frustrated with. If I push it, we get into an argument. He yells, and it scares Charlie. His reaction makes it worse. It's like reinforcing he doesn't care about me anymore. Not enough to have a hard conversation let alone try to change. He's traveling again next week, so we won't have a chance to talk face-to-face after Sunday."

"It's gotta be hard not being able to speak your piece. Then, sitting on it while he's away. The whole situation sucks."

"Exactly! I don't want to be separated- divorced. And Charlie. I know we would co-parent, and Chad would be in his life, but being in a broken home. My kid being raised in a broken home?" She shakes her head as if the idea is unfathomable. "I never wanted this."

"What *do* you want?" During these heavy conversations, Emma is usually adamant that she wants Chad and her to be happy and in love and to live the picket fence dream of her childhood.

"I want... authenticity. I don't want to wear makeup and do my hair to go to the post office. I want to be silly with Charlie and not worry about what other people think. It would be great to be with someone who thought I was beautiful in the unfiltered moments, but I would take just the moments themselves." When she finishes, she looks shocked. Then tears do well in her eyes.

I grab her hand from her lap and squeeze, holding it tight, focusing on being an anchor for her. "You deserve to be you, without any airs. Have you met you? You're an amazing Mom and friend; you're funny, smart, and kind. I mean, who goes out of their way to save house spiders? Not to mention…" I ogle her up and down and, in my most over-the-top voice, exclaim, "GORGEOUS!"

Emma laughs despite herself. "I pay you to say that."

"Uh," I furrow my brow and scratch my temple. We'll have to talk about my wages then."

THE NIGHT SPEEDS BY, and I ignore the clock until I absolutely can't. I don't want Emma to leave, but I have to work early today, and she, Charlie, and Mom will be driving back to Marysville. I turn off my alarm as soon as it sounds, praying it doesn't wake Emma. We're both operating on two hours of sleep at most.

I'm pouring my coffee into my trusty travel mug when Mom pads into the kitchen. "I want a hug before you go to work."

I open my arms, and Mom embraces me; she's much shorter than me, and I can almost rest my chin on her head. "Thank you again for such a wonderful birthday visit. Really."

We break apart, and Mom smiles at me. "Thank you for hosting us. I want to tell you, Bet, even though I don't always understand your decisions or always agree with them. I see how you're doing good for yourself. You're supporting yourself. You seem happy." I can hardly believe it. Mom's behavior has been unusual these past few days, but now... I think she's trying to accept who I am?

"I am happy, and thank you. For calling me Bet."

She waves her hand. "That will take some getting used to."

I smirk. "Well, I do have to roll."

"Are you going to ask out that boy? Ted?" She says it fast like it's all one word.

"I don't know. Maybe."

"I hope you do."

"Have a safe drive back, Mom. I love you."

"Love you, too."

My brain feels off-kilter under the strain of many things demanding attention. Emma and Chad. Mom trying to do... What? Turn a new leaf? The Fall Festival and Ted. Woven through everything, Ted.

26

TED

Thursday is quickly becoming my favorite day of the week, though it's in stiff competition with Tuesday. Waking up this morning feels like being a different person. Or maybe it's more like being the old Ted from when Phil was alive, and things were simple. What I know for sure is that I woke up rested, happy, and looking forward to the day. Yes, Bet will be in class tonight, and we're meeting afterward to plan out the Chamber of Commerce meeting. I even have a little surprise planned for her, but it's more than the prospect of seeing her. Since getting Connie's sign-off, everything feels hopeful. Achievable. It's amazing what two days of carrying a tiny seed of hope will do for a person.

Everything has been so rushed recently, but I intentionally take my time before heading to Noble today. Pure decompression, I flick through videos in my TikTok feed while sipping coffee, my feet propped up on a table. Until one advertises a free yoga class online.

Bet does yoga.

I click the link, and it opens to a site touting a subscription service, but there it is, a free video front and center, so you can try before you buy. I note this as a promising strategy I may be able to use for Noble and open the video.

A cool, calm voice gives an introduction to the class. Nobody talks like this, and it gives the video an inauthentic feeling. Things get more interesting when the moves, or they called it a 'flow,' begin at least. The first few steps are easy until the annoying, tranquil voice addresses common form problems, and I start correcting my posture. How am I supposed to breathe deeply and hold the proper position simultaneously? There's too much to focus on. Plus, Hitch keeps winding his body through all the positions. The serene instructor announces she'll demonstrate advanced moves in the last ten minutes. I admit, when I started this, I didn't think yoga would be challenging, but my muscles are spent. I'm a long way from achieving the King Pigeon and Twisted Bow Pose.

"I think Bet might be stronger than she looks." Hitch replies with a chirruping purr-meow hybrid and bumps his head against my hand.

By the time Advanced Class starts, I haven't lost the feel-good energy of the morning. There's been even more sign-ups for Parents' Night Out, and I have something with fluttering wings popping in and out of me, knowing that Bet will walk in any minute. When she does step in, the light shines off her inky hair. How would it be to run my hands through her hair? We could lay beside each other, and I'd count every strand. She smiles and waves at me before gearing up.

The class is going smoothly, and though I'm enjoying it, I have to resist counting down the minutes until I meet with her. We've got 20 minutes left when the front door opens. I glance through the lobby window, and my heart drops through my feet. It's Phil. Except it can't be. I jog closer, and the change in distance reveals the differences. This man is shorter and rounder, and there's a subtle unscrupulousness about his expression that I never saw on Phil. "Mark, I didn't expect you until next week." I hold out my hand to shake his. He looks caught off guard that I've recognized him, but it only lasts a moment before he's sneering at the hand extended toward him. Despite the reaction, he does return my handshake. His hand feels oily in mine, but I'm unsure if it's in my head.

"You claimed there was nothing you needed to do to prepare." It's an accusation. He must think he's about to discover the school is in shambles.

I make the instant decision to be as nice as possible because I think it will piss him off. "There isn't! I'm truly glad you're here; I can't wait to show you around. Do you want to see a class in action? Our Advanced Class is happening now, and they're exciting to watch."

"I can see them fine from here." He points toward the window.

"Then you can see how talented they are. Would you like to see our computer? I could show you the calendar, student roster, financials?" These are all things I've shown and discussed with Mark before via email and phone call. "Or I could give you the tour of the building and our equipment? I think you'll find it all in good condition."

"Computer first." Mark's voice couldn't be more different from Phil's. I'd already known that, but seeing how similarly they look makes the gruffness of his timbre stand out even more. Perhaps he started smoking young.

"Right this way." I lead him around the front desk and log in.

"What's the password?"

I struggle for a fraction of a second. I don't want to give it to him, but I can't think of any reason to withhold it. "It's noble life but spelled like capital N - o - b - l - e - capital L -

the number 1 - f - number 3 - exclamation point." He doesn't write it down. Maybe he won't remember.

The Calendar loads on the screen automatically, so I take Mark through it first, pointing out the Parents' Night Out addition on the 3rd Friday of each month. He grunts at this, but when I get to the financial reports, which show the additional $350 for this week, he points a finger and asks, "What's this line from?"

"That's from the Parents' Night Out. I put up the offer earlier today but already had 14 families sign up. I'm charging $25 per family. There'll be something like 20 kids here. I think it will get more popular over time and with the consistent scheduling. Good, right?"

"That… is good." His response is reluctant. I swear he seems upset he can't find a reason to complain.

Moreover, I'm not sure he knows why he's here. He had nothing to add regarding what I showed him on the computer. This meeting feels directionless. "I can show you around the building if you'd like?" I offer.

Another grunt before acquiescing.

"This is our lobby, of course, and we have a small…"

"It stinks in here." Mark's eyes travel to the pile of shoes in the far corner.

"Yes," I agree, sticking to my killing him with kindness approach, "I do clean every night and spray air freshener between classes, but the smell of shoes and sweat is unavoidable in our business." When he doesn't reply, I resume the tour. "This is a small conference area we use to talk privately with people. Usually with new clients who have questions but also parents who want progress updates on their students. I also keep the gear we have for sale in this locker." I knock on the dark blue metal. "This is a convenient place so students can try different sizes if they aren't sure before buying."

Mark scrutinizes the gear within the locker. The uniforms are tidily folded and organized by size. All the other gear (helmets, gloves, shin pads, vests, mouthpieces) has its own bin. After a long moment, he asks, "What's the margin on these?"

"Margin is favorable. Depending on the gear, it's anywhere from 60-80%." His eyes widen. Impressed despite himself.

"How often do students need to buy new gear?"

"Not often. For adults, rarely if they take care of it. For kids, they may need to size up as they grow."

Mark twirls his finger around his stubbly goatee. "Anyway we can sell more would be good. Maybe they should expire after a year?"

My blood is boiling. I want to yell that I would never take advantage of our students, but I swallow the biting words rising in my throat. "Our specialized weapons class works similarly. We study a new weapon each quarter, so students purchase those until they have a full collection." A thoughtful expression crosses Mark's eyes, and he asks to see the weapons. "Sure, I keep them in the back office." He follows me through the class. Bet shoots a questioning look at me, and I shake my head slightly in answer. As we exit the class through the back door, I resume giving the tour. "The bathrooms are here," I point to the left, "over here is the equipment we don't use as often, but is still good to have handy, "I indicate the folding table with medicine balls, ropes, and rope ladders beneath it, loaner gear lays on the top, but I decline to explain what it is, "and this is the back office." I switch the light on as we walk through the door to the small room. "I use it mostly for storage since the computer is at the front. The weapons stay here because of their size and to keep them out of the eyesight of passersby."

Mark walks the perimeter of the room, touching everything as he goes. He slides a finger up a bo staff, sets the hanging nunchucks to swaying, and picks up a sword. He admires it until he sees the kamas, then carelessly drops it back into its bucket and hungrily picks up two kamas. "What are these?" The air before him cuts with a 'whoosh' as he swipes the blades viciously. I take a step back.

"They're called Kamas or Sahn Knat. They're inspired by sickles."

"Like the Grim Reaper." It's the most excited I've ever heard him sound, and the pleasure he takes in the analogy turns my stomach. Not for the first time, I wonder how Phil was so knowledgeable and involved in martial arts while his brother appears to know nothing.

Our interaction is going well enough so far, so I dare to ask, "So, why didn't you learn this stuff with Phil? He started as a kid, right? Did you take karate together?" Mark's smile slides off his face, and he pushes the kamas back onto the shelf.

"No," he states definitively. I don't think he'll share anything else, but then he continues: "Phil was always the special one. Even now, everyone thinks so, and he's dead!" Mark is shouting, and I pray the class has already been dismissed so they can't hear him. He steps directly in front of me and pushes his finger into my chest. "And you. You think so even after he betrayed you!"

I step back toward the doorway reflexively. "What do you mean?"

Mark sucks his teeth. His voice is suddenly lower as if he, too, is aware others may be listening. "You know what I mean. Supposed to leave you this school, wasn't he? Promised it to you." My breath stalls out. I'm so shocked the room seems to tilt. How does Mark know? He relishes my reaction and chuckles softly before clicking his tongue and adding, "He didn't, though. I'm here now, and you must do exactly what I say."

"Is everything okay?" Bet walks into the back, sweat dripping down her brow, followed immediately by Cooper. "I thought I heard something."

I'm gripping the doorframe so hard my hand aches, and I quickly let it go and stand upright. "Everything's fine." I try to convey more with my eyes. "Just giving Mark the tour. I think we're wrapping up now." I look at the man, and he nods, but not before I notice the glance he exchanges with Cooper, which weighs heavily with the unspoken. Great.

The four of us walk to the front lobby. We're the only people left in the building. Mark turns awkwardly at the door. "Thanks, uh, for showing me around. I'll be in touch." His final words sound more like a threat than they have any right to. He leaves, and Cooper follows him into the parking lot without a word.

I watch them from the window. They briefly exchange words before Mark waves Cooper off dismissively, and he jogs to his truck.

Bet stands beside me, taking in the same view. "That's Mark, huh?" I dip my chin, still gazing out the window. Both men have driven off. "He seems like a real peach." I want to say something. I know I should reply in a lighthearted way. I know she's trying to break whatever tension she's picking up on, but his words are pounding in my head on repeat. *He promised the school to you. He betrayed you.* Everything happened so fast. How did we even get there? To that conversation?

My hand is suddenly warm, and I see Bet twining her fingers in mine. At my glance, she hesitates and sucks in a breath. My eyes find hers. "Is this… Are you okay?" Is she seeking permission to hold my hand, asking about me, or both?

Her touch lightens the heaviness on my chest, and I'm able to reply. "Yes. No. He... Things were going okay at first."

She squeezes my hand. "It's lucky he came in early, in a way. Tonight, of all nights, right before we practice. Now we have the fuel to be more determined than ever."

27

BET

*T*ed was so shaken after whatever happened in the back room I wondered if he would cancel our meeting tonight. The whole thing was strange. When Mark entered, it was like he saw a ghost- or even became one. His face went so pale, but then he went to greet him, and when he came back through the classroom to the back, he looked fine. He even winked, indicating he'd tell me more later. When Mark started yelling, the class had been dismissed, and it was only Cooper and I sitting in tense silence, waiting. But truthfully, Mark's yelling shouldn't have stolen Ted's spark. It sounded more like a man-sized hissy fit than anything else.

I thought of what might have happened all the way home, Ted driving behind me. How did Cooper fit into everything? I tried not to even look at him for the few minutes we were alone together and felt he was doing the same. Cooper had asserted that someone else could take over the school if Ted were let go, and the way he said it screamed that he was interested. Would he go as far as colluding with Mark? Thinking of it makes me feel dirty for having dated him. I wondered about nibbling on his muscles, for Christ's sake. Gross.

Ted carries in a folder and lays it on the kitchen table. His color is back, but there's still something hollow about him. "What happened back there? You said things had been going well?"

He shakes his head, and the perpetually misplaced curl of hair sweeps his brow. "Can we talk about the Chamber instead?" He asks so delicately it cracks my heart.

"Yes. Of course."

Ted extracts a small stack of papers from the folder and pulls a laptop from a bag I hadn't noticed. "I started making a presentation. They have a projector I can use with my computer, but I've never done anything like this before. I want to make sure I'm not missing anything and that it makes sense and looks at least halfway decent?" I laugh, and he chuckles at my reaction. His shoulders relax, falling an inch. The muscles along his neck elongate with the motion.

"I've never done anything quite like this either, but I'm sure we can do it. Then Abby can tell us where we royally fucked up and fix it." His lips curl upward, and gods, they are full.

"You're right. Okay, these papers are all the plans Abby had jotted down. If we go through them together, I'll show you the presentation, and we can compare."

We flip through Abby's outlines, spending the most time on the financial proposals. Her wording about *taking a stab* at putting them together was a gross misrepresentation of what we were looking at. These were thorough. Professional in a way I've never seen before, even from Lily's bookkeeping (which perhaps shouldn't be a shocker, but it's my exclusive source for comparison). She'd even gone as far as to make three projections, each calculating profitability based on a low, medium, or high number of vendor participants and what we should charge them to be profitable under each circumstance. Ted squints at the estimations, his thick eyebrows drawing together to form a severe line. "Hmm. We won't know how many will sign up, and we can't exactly change the cost of participation after the fact."

"True. Could we take a tiered approach? Early sign-ups start at a lower rate, but it hikes up two weeks before the festival. It makes sense because we'd probably have to edit the mapping. More labor."

"Hmm, Ted nods to himself, "I've seen karate camps do something similar to encourage timely replies. Yeah. Should we start at the middle fee? I want to maximize vendors, but I just don't know how the response will be."

I lean over to review the cost difference and try to think about Daisy's. "It's only a $50 difference between low and medium. I don't think $50 would deter signups. It's so low to a business that it wouldn't matter. So yeah, I'd start in the medium."

Ted types on his laptop; the screen's glow softly illuminates his face and reflects off his glasses. Full of concentration, his jaw flexes, causing a shadow to fall under his cheekbone. "Got it in. You said two weeks before the festival, which is October 1st. Let's go with September 27th then, the start of the week." He lifts his eyes to mine, and I fall into the dark brown behind the lenses. "Ready for this?"

I know he means the presentation, but my heart flutters like his question is full of possibility. "Yeah, run me through- I mean give me the run through- I mean... I'm ready." My cheeks are on fire with embarrassment. Ted glances down, but I still see the left side of his lips quirk up in a smirk. Before I can process this reaction, his chair scrapes back, and he turns the computer to face me. He stands directly behind my chair, leaning over me to reach the laptop's trackpad. Though he changed out of his uniform, his scent is intense after a day of working out. Not unpleasant- he smells like himself, but more, and I wish I could bathe in it. Huff his neck. A tingling sensation starts between my legs, and I clench my eyes closed, pushing my desires aside so I can focus on this presentation.

"I'll start by reminding everyone what the Fall Festival used to be like. My mom found some pictures, and I got some online, too." Ted flips to a slide covered in photos.

"Oh my God, is that you?!" I don't have to ask. It couldn't be anyone else. In the picture, Ted must be around eight years old and looks exactly like a kid version of himself. His dark locks were messy back then, too.

"Yeah, and that's my dad," He points to the adult behind him, "I was waiting in line to get my face painted. I can't believe you could tell."

"It would be stranger to miss it. You look exactly like a younger version of you."

Ted scrutinizes the photo, insists he doesn't see it and moves to the next slide. "Then I let them know we're reviving it. I've got all the details, the date, location, which will be familiar, the cost to rent a space, how to sign up, and what to expect after..." His sentence has the feeling of hanging.

"What?"

"It seems too simple. What am I missing?"

I relax into my chair, thinking, my hair brushes against Ted's chest, and he takes a seat again. "You've got all the information needed, for sure, and even a sort of nostalgic plea with the photos. This is really good!" I can see his ideas racing behind his eyes. "You know what helps me think?"

"Hmm?"

"Baking."

My legs tremble at the smile that erupts on Ted's face. He raises from his seat before I do. "It's still cake today?"

"Yes. Chocolate Cupcakes! Mmm, you're going to love them." I roll my eyes back in faux ecstasy for emphasis.

The most complicated bit of the batter recipe is making the vegan buttermilk, which is easy. So it isn't long before four batches of cupcakes are in the oven, and we start whipping up the icing. Despite his smiling and our easy conversation, I can tell something is bothering Ted. He seems on edge. I want to ask again, but he said he didn't want to discuss it. So, instead, I ask, "So, what did you get your face painted as?"

He stifles a laugh, "I asked for Bart Simpson, thinking she'd do a Bart cartoon on my cheek with a skateboard. She interpreted the request... differently." I stop my mixer and turn to him in question. "She..." He laughs in earnest, "My mom was so mad. She painted my whole face yellow and made big white circles around my eyes. It was so bad, and the paint got everywhere! My hair, my shirt."

"Where? Ted... This is important. Where is the picture of that?"

Ted laughs again, and it's unbridled, almost a fit. "No. That doesn't exist. I mentioned Mom was mad, right?"

"I cannot believe your turning into real-life Bart Simpson wasn't documented. This is a travesty! A complete miscarriage of justice!" I'm laughing now, too, and Ted seems a little better. Lighter than he has since Mark left, to be sure.

Ted reaches over me to turn the stand mixer back on and asks, "What about you? Any face painting mishaps in your childhood?"

"No," I shake my head, "well... No, it's not the same."

"Spill the beans, Bet. You owe me a story." He tilts his head down, and I avert my gaze so I don't drown in those deep brown eyes. Maybe the spears of gold could act as a floatation device?

"When I was a kid, we had azaleas all over; everyone grew them, and they were at our school. These huge azalea hedges were big enough to crawl into, and it was like our own little world inside of them. Me and my friends would crush up the pink flowers and use them as blush and lipstick." I trade out the bowl to start making the second batch of icing. "When I was older, and all my friends started wearing real makeup, I wasn't allowed yet. I was supposed to wait until I was 15. I was getting teased about it, and one day, I had the idea to crush up an azalea like we used to. Except my memories of how we used to look so elegant were absolutely influenced by my child eyes. The color was so bright and didn't come off; it was like a stain everywhere it touched. I probably looked like you did, only pink, so I was a laughing stock all day, and when I got home, my dad said I deserved it for trying to skirt his rules." Ted presses his lips so firmly together that the skin around them is white. I roll my eyes and tell him, "Go ahead."

He lets loose, and I secretly bathe in his mahogany baritone laughter. "I'm sorry; yours is so, so much worse than mine."

"Is it? It probably looked like you were jaundiced as hell." I smile coyly at him. "Oh! Oh!" I grab his forearm, and he looks at my change of tone with alarm. I spin toward the table, but the oven alarm goes off at the same time. "Ugh!" I circle back up and retrieve the cupcakes.

"What's up? What is it?" Ted asks.

"I know what's missing! I've got it!" I practically fling the trays of cupcakes onto the counter in my haste to see the slides.

"Hey! Don't abuse the baked goods, Bet. Don't you want to poke them and test for readiness?"

"Don't be silly; they're perfect." I finally twirl back to the computer and slide to where it should fit. "Here. Right after the details, but before you tell them how to sign up, explain why it's beneficial for them to do so. Sell it."

Ted's eyes widen, and he slides into the chair beside me. "Of course!" He starts typing, and I get up to test the cupcakes. "I thought they were perfect?" He hasn't even turned around.

"They are… but I gotta check." After confirming and finding them flawless, I take each cupcake out of the tin and place them carefully onto the cooling racks on the counter. The sound of typing on and off reaches me from the table. When I turn to rejoin him, he's turned around in his chair, looking at me. Was he biting his lip? Bright headlights flood through my window, and his face changes so fast it's probably a trick of the light.

"Alright, how's this?" He gestures to the new material, and we hone the wording and do a few run-throughs as the cupcakes cool.

Usually, letting baked goods cool seems to take forever, but tonight, the time flies by, and when the alarm goes off, it startles me. I think Ted is reaching for my hand, maybe to calm me down, but then he's digging in the computer bag, and I'm up to load the piping bags. "Have you ever used one of these?" I hand Ted a filled bag.

"That's a big negative. Should I not do this part? I know it's important they look good."

I swat his question away. "No, you're going to be a natural. Besides, you can at least try on our couple of test cupcakes, and if you're awful, we'll reassess."

He chuckles and follows me to the counter. "You're the boss."

I demonstrate how to grip the bag, pushing the icing down toward the tip, then apply a wide circle around the perimeter of the cake and increasingly smaller circles traveling upward to make a classic swirl effect. "Tada! Now you try."

The level of concentration on Ted's face rivals the time I

saw him beating that bag to a pulp. I can't peel my eyes away from him to watch the results of his efforts, so the first time I see his cupcake is when he pulls back and announces he's done.

"Alright!" I pick up the cupcake to see it from each vantage point. "This is a great first attempt, Ted. I'm impressed. Let's try on..." I start to say another, but Ted has put a candle in the top of the cupcake and lit it.

"Happy Birthday, Bet." His voice is a rumble, and he's suddenly very close.

"I... Where did this candle come from?" The glow from the flame flickers across him; his throat bobs, and he steps closer still. His hands are on my hips.

"Make a wish." I am too stunned to actually do so, but the swooping feeling in my stomach makes me believe it may come true anyway. I lock eyes with him and blow out the candle.

He gently pulls me toward him, and I set aside the cupcake without regard for whether it lands nicely or crashes to the floor. Ted presses his forehead to mine. I relish his ability to do so, that he's a little taller than me. My hands stroke up his back, and then, as if on cue, we angle our heads up so our lips brush against each other. I can barely breathe. His lips are full and firm, and when he deepens our kiss, our tongues exploring each other, I feel like I'm melting into him. He cups my cheeks with his hands, tenderness at a juxtaposition with the passion of our mouths. His beard scratches against my skin, and I crave the roughness of it.

Bright lights flash through my window. On and off. On and off. How long have they been there? It disrupts everything- everything, and we pull away from each other. Ted stares at the window, "What is happening out there?"

I'm already storming toward it to find out. "No clue." It's dark outside, and there's no vehicle in the space in front of the window. I just make out a truck exiting onto the street in the distance. "Nothing out here." Whatever was flashing is gone, and many more important things are on my mind. I whirl toward Ted and find he's followed me to the window. "You brought me a birthday candle." It's an accusation and a question.

"I did."

"You kissed me."

"I did. I… I hope it was okay. It just felt like…," but my mouth is on his before he can finish his sentence. Let there be no doubt that it was okay. Zero.

28

TED

The sky outside is growing the slightest touch lighter. I check my phone, it's 5:23 am. I've been at Bet's house for approximately seven hours and twelve minutes, and I'm horrified it will have somehow been a dream if I leave. No, staying here is the thing to do. If I stay, the sound of her sleeping in the room next door reassures me that I haven't made anything up. Last night was real. We kissed, and the absolute thrill of it was like being a teenager again, except we were much better at it than I remember from those days. We'd kissed, then spent the entirety of the night talking about everything. The story of our lives unfurled around us as we sat, legs entwined, on the couch.

I hear the sound of sheets moving from the bedroom. Bet had fallen asleep on the couch at 4:30 am, practically mid-sentence. I'd scooped her up and carried her to the bed, hoping she could rest better there, then returned to the couch. I should have tried to sleep here, but my brain won't stop. We kissed! And what does it mean? Plus, the countdown to the Chamber and today's schedule. It's the first Parents' Night Out, followed by Dungeons & Dragons. Bet offered to help me with PNO when I mentioned it last night, but I'm not sure if she'll remember. And finally, sneaking in side blows amongst all the wonderful things, Mark's words. *Phil promised to leave you the school and betrayed you.*

"Ted?" Bet's voice sounds croakily from the bedroom. The question in it makes me smile.

"I'm here." I walk the short distance to her bedroom doorway but don't enter.

"Oh." Her hair is sticking this way and that, and she is so beautiful the air is sucked away from me, and I can barely breathe. "How did I get in here?"

"You fell asleep on the couch, so I carried you." Her expression is hard to read for a beat, then she laughs. "Can I make you some coffee or breakfast or anything?"

"What?! Ted, you don't have to…"

"I want to."

She looks around the small room. "What time is it?"

"5:30ish, probably. You can go back to sleep if you need…" Yet as I speak, she's hastily getting up.

"I need to get ready!" Bet looks at me, "I… You… Last night was amazing. I wish I could stay and have a lazy day with you."

My heart is somewhere above the building. "Yes. It was amazing for me, too. I understand you have to go, though. I'll see you later tonight."

"At Parents' Night Out and D&D! Definitely." She does remember. "Um, I'm going to take a quick shower. You can too, I mean, after- or you could have before, I wouldn't have minded."

I shake my head. "It's okay. I've got time to check on Hitch and clean up before Noble opens."

Bet is walking into the bathroom with a handful of clothes but stops to swoon over Hitch. "I'm so jealous! I can't wait to meet him, the little hitchhiker." We'd talked about Hitch and how I'd come to adopt him last night.

The bathroom door clicks shut, and I wander into the kitchen. I'm not totally unfamiliar with the small room, and luckily, I find it easy to get coffee going and start some fried eggs and toast. When Bet emerges from the bathroom, fresh-faced and hair wet, I'm already tipping the eggs onto a plate. "Voila!"

She looks conflicted about something for half a second before it passes into a smile and thanks. Bet dips a bit of toast into the yolk and says, "I never thought about how different our schedules are. You get to sleep in if you want; when is the first class?"

I nod. "True. Unless there's a special event, my earliest classes are at one. You wake up this early every morning?"

"Most days, yes. It's a bit more volatile depending on what orders are like and when they need to be delivered." She shrugs. "It works out for me. I can deliver the baked goods bright and early to Gerard. Did you get any sleep?"

I scoff. "Are you counting the one hour you got as sleep?!"

"Better than nothing."

"Yeah, I might. I'll probably text Abby to let her know we're ready for the Chamber of Commerce, get washed up, feed Hitch, and maybe try to rest."

Bet stands and grabs her purse from the back of the chair. I take the cue, grab my computer bag, and follow her out the door. "Thank you for breakfast. I hope you do take a nap, and I'll see you later."

I want to kiss her goodbye but instead reply, "Anytime. See you soon."

I shoot Abby some messages before driving home, then do exactly as described: Shower, brush my teeth, feed Hitch, and pass out.

. . .

PETALS & PUNCHES

THE ALARM SOUNDS TOO SOON. My eyes are the only heavy thing about me, though; the rest of my body still feels elated. Though I still don't know what last night made us, Bet said it was amazing, and more than that, she was looking forward to meeting my cat. That has to mean something good.

As I turn off the loud jingle on my phone, the red dot on my Messages app catches my eye.

Ted Dawson

> Bet and I met and I think we're ready for the Chamber next week. Sending a presentation I made. 5:55 AM

ABBY Taylor

> FFS why are you texting before 6? 9:23 AM

ABBY Taylor

> Oh, this is really good! Great job, you two! 9:40 AM

ABBY Taylor

> Wait... Why WERE you texting so early? 9:42 AM

The smart thing would have been to wait to send those out. Do I want Abby to know I stayed over at Bet's? Nothing happened- or everything happened. But Abby will pump me for every detail, and I don't know...

Ted Dawson

> I'll explain later 10:01 AM

I suddenly realize I need to be clearer, unless I want to tell the entire gang in front of Bet.

Ted Dawson

> NOT AT D&D 10:02 AM

Abby Taylor

> lololol OKAY 10:05 AM

Despite my exhaustion, the day speeds by. Pleasant recollections of things Bet shared with me interrupting my routine. Her favorite color is forest green. Her favorite subject in school was Science, and she'd fallen in love with baking in Home Economics. She attributed her vegan baking and enjoying floristry as the intersection of those things.

She'd wanted to go to community college but could never afford it, which used to be a point of shame. Now, after years of on-the-job business experience, she feels better about it. She's fiercely independent, which I already knew, but her awareness of it runs deep, and she'd talked about how she sometimes struggles with accepting help.

I wonder if she's recalling our late-night stories, too.

Bet arrives a few minutes before Parents' Night Out begins. I raise a coffee cup in greeting, and her smile stops my world. Her white teeth always seem to shine compared to the blackness of her hair. "You're a lifesaver!" She grabs the cup and immediately sips from it, bouncing on the balls of her feet.

"I can't believe you're still upright! You… you don't have to help or hang out tonight. You should get some sleep."

"No, no. I'm okay. I'm not saying adrenaline isn't the only thing keeping me going, but I'm okay." She pauses, then adds, "Plus, I couldn't miss this."

The door opens and the first few families stream in behind her. "Sarah, Mo, Paul, I hope you're ready to have some fun."

Sarah clings to her mom's pants. When she doesn't let go, her mom leans over and they exchange words, but it must not have been what Sarah wanted to hear because she starts crying and whines, "No! Mommy, I don't want to!"

Recognizing the familiar scene, I start toward them from behind the counter, but Bet beats me to them. She kneels in front of Sarah. The light sparkling in her eyes doesn't betray her lack of rest. "Hi, I'm Bet. What's your name?"

Sarah sniffs and looks apprehensively at her mom. "Sarah."

"Sarah, what a beautiful name! And are you… four years old?" She nods. "Oh wow, I have a nephew named Charlie, and he's three years old. Do you remember being three?"

"No."

Bet shakes her head. "I don't either. I bet you can do a ton more stuff now that you're four, though! Have you ever played hopscotch?"

"I can!" Sarah's grip relaxes, and she drops her mom's clothing. "I can do lots!"

"Because you're so smart and strong, Sarah! Could I ask you a favor? Could you help me set up a hopscotch game in there?" She points to the classroom. "Maybe we can even make a whole obstacle course." Her eyes shoot to mine in question, and I nod. "Ooh! Mr. Ted approves!"

"I can help!" Sarah is positively excited now and takes Bet's proffered hand. "Bye, Mom." Sarah's mom mouths a thanks to Bet and waves as the two enter the classroom.

"She's great. New teacher?" Her mom asks on the way out.

"No, she's an adult student helping for the night."

"Hmm, too bad."

Am I surprised Bet is incredible with kids? No. She's incredible at everything, but seeing her jump in to help someone and forge an instant connection with them. I was not prepared for how much it would affect me. This was a woman with whom I would raise children. Maybe it's an insane thing to think after just kissing last night and being unclear on our dating status, but fine. I'll own my unsound mind.

Her prowess didn't stop there. The obstacle course proved to be an outstanding hit, entertaining the kids for over an hour, and by the time they grew bored of it, she was ready with another idea. "Bring me that pool noodle." Sarah obediently jumps to the task. "Hmm." Bet rolls the foam in her hands. "Will anything fit snuggly in the middle?"

I jog to the back room and bring out a bo, a nunchuck, and a combat stick to test. The padded bo works well, and she brings her new gadget to the middle of the floor. "Everyone make a circle around me. If you get hit with the noodle, you're out." Bet spins with the noodle on the ground, and everyone tries to jump it. Then she raises it, so they have to duck instead. Once they all get the basic rules, she leaves her post so someone else can be in the middle and returns to my side.

"You're a genius. How'd you come up with that?"

Bet shrugs. "It's not my idea. I've seen it somewhere before."

"I was just going to play a movie. This has all been so much better."

"A movie is good, too!"

"Yeah, but they've been busy all night this way. I enjoy watching out for them and talking to you." I lean toward her, nudging her with my shoulder. She returns the pressure.

The kids modify the rules by themselves and play until their parents arrive to pick them up. Bet and I chat casually about our days between minor interventions needed to keep the peace and good times going. It's not a deep conversation, not like last night, but it's as natural as coming home from work would be any time. It's like I remember my mom and dad doing growing up.

When everyone is gone, Noble is cleaned and locked, and I've changed into jeans and a T-shirt, we head to Mitch's house.

29

BET

Okay, so I'm exhausted (yet again), but I can't stay away. Thinking about skipping D&D is a nonstarter. Ted is some drug, and I'm totally addicted. Besides, I'd just be baking at my house.

When we pull into Mitch's driveway, Ted comes to help me unload all the ingredients and cooking supplies from the car. Pumpkin pie is on the menu tonight. I chose it because it's not too fussy, and I can use some of the pie crust I keep on hand in the freezer. Fun fact: You can freeze homemade pie crust for up to three months. I always keep a few recipes on hand in case I need an easy night.

Ted leads the way up the ramp to the front porch laden with a bag full of pie plates and flour over a shoulder and a stand mixer and bowl in the other hand. His jeans are hugging his ass in a way that makes me want to hug his ass too, and I consider pinching him for a moment, but the door opens, and Abby steps out. "Can I help carry anything?"

"Sure, thank you! There's a blender and, I think, one more bag in the back seat." She winks at me on her way to the car. Suspicious, but I could be misreading a friendly gesture.

Though, if Ted did fill her in on our kiss, it's probably a good sign. I know I've been stealing texts with Emma all day. Would our conversations with our friends have been similar today? Emma and I dissected everything, but in the end, we still aren't even dating... If he had talked to Abby, maybe he was thinking the same thing. We'd have to remedy this soon. For once, I don't want to be hesitant or noncommittal. Emma had pointed it out happily. I don't know what the difference is. Ted just feels right. A buzz issues from my right back pocket. No doubt Emma is checking in on me again.

The pizza has already been broken into, and half-empty beers are scattered across the table. PJ says, "Finally! Hey, Bet, good to see you."

Mitch rises to help me set things up in the kitchen. He doesn't have to go far; the kitchen is directly on the other side of the table. Ted has already plugged in the stand mixer, unpacked the bags, and organized the items on the counter. Mitch says somewhat lamely, "Looks like you've got it. You're welcome to use anything in the kitchen. If you have any questions or anything, I can *try* to help."

"Thanks, Mitch. I appreciate you offering your kitchen for baking. I've never been able to hang out and get work done like this unless everyone comes to my tiny apartment, which you wouldn't fit."

Mitch smiles behind his scraggle of facial hair and seems pleased. "Y'all should catch up. Grab a slice while you're setting up there. Beer is in the fridge."

Despite having never been in this kitchen and no indication that Ted has done anything here besides raiding the refrigerator and fetching cups and plates, we work around each other as if we've choreographed a routine. I turn on the oven and start unwrapping the pie crusts, but Ted places his hand on the small of my back and says in my ear, "Preheating is the perfect time for some pizza." He slides an open bottle of Dos Equis to me, and I can't help but grin. I accept the perspiring bottle, and we clink the necks together.

A male voice, PJ's, I think, breaks a silence I wasn't aware of. "You two seem… good?" The question dripped with intrigue, and it wasn't until I turned to face the table that I noticed PJ, Abby, Melissa, and Mitch had their eyes glued on us. "Come sit down. Catch up with us for a minute."

As we approach the table, Melissa gets up and moves closer to Mitch so Ted and I can sit together. A hint of pink rises in her cheeks. Sweet Melissa, I think she would blush at anything.

"Did Abby already tell you about the presentation?" Ted asks as he scoots over on a bench, giving me room.

PJ replies, "She did. It sounds like everything is going to be gangbusters."

"Yeah, just don't fuck it up when you're actually there," Mitch adds. He winks at my wide-eyed accusatory look — Abby and PJ chuckle.

Ted shakes his head. "I won't. I mean, I can't. It would be a disaster if I did. Mark came to the school for the first time yesterday, and it went about as well as you'd expect." I double-take at the reminder that it *was* yesterday. It seems like last week.

"So, not well at all then?" Abby asks.

"Yeah." Ted lets his cheeks puff out with a long exhale. "Some of the things he said make me wonder what his motivations even are. I don't know. He's obviously into money. Maybe I'm overthinking the whole thing."

Mitch reaches across the table and picks up another slice. He gestures to Ted with it. "You're always overthinking."

Ted rolls his eyes. "You're always underthinking!" Everyone laughs, and Mitch nods in agreement. "What has everyone else been up to?"

I try not to impersonate a pig as I gobble down two slices

of pepperoni while the group updates us on their activities. Maybe it's from the fatigue, but I'm starving.

Abby starts the conversation with an update on Wes, who has yet to propose. She waves an unadorned finger and earns an eye roll from PJ and Mitch. PJ reports low spirits at work and looks forward to the winter break. Mitch gives a non-update of, "Delivering packages hasn't changed one bit."

I swallow a too-big bite and ask Melissa, "How about you?" Melissa is stunning, with long blonde hair and an upturned button nose. I muse about why she's so shy, even around her friends.

Asking her directly does appear to permit her to speak. "Things are good. I'm booking more events than last year, and my ratings online are high. I've been wondering about hiring an assistant photographer."

"Wow, Melissa! That's a major step. Congratulations."

She shrinks slightly. "Yeah. Thanks. I'm not sure yet; it's just that if I get any more inquiries, I'll have to start turning people down."

Abby jumps in and says what we're all thinking. "Then it's the perfect time to expand, but why do you seem bummed?"

Melissa pushes the empty plate away from her. "I don't know. I don't know how to hire someone and trust them. I'd have to really, *really* trust them. I can't mess up and take on the wrong person."

Mitch has been watching her intently. "Sure you can." The daggers from Abby's eyes do not go unregistered, and Mitch puts his hands up as if in surrender before continuing. "I'm not saying she will!" He turns to the left so he's facing Melissa. "What I'm saying is, if you did hire the wrong person, it's not the end. You'd tell them they aren't a good fit and find someone else who is. One bad hire won't sink you. You're an incredible photographer, and everyone knows it."

She goes bright red from her forehead to what's visible of

her chest. Mitch sucks in his cheeks, again pleased with himself.

"Thanks, Mitch," Melissa mumbles.

Mitch, the asshole, says, "Hmm? What's that?"

To my shock, Melissa raises her head to meet him, the ruby hue slowly receding. She clears her throat and says, "I said thank you. I appreciate your perspective and the compliment."

Mitch starts to say something, but PJ kicks him beneath the table, and he recoils, glaring at PJ.

I make a mental note to talk to Ted about Melissa and Mitch. Melissa is obviously into him, and Mitch is giving off some signs to me, too. The look he gave her when she blushed was not so innocent. "I better get the pies going so we can play." Ted follows me into the kitchen, and I see sidelong glances follow us as we walk past the table.

"How do we start?" Ted acts as if it's a given that he's my assistant in this and not the DM, who could easily get the game going.

"We need to roll out the dough and parbake for a few minutes. While the crust is in the oven and cooling, we can mix up the pumpkin and start the topping. It shouldn't take too long- the blender and mixer do most of the work."

Ted follows directions meticulously and asks for feedback on the evenness and thickness of the crusts he tackles. They're perfect each time, and it's enough for me to wonder if he's been practicing. It takes about ten minutes until we're par-baking. By this time, the rest of the gang has joined us in the kitchen to watch and visit, so six of us are standing around a small space.

I'm adding pumpkin to the blender when Abby asks, "Can we help?" I put on a thinking face so she knows I'm considering. I don't prefer too many hands on a recipe, but I'm also not keen on shooting down an offer with my new friends.

New friends. The words catch in my mind.

"Yes. I think we can assembly-line this part, but don't hate me if I oversee all of you. It's important they come out uniform."

Abby salutes. "Tell us what to do."

I organize everyone in a line and hand them the necessary measuring tools and spices. Ted is at the end, so he can empty the blender into the crusts. It's the most important job, and I hope he knows it. He's proven he'll take as much care as I do.

The production becomes a game, with people dancing around each other, re-ordering themselves, and measuring teaspoons of cinnamon, nutmeg, salt, and baking powder. Everyone, even Mitch, performs their tasks attentively.

It's a short time before everything is in the oven or a holding pattern. As we return to the table, Abby comments, "You and Ted make a strong team in everything you do together, huh?"

Which is true. So true.

I am wholly distracted during my first real game of Dungeons & Dragons. First, I dwell on Abby's comment; then, I relive last night. Not helping my focus is the fact that Ted is an insanely good DM. He's helping me along as we go, and the story is captivating and funny. So far, the team is pretty sure we're walking into a trap, and I think something is up with Lore's harmonica.

The thing is, seeing Ted in action, commanding a room by storytelling makes his face even more handsome than unusual. Or maybe it's the low light? I catch myself staring at him multiple times before, finally, my mom's voice starts repeating in my head. Should I ask him out? I want us to be something, anything, official. If it's an official one-time coffee date, I'll take it. Please let us get started. I could do it. I could ask him. He'll say yes; I know it.

"Bet? It's your roll." Melissa's gentle voice interrupts my self hype-up, and shit, I'm staring at Ted again, and he's grinning back at me.

"I'd like to roll for a mystery initiative." Every expression is confused.

"What is a mystery initiative?" PJ asks with such a diplomatic tone that I can imagine him being at the head of a classroom.

But I am chickening out, and if I don't do it now... I roll the giant 20-sided die, and it lands on 18. All eyes are on the die. I could just pretend I have no idea what I'm doing. It would be easy; it's my first game.

I look at Ted. He's patiently waiting for me to speak, and though my heart is beating and beating in my throat, I somehow get out, "Go on a date with me?"

The table explodes. Ted and I are the only two people still sitting. Everyone else is on their feet, hands in the air, whooping as if their favorite football player has made an impossible save. Notes and pencils flutter across the table. PJ's beer mug is knocked over. Motion is all around us, but my senses are locked on Ted. I've never seen an expression on any person that is so purely happy.

"It would be my greatest honor, Bet, to go anywhere with you."

THE REST of the night is filled with laughter and learning curves (my character nearly dies twice trying to keep up with the more advanced players). I had a wonderful time and felt grateful to have met Ted and his friends, but I was still glad when the night came to an end. I am so tired- It's a miracle that I manage to unload all the pies into my fridge and brush my teeth before passing out. By the time I'm in bed, my strength is rushing out of me like the sand at the end of an hourglass. I feel myself fade. There's just one thing left to do before blessed sleep, and that's texting Emma. She's going to freak.

Coupé de Ville

> Grab a drink with me tomorrow? 9:16 PM

30

TED

When had communication become so casual with Bet? Since Friday, we'd only spent time apart while at work or asleep, and in those times, stolen moments for texting were regular. But it started before then, right? Smiling, I scroll up our message history and register the increasing frequency. So many of the past few days have felt like the best dream, and the evidence, the trail on my phone proving it's real, is meaningful.

Yet, there's a small voice within me I don't dare vocalize. What if Mark fires me or Noble closes? Despite feeling energized and happy, for the first time in a long time, I know the possibility is still looming. If I lose my job and Noble remains open, well, Haven Cove isn't big enough to support a second martial arts studio, and even if it were or if Noble closed, I don't have the start-up capital to open one. If I want to keep my job as a teacher, I'd have to move.

I'd have to move even though everything - life - is beginning.

Maybe I could do something else for work. I've offered the idea to the small voice but without much enthusiasm, because the truth is that I know teaching is what I'm meant to do. If it weren't for Bet, there would be no question. It makes me sick to admit it; I can't imagine giving up my dream job for someone I started dating so recently—even if it is... Even if she is... Can I?

Bet knows it, too. Our past few days have been blissful, yet there's an emphasis on the if of *if the Fall Festival is successful* that makes me want to scream. Can't anything be easy, and of all things, my relationship with Bet should be easy. It is in every other regard aside from this hellacious complication.

After Advanced Class wraps, Bet comes over for the express purpose of meeting Hitch. It's the first time she'll be in my home, and though I keep a clean space, I panicked before heading out and tried to make it feel inviting. Curse me for not having pillows on my couch.

The class went *mostly* as expected. Cooper was mysteriously gone, and I noticed Roy and Brian kept to themselves despite his absence. Usually, when Cooper isn't there, they lead the class more, but not today. Bet's movements have gotten cleaner and swifter, making her a standout when we spar, even amongst the students who outrank her. Quickness is hard to achieve with such length, but she seems to come by it naturally. It's like watching a swan on the attack.

I push the headshot she landed with a number three round kick out of my mind so I can exit my car without an obvious erection and direct Bet to the parking space beside mine.

"This isn't an apartment. You have a house?" She appraises the exterior. "Except there's a parking lot…"

"It's a duplex. It was a house, but it's kind of divided up into two houses on the inside." I point across the lot. "Same thing over there. Stanley is my neighbor. He's an older guy who's lived here forever. Across the lot are some young families, the Pattons and Murphys. Their kids play in the side yard, and it drives Stan crazy."

She cocks her head to the side. "Typical old man vibes. Stay off my lawn!"

"Yeah, kinda. I like Stan though, his heart is in the right place, I think mostly he's worried they'll get into the parking lot." I open the door and sweep Bet inside, "Welcome to my abode."

As she crosses the threshold, I see her eyes marking things, and I wonder if she's having the same experience I had when entering her apartment for the first time. Everything, no matter how small, spurs a question or even answers some. "Wow, Ted, this is nice." I start to reply, but then, "Oh my God! Hitch! It's Hitch!"

Hitch has jumped onto the back of my tan couch and keenly observes Bet, orange ears and whiskers, doing a jig. Bet approaches slowly and offers a hand for him to sniff. Before I can worry about his reaction, he rubs his head into her proffered hand, and she starts cooing at him and scratching his ears. "Speaking of typical behavior. That's Hitch for you, a total love sponge."

"He's so soft! And he's purring! Oh, I love him!"

"Hitch is also obviously a big fan of yours. Little eager there, bud." I chuckle at the pair. Hitch has always taken to guests, but I've never seen him roll over and offer his tummy up for rubs so quickly.

"Can you blame him?" Bet smirks.

"No. No, I cannot." I run my fingers down her arm. Being able to touch her is new but feels as old as time. "Needless to say, this is the living room. The kitchen is around the corner, and down the little hall are the bedrooms and a bathroom in the middle. Feel free to explore."

Bet takes the invitation and reluctantly steps back from Hitch, who chirps in question, but she doesn't investigate the living room further and instead takes the turn into the kitchen. "Ooo, it's big in here. Are these herbs?!"

"In the window? Yeah, just a little basil, parsley, and thyme plants."

"I should do that. Geez, why haven't I thought of growing fresh herbs for my savory stuff?"

I lean against the entryway to the kitchen and watch her. I only use it to feed myself, but my kitchen is indeed larger than hers- not huge, but hers is teeny. It's an injustice, really.

"Is it too weird if I..." Bet mimes opening a cabinet.

"Nope, not too weird. Not for you anyway." I quip. She shoots a quick glare at me but then opens cabinets and drawers as she moves through the room.

At the end of the counter, she closes the last drawer and says, "This confirms it. I've wondered for weeks how you seem to know where everything is in my kitchen, but now I see we have a similar way of storing items."

"Funny enough, I've noticed this too. It's easy for me to predict where things might be in your place because it makes sense." We stare at each other for a second; her mouth quirks up on one side. Then she heads back to the living room, giving me a quick brush across my abdomen as she passes.

"Where'd you get this artwork from? I like it." She eyes the abstract colored canvases on the wall.

"Oh, it's just from Walmart or somewhere. When I moved in, I was dating Abby, and she tried to help me—how'd she put it, 'not live in a man cave.' We only got as far as some paintings, I'm afraid."

Bet shook her head. "The herbs count as non-man-cave. Plus, you've got this throw blanket." Bet's expression changes to one of horror. "Actually... I think my place is more man-cave-ish than yours. Oh no."

I can't help but laugh. She has a point. "You're utilitarian, and I'm not sure we can count this place as posh either."

She sighs. "I'm mostly just broke, and when I see something decorative that I like, I tell myself that all I do at home is sleep."

"How will you decorate in the future when life is easier?"

Bet doesn't hesitate. She's thought about this. "Colors. I'd love the kitchen to be a lovely mossy green and maybe lavender in the bedroom. I'd have art, too. Walmart art is fine. A bookshelf for all my cookbooks. Two bookshelves! One for cookbooks and the other for all the other books I'd have time to read. I'd have one of those soft round chairs to squash down into, too." Her face slackens as she talks as if imagining the scene.

"That sounds beautiful."

"Yeah." Bet breaks from her reverie and walks down the hall. She doesn't go into my bedroom but peers inside.

I pass her through the door. "You can come in."

"I'd have pictures, too." She points to my dresser. On top are several pictures of my mom and me, my dad, and one of my friends. She picks up the book on the end of my bed and reads, "How to Win Friends and Influence People?"

"Don't judge me. It's supposed to be a classic, and I'll do anything to make things easier with Mark."

Bet puts her hands up. "No judgment here. I'd do anything to make things easier with Mark, too." There it is. The unspoken acknowledgment that not all is well. "Your house is lovely. Um, what's in the other bedroom?"

"Let's see." I walk the couple steps to its door, open it, and flip on the light. There are some large Noble signs and holiday decorations in boxes stacked up in the corner. "Basically nothing, but maybe like an office? It's all supplies I use to decorate Noble for the holidays and some old signage we used to have up in the windows and lobby—old gear in the closet. You know. You could bake over here any time you want. I'd even let you use my herbs."

"Not the herbs!" Bet grasps my wrist in mock shock but then says thoughtfully, "You are too kind. I'm sure I'll take you up on it. Especially now that Hitch and I are BFFs." She bends down to pet Hitch, who is aggressively marking her legs.

"Traitor!" I shoot at the cat.

"Should we do a final run-through for tomorrow?"

"Definitely." The Chamber of Commerce presentation was in less than 24 hours, and though we'd practiced ad nauseam, I couldn't stop myself from practicing more. Having Bet as an audience was an advantage. Her physical presence made me sharper. When I went through without her, I tended to stumble or miss critical things I wanted to say and have to go back.

How would it be in front of all the business owners? How many people would be there? The unknown and the prospect of speaking in front of a large group of people when what I said mattered so much was stressful. Anything could happen. What if I couldn't do it at all and froze? I'd seen it happen in karate competitions and belt tests before. Even the most prepared students could freeze up before an audience or a panel of judges. It had never happened to me, but then I'd never been speaking in front of an audience who unwittingly held the future of my career in their hands either.

31

BET

Walking into the Chamber of Commerce meeting was jarring. I carefully search Ted to see if I can divine his feelings; if he's expected this or is as thrown off as I am, I can't tell. We've arrived early, yet plenty of people are milling around the large hall. There are rectangular tables up and down either side of the room and a large screen at the end where presentations would be made. I wonder if they expect to fill all the seats, but answer my own question when I see a printed agenda page in front of every chair.

"Did you know there'd be an agenda?" I pick up the nearest paper. Ted shakes his head. "It makes sense that there would be. I guess I didn't know what to expect at all. Oh, you're the first speaker under the New Business section." I hand the page to Ted. His throat bobs as he takes it, and my heart aches at the show of nerves. I grab his hand and lead him to the first table next to the podium and projector.

Ted is still silently observing the agenda as we sit. "I didn't." He swallows again. "Know there would be an agenda. Like you said, it makes sense. It seems so formal." Panic rises in his voice, and he whispers, "Am I dressed how I should be?"

I try to be confident for Ted and squeeze his hand. "You are. You look professional. Most other people here are wearing a similar outfit. Only you make it look better." Ted looks up at me but doesn't quite smile. "You're going to do great. You're prepared. You've got a great presentation and have practiced. Besides, if anyone gives you grief… well… you know I study karate, right?" This quip succeeds in earning a huffed laugh.

"Ted Dawson?"

We both twist in our seats at the voice. A woman in a turquoise dress and blazer smiles at Ted and shakes his hand. "I thought that must be you. I'm Chief Officer Stephanie Hayes. I wanted to welcome you and answer any questions you have."

"Thank you. Um, I do have a question about my computer. I have a presentation to share. How do I hook it up?"

Stephanie nods her head, her poofy bangs following the movement. "Great question, I'll show you. Bring your computer up front." Ted obediently grabs his laptop and follows her to the podium. When he returns, Stephanie calls the meeting to order.

Ted's leg bounces up and down with nervous energy. I glance behind us to find we're nearing full occupancy; there must be at least 50 people here. I put my hand on his shoulder and massage it. It's the only way I can figure out to offer him solace without being rude and talking during the presentations. His shoulder muscles are so tight it feels like rubbing a statue.

I try to catch Ted's eye, and seeing his handsome profile nearly makes me laugh. It's a little funny. Endearing, even. Here is a beautiful man, big and strong, who has competed in countless martial arts events in front of thousands of people. His nerves are out of place in that context, though I understand this is different. Ted finally turns his head to face me, and I try to communicate all the encouraging words I want to remind him of with my eyes.

His foot stops shaking as rapidly, and I smile. His lips gently turn up in reply but then crash at the sound of his name from the front. "Our first new business today is from Ted Dawson, who is speaking about the revival of the Haven Cove Fall Festival. Come on up, Ted." Stephanie's voice is inviting, and I'm grateful for her demeanor.

I give his shoulder a final squeeze. He takes a deep inhale, then stands as he breathes it out. At the podium, he squats down to hook up the computer. He should have introduced himself or indicated what he was doing first, and the silence feels awkward. He does get the presentation on the screen in short order, though.

Ted stands up from behind the podium fast and starts to speak at the same time, "Thanks for…" comes through, except he's risen so quickly he must have yanked the computer cable somehow, and his laptop crashes onto the ground from the podium, coming unplugged in the process.

Some of the audience gasps. Ted sinks below the podium again, then holds up the computer, announcing, "It's okay!" He plugs it back in and rises more carefully this time.

"Um, as I was saying. Thanks for having us, I mean me, today. Um, I'm happy to share with you that Noble and all the businesses in the Haven Cove Mall will be hosting the Fall Festival this year on October 15th." Ted pauses, staring at the crowd, but the pause lasts too long.

Someone in the audience coughs. Come on, Ted, look at the computer. If he follows his presentation, he'll be fine, but he doesn't. He stutters, "I, um. I…"

I raise my hand in the air and wave it around.

Ted looks at me, and it's enough of a cue for me to ask, "It sounds like this is a revival, but I'm new to town. What's the Fall Festival like?"

Ted keeps his eyes locked on me while he answers. "Great question. Haven Cove hosted an annual Fall Festival for 60 years, but it stopped being held in 2005 due to the hosting businesses' inability to support it that year." He progresses the presentation to the photos from prior festivals and faces the crowd again. "If you weren't around for the festival back then, here are some pictures from the event. It was consistently well attended by Haven Cove and the families in the surrounding area. It was a great way for businesses to make connections within the wider community and downright wholesome family fun."

He had found his groove. Ted didn't falter the rest of the presentation, and when he opened the room to questions, he received only a few.

"Where did you say this would be?" A man's voice shouts from the back.

"It'll be in the parking lot of Haven Cove Mall, the same place it used to be held."

A woman who was more dressed up than the rest of the attendees stood and pointedly asked, "How much profit do you anticipate vendors getting from the event?"

Ted's no-nonsense answer makes my chest swell with pride. "I'm afraid it would be irresponsible of me to guess. Many factors could affect that. Earlier sign-up times allow for heavier advertising. I don't know your wares or margins; interaction at the event will also be crucial. What I can say is, as you've seen, vendor costs to sign up are reasonable, and that is purposeful. My goal is to see our town have an enjoyable time and expand our businesses so everyone wants to return next year."

Finally, a voice I'd recognize anywhere. Lily. "Can I sign up right now?"

Her question elicits some chuckling and some agreeable comments, too. "Yes, anyone who wants to sign up today can find me after the meeting. I'm right here at the front table."

Stephanie sweeps in and ensures there are no further questions from the group, thanks Ted, and explains the next new business on the agenda: A new restaurant offering a Chamber Mixer Event the night before their grand opening.

"You did great," I whisper in Ted's ear as he joins me.

"We'll see. I'm just glad it's over." I feel the change in him, though. He's positively relaxed compared to when we got here.

The Fall Festival was the most complicated topic discussed, and the rest of the meeting concludes shortly. When Stephanie closes the meeting, Ted and I stand and turn to face the room. I was expecting Lily and, hopefully, a couple of other people to come up, yet the majority of the crowd was moving toward us. More people were coming to our table than were exiting the hall!

"If you'll greet people and take questions, I'll help them sign up on the web form."

Ted nods, his face disbelieving at the approaching hoard. "Good idea. Divide and conquer." He breathes, "Wow," under his breath before raising his voice and saying, "if we can form a line here, I'll answer questions, and Bet will help with signups!"

We work our way through the line. Not everyone signs up immediately, but 25 businesses do, and everyone else takes Ted's contact information. Lily is the last person in line; I'm confident her placement is purposeful. "Little bit of a rocky start, but you pulled it together. How many people signed up?"

Ted raises a heavy brow at me in question, his glasses sliding down his nose.

"Twenty-five."

His mouth falls open slightly. "Twenty-five?!"

"Better make it twenty-six." Lily cackles.

While I turn the computer toward her so she can fill out the form, Ted says, "It's thanks to you both. I don't know if I could have recovered if it weren't for Bet. And Lily… you did magic helping me get Connie to agree, then asking to sign up. I think your question influenced everyone else to come up."

Lily waves her hand to dismiss the compliment. "Bet and I are a good team. Bet and you are a good team." She winks at me. "I think you'd better take tomorrow off."

I start to protest, but she raises her hand again, this time to stop me. "As your employer, I'm telling you to take the day off. You've got to go out and celebrate tonight, both of you." With that, she spins on her heel and exits the hall.

"I KNOW where we should go. It's easygoing, and it's guaranteed we can both find things we like. There's probably music. I can drive us." His speech is fast with excitement.

"Sounds awesome. What's it called?"

Ted swings his keys around his finger and catches them as we walk to his car. "Trust me."

I skip to catch up to him and sing back, "Okayyy."

Now that the presentation is complete, I can appreciate how handsome Ted looks in his business casual outfit. His attention is on the road, so I let myself feast a bit. His shoulders are broad, and his blue shirt tapers in with his body until it tucks into slim-fitting black slacks. The bulge beneath his belt buckle keeps catching my eye.

In a few minutes, we're pulling into the grassy lot of Food

Worx. A silly part of my brain is worried that Cooper could be here because we went on one date here a long time ago. It's illogical, and I know it. Cooper is the last person I want to think of right now. This is precious time with Ted for us to enjoy together. I'll have to figure out a way to thank Lily; she is absolutely the best boss.

"Have you been here before? There's all these food trucks. It's pretty cool."

"Just once. It is cool. Good idea!" The walk to the trucks is much less of an ordeal in the black flats I'm wearing today.

People are buzzing around, and a bluegrass band plays on the little stage beyond the trucks, but Food Worx is less crowded than my last visit. The level of activity is perfect. I can hear Ted easily, and we won't have to wait in line for long.

We stop in the middle of the trucks to consider our options. "Yes!" Ted pumps his fist in the air. "I can't believe they're here. We have to get this strawberry shortcake beer. It's brewed by a place in Tampa, but you can find it up here sometimes. It is so good!"

"A rare treat beer *and* 26 vendor signups!"

Ted takes my hand and spins me around out of the blue. "And a surprise night off!" He stops the spin suddenly by hugging me against him. His muscular body beneath his polo and the hard metal of his belt buckle give me half a mind to say we should get out of here.

Instead, I say, "You pick the beer; I get to choose the food, and it's looking like ramen tonight."

Ted's eyes go wide. "I love ramen."

We join the short line for our noodles first, recalling some of the vendors who had already signed up. We'd have plenty of food at the festival but the vendor list also included a dance academy, jeweler, comic book shop, and even a farm.

"We'll have to send all the info to PJ and Mitch so they can start assigning places."

Ted agrees but suddenly looks horrified. "Oh no! I haven't texted Abby. She's going to kill me."

I shake my head slyly. "I texted her. You're off the hook."

Ted opens his phone screen and laughs. He flashes the screen to me.

A<small>BBY</small> Taylor

> Good thing Bet's on top of it. I was hanging from the edge of my seat over here! Congrats, even though your update game is WEAK. 6:10 PM

"H<small>AH</small>! I guess my update game is strong, then."

We pick up our bowls and walk up to Zippy Brews. Ted orders the strawberry shortcake beers, and they hand over two dark bottles. I open my purse so Ted can put them inside, and we find a table.

Ted sits on the table and puts his feet on the seat facing the band, so I follow suit. Our legs touch, and our arms bump against each other as we eat the ramen, but we don't move apart. I take the first taste of the beer and can hardly believe how delicious and true the flavors are. "Wow!"

"I know, right?" Ted looks over at me and swigs from his bottle. "It tastes exactly like a shortcake."

"Even the texture is incredible. How is it… velvety? Yes, velvety."

Ted's eyes crinkle at the corners. "I know what you mean."

I take another glorious swallow. "I fear I must admit something." I aim my head down to look at my feet.

"What's up?" His tone is immediately one of concern.

"I... This is hard, but... I've been checking you out all day, and you clean up super well. Too well."

Ted pushes me playfully, but his voice is low and laced with challenge when he speaks. "You've been checking me out, huh?"

"Mmhmm." I lean into him and kiss him deeply. His hand gently traces my jawbone and chin, sending tingles down my spine.

A loud knock sounds from behind our table. "Owww! Ugh, that hurt."

Our make-out session ends too soon as we turn to the source of the bang. "Chuck?" I recognize him instantly, but don't know why he would be right behind me and Ted.

His round cheeks redden. "Yes, um. This is embarrassing. I thought I saw you and wanted to talk, but by the time I got here, you were, ah, you know. So I turned to leave, but my knee hit the table."

"Are you okay?"

"I think so. Sorry for interrupting."

"It's okay. Is Cooper here?" I scan the crowd beyond him.

"Not that I know of. I'm here with the fam. Megan and the kids are right over there." Chuck smiles and waves at a woman with long, wavy brown hair and dramatic lipstick. She waves back and returns to attending to two very active kids around her.

Ted clears his throat next to me and I realize how strange this interaction must be to him. "Ted, this is Chuck. Chuck is one of Cooper's friends. He's the head baker at Casa de Pan. Chuck, this is Ted; he's the lead instructor at Noble." They shake hands and offer polite greetings.

Chuck addresses me again, "Casa de Pan is why I wanted

to talk to you. I remember you do the baking for Gerard's. I'm not going to pretend I haven't done some taste-testing research. You're a great baker, and one of my bakers is moving in November."

My face, I'm sure, is utterly slack with shock. Is he offering me a job right now? At Casa de Pan? The best bakery in hundreds of miles? Except he stops there. "So, you have an opening coming up, and you wanted to let me know. Chuck, I am so flattered that you'd give me a heads-up. I can't believe you tried some of my stuff."

"Did you try the Peanut Butter Chocolate Chip Cookie Bar? It's my favorite." Ted's hand is gentle on the small of my back, his fingers circling slowly.

"As a matter of fact, I did. It's exceptional. How do you get the middle to be so moist while the bottom retains its solidity?" I start to reply, but Chuck stops me, "Don't tell me. Teach me. We'll both learn from each other. I'm not rushing you, but here," he hands me his card, "take this and think about what questions you have, then call me so I can bend to your every whim and convince you to come work with me." He saves me the dignity of having to emerge from my stupor by waving goodbye. "Hope to hear from you soon."

Ted lets out a long whistle. "That was unexpected."

I stare at the light brown card in my hand. It's the exact color of a crusty sourdough boule. "This isn't a good way to thank Lily."

"So you're going to take it?" Ted asks.

"I don't know." I bite my lip and glance over to see Ted observing me. "I have to think about it more. Casa de Pan is an incredible bakery. Even being invited is a huge compliment. Geez."

Ted traces my shoulder. "If I can help you think it out or just listen, let me know." My eyes are glued on Chuck's card.

Do I want to bake, or do I want to be a florist? Could I leave Lily? She needs reliable help, and I can't put her in a bind.

On the other hand, working at Casa de Pan would simplify my entire life. Even without asking, I'm sure the salary would be higher, and I wouldn't have to bake on the side. Plus, baker's hours are early, so I could attend a proper level karate class. I nearly giggle at the thought, but Ted snags my attention. "You said that guy is friends with Cooper?"

His tone is so skeptical I snort. "I know exactly what you mean, and I thought so, too. Different vibes, right? All the other friends I met were like mini-Coopers. I'm not sure how he fits in. I should have asked him about that text."

The last part is more me thinking aloud, but Ted doesn't miss it. "What text?"

"It was some weird text Cooper sent the other day when we were at D&D. I had forgotten about it. I don't think it was for me. He was trying to ask someone out for a drink and sent it to me by mistake. No follow-up, see?" I open the old message and show Ted.

"Weird."

"Yeah. Also, let's not forget we're celebrating."

Ted raises his beer. "Celebrating your job offer now, too! Even if you don't take it, like you said, it's some well-deserved recognition." He drains the end of his bottle.

"We're going to need two more of these, stat." I hop down from the table and reach toward Ted, who accepts my hand.

On the way to the truck, Chuck passes us going in the other direction, a plate of pizza and french fries stacked on top of each other. I steer us to meet him, wanting to thank him for the offer more appropriately, but also with curiosity about Cooper's text. "Chuck, hey, thank you so much. I was a bit too stunned to speak back there and didn't express my gratitude the way I wanted to. Your offer is a huge deal to me. I will think about it and come up with some questions for you."

"Oh, don't worry. It's my fault. I shouldn't have snuck up on you in the wild and sprung something like that. I'm glad to hear it, though. Call anytime."

He takes a step toward his family, and I cringe before stopping him. "Just one more unrelated thing? Um, Cooper texted me last Friday. It was kinda strange. I'm not sure it was even for me, but…"

Chuck interrupts, his brows shooting up. "Oh, it was for you." He sighs, and his eyes travel to Ted and back. "Listen, the moment I met you, I knew you wouldn't put up with Cooper for long. Shoot, I barely do. In any case, I wasn't there, but I know about the message. He was trying to prove you were, well… He said you were… promiscuous."

"What?!" I exclaim, and Ted's hand tightens around mine so hard it hurts.

Chuck continues quickly, "Nobody believes him. I'm so sorry. He has never handled breakups reasonably. He was trying to show that you wouldn't text him back, and that, in his mind, is proof to everyone that you're, whatever."

"But we broke up weeks ago and only dated for a few weeks!"

"I know." Chuck shakes his head. "The older I get, the more I don't understand him anymore. Anyway, all the better for you, and it was nice to meet you, Ted."

32

TED

*E*verything feels like a countdown that I'm battling against. What happens when we reach zero?

"That's the 17th sign we've passed. They're everywhere! This is really happening." Bet points to a Fall Festival sign. This one is laminated and looks like something you'd see for a politician sticking out of the grass on the side of a road.

"This one is fancy. Who do you think paid for it?" The previous 16 were posters in shop windows, chalkboard sidewalk signs, or even pasted onto street lamps.

"Didn't we have a sign shop join? I bet it's them."

"Good point. There have been so many, it's hard to remember anymore." I sip the latte we picked up at the beginning of our walk. It's not great, but it's also from the last shop open this late.

We walk the quaint downtown street of Haven Cove, counting more signs until we reach Bayside Park. Bet and I have been stealing down here for short walks before baking into the night, and this is where we usually turn around. We both stop, but Bet says, "Let's go this way," and points to the right with her half-empty cup.

"Look! They're in the park, too!" Her excitement crumples something inside of me. I had shared in it until this morning when I sat down to do the math. I peer out over the water so she can't see my face. The days are getting shorter, and the light is almost gone. Another countdown. Maybe that's what happens at the end. Just dark.

It's a beautiful evening, and I'm trying to be present. I focus on the briny smell coming in from the bay, and as I start to get curious about where we're going, Bet takes a few leaps to the top of the small footbridge in front of us and leans against the railing. Only a sliver of the sun remains over the watery horizon, casting orange light over Bet's delicate features. "I wanted to tell you I've made my decision."

I sidle up next to her to watch the sun sink. "Yeah?" The past week had been a flurry of what-if scenarios, weighing pros and cons, and daydreaming about her career options. The whole process makes me grateful. I was lucky enough to land right where I wanted to be with Noble from the start. Her decision was hard and complicated by feelings of love and guilt.

"I'm going to call Chuck tomorrow and take the job. It's too good to refuse. The salary, the hours, the team, and the flexibility to start after I get Lily situated—I just can't pass it up." She sounds sad.

I bump her with my hip. "Are you apologizing for taking a dream job?"

"No, it's… I don't know how I'm going to tell Lily. After all she's done for me, I never imagined hurting her."

Bet is still looking over the horizon, the light of which shimmers a tear on her cheek. I wipe it with my thumb. "You deserve to feel happy about this momentous event. I don't know Lily nearly as well as you do, but I have a feeling she would want you to be happy—that she'll be happy for you."

Bet lets out a single wet laugh. "Yeah, she probably will. I still worry, but maybe everything is working out." She turns a shining smile at me. "Good things are happening for both of us."

I almost tell her. Part of me wants to, but I can't bear to sully her optimism, not when she's digesting her huge decision. The truth is, even when we have every vendor spot full, we'll be short by Mark's standards. Even if I recruit fifteen-*fifteen*- new families at the event with the new higher tuition, compared to those who told me they won't renew, the numbers won't work in his eyes. The feeling of being closed in on grips me again, but I shake it off. The smile I return to Bet is genuine despite the sadness beneath, but oh, I feel like my muscles are shaking, trying to lift some crushing weight. "You're right. So many things are in motion, but they will all work out."

Bet kisses me on the cheek, and we trek back to my car. Main street foot traffic has decreased. Only the late crowd at restaurants and a few bars are open, and the sounds from within them swell as we pass. We're across from Willie's Tiki Tavern, and I'm listening to catch snippets of conversation from the crowd to compare with Bet when she asks, "Is that your phone?"

I hadn't registered the ringing above the din of customers, but now she's said it, I fish the phone from my back pocket. "It's Mark."

Bet protests, "It's after 10!" but I've already clicked to answer.

"Wait, I'm sorry, Mark. Give me a minute. I'll get somewhere quieter." I nod to Bet to make sure she heard me, then run to the end of the block. "Okay, this should be better."

Mark is perturbed. "I *said* I'm having a new teacher start. Their first day is October 16th. You can figure out the schedule between the two of you."

Chills run down my body through my feet straight into

the pavement. "Mark. Wait. Why? Isn't that going to cost more?"

"You gotta spend money to make money. Everyone knows that. You'll add some new classes. God, but you are slow." He chuckles at his insult. "It's late. I gotta go."

"Mark, wait. We have to do a background check and a W4. Did you interview this person? Do they have experience? What's their availability? I need more information. You can't just dump something like this on…"

"I can, and I did. We need more classes to support more students. Don't get your panties in a twist." His voice curls with relish. "Besides, you know him." The earth is spinning too fast. "Cooper is what the school needs."

Mark hangs up, but I can't lower the phone from my ear. Bet watches me cautiously, waiting to hear what's happening. How my feet are still on the sidewalk when the planet is trying to fling me from it defies my novice understanding of physics. My hand drops. Bet steps forward, wraps her arms around me, and squeezes tight. She doesn't ask what happened but whispers in my ear, "It'll be okay. Everything will be okay."

Her breath in my ear unleashes me. The world's rotation returns to its usual clip, but I shudder in her arms. My face is wet. Bet holds me and continues her soft and soothing reassurances. Her hand runs through my hair every few seconds. I steady my breathing and focus on my heart—or is that Bet's heartbeat in my ear?

It's not until I pull away that she asks—not what happened, but "Are you okay?"

I shake my head. My voice is hoarse when it comes. "No, I… Mark hired Cooper as a teacher, but there's more. I didn't want to tell you yet."

And it all came out. Everything.

I swallow hard. "Phil was supposed to leave me Noble in

his will. He told me for years, even before he was sick. I haven't told anyone that before." I had outright refused to think about it at all. "Mark knows."

Bet squeezes her eyes shut. "Oh, Ted."

We bake at my house for the first time so I can show Bet my calculations from the morning. Those, in conjunction with Cooper's suspicious start date, leave both of us feeling uncertain. Bet is mid-fold when she exclaims, "He hasn't even been coming to class!"

"I don't think Mark cares about his attendance."

She stops folding the dough and puts her wrists on her hips, fingers turned out to avoid getting a mess on her shirt. "Is he *trying* to hurt you, and if so, why? Could he know about your relationship with Cooper somehow?"

I shrug. "I don't know. I've always assumed he was a greedy asshole. I never even knew him until after Phil passed. I don't know how it could be personal. What worries me most is the start date being the day after the Fall Festival. Is that a coincidence, too?"

"Hmm," I can tell she's not entirely convinced. "If he's just into sapping all the profit from the school, you've got a leg to stand on. Yes, you probably won't meet his goals, but the festival and Parents' Night Out are profitable. You're set up to make much more money this year than last. Show him *that* math."

"He was happy about the PNO profit when he visited that day."

Bet resumes folding and gestures for me to do the same with a half-grin. "If he sees what you're pulling from the festival, he should be pleased. $8,000 is nothing to sneeze at."

I'D PREPARED a spreadsheet comparing last year and my projections for this year to show Mark the monetary progress Noble was making easily. It may not be the progress he prefers, but I need Mark to buy in. The more I think about it, the more I'm convinced he's trying to replace me with Cooper, not hire an additional instructor. Of course, he'd waited until 15 minutes before my first class to reply.

MARK DAUGHTRY

> No I can't meet you. I'm not making the drive for whatever chat you want to have 11:43 AM

Ted Dawson

> FaceTime, then? I have good news but I want to show it to you. 11:44 AM

A FACETIME REQUEST immediately comes through to my phone, and I curse to myself. Sure, call immediately. Don't think about whether this will work for me. I should have specified a time. "Thanks for calling, Mark. I don't have a lot of time right now. Could I call you later?"

Mark is poorly lit, but he clearly shakes his head before I finish the sentence. "I'm a busy man. Better make it quick."

The effort it takes to keep my eyes from rolling physically hurts. "Okay, let me share this with you. In the left column is Noble's profit broken down by month. On the right is where we're at so far this year and my projections for next. You can see that we're more solvent than ever. I also have a breakdown of what our take-home from the Fall Festival will be. All our vendor spaces are full. It's already a success, and I expect to be able to recruit new students with our Demo Team at the event in addition to the fees."

Mark rolls his tongue across his teeth. "Is this some pig-in-lipstick way of telling me you can't hit the annual goals I set?"

My fist clenches around the pen I'm holding. "It's my way of showing you the progress we've made," I say, seething. "Those goals are not attainable, and you know it. Why are you doing this?"

He leans back from the screen, casting him further into darkness. "This festival is your last chance."

The first students enter the door, and I wave at them, lowering my voice to hiss, "So that's it. You're going to replace me with Cooper? Why?"

"You said it, not me. All the better; I'm shocked you're still here." The lobby is growing louder with happy chatter, and I'm having trouble hearing Mark. It sounds like he says, "You're a risk I'm not willing to take."

I end the call. I have a class to teach.

33

BET

I'm going to kill him. I. Am. Going. To. Kill. Him.

Fucking, Chad. I'm going to rot in prison for murder and it's going to be because of Fucking Chad.

I purse my lips to keep from absolutely going off. The things in my head can stay there, but I can't prevent the wrath from showing on my face.

Emma is lifeless on the screen before me. I've never seen her this way. She's drained like a victim of a vampire would be portrayed—a shell. I guess the comparison is not too far off. She barely looks like herself. She's colorless except for the heavy red around her eyes; her hair is flat and stringy on either side of her face; even her movement (or lack thereof) isn't her own.

"So this all just happened?"

Emma slowly shakes her head and sniffs. "Sort of. It was late last night." That tracks. She isn't crying now, but it's clear she has been prior. Silence falls between us, but I'm unaware until she breaks it, "Say something."

I look around the room. I don't know what to say. My

mind is a fuzz of fury. I decide to focus on her. "You don't deserve to be treated this way."

She laughs. Emma actually laughs. "Say something I don't know. I know you're thinking. Say what you're thinking." I lean my head toward her in question. She confirms, "Do it."

"Chad is the biggest piece of shit I can imagine. Always has been; some turds are just born that way. Even when you were dating, he never treated you well, and it's gotten worse and worse. Who the fuck does he think he is? He's so untouchable he believed he could abuse you, ignore your pleas for respect and help, barely be a father, and that you'd stay under his thumb. Arrogance and entitlement don't even cover it. He disgusts me. His actions and his cowardice these past few months? He's a fucking parasite gas-lighter. I have never been so angry in my life!" I stop talking only because I run out of breath, but I realize what I've said during my inhale. "I'm sorry." My hands are shaking.

Emma smiles weakly. "No you're not. Don't be." She sighs and closes her eyes. Silence resumes.

Chad is away at work. Fucking Chad. Emma noticed something off with their bank account. His paychecks had always been deposited in their shared account automatically, but there weren't any deposits for the past month. Upon asking Chad about it, Fucking Chad told her he couldn't trust her anymore with their money and had taken out a personal account. A heated discussion ensued, ending with Emma saying she couldn't do this anymore. Fucking Chad was *relieved* when she said those words. Relieved! He used the word! Emma said it was as if he'd been waiting for her to say something like it and jumped on the words, agreeing that he felt their marriage was over.

"What am I going to do?" She barely whispers the question. This one, however, I know how to answer. At least partially.

"You and Charlie are going to be fine. You're smart, talented, hardworking, and a great mom. You're going to do exactly what needs to be done to ensure you both thrive." She casts her eyes down. "Look at me." Her blue eyes find me again. "I have zero doubt about this. None."

Emma turns away from the camera suddenly. It's the most natural movement she's made so far, and I'm sure Charlie has made some noise in his sleep that she's tuned into. "See? Your instincts are good even when you're exhausted and sad." Hadn't Lily given me similar advice recently? Hearing myself say it reminds me of her, and a spark of an idea flashes in the depths of my mind. It's a pipe dream, and now is not the time, so I file it away.

"It sounded like he got out of bed, but I guess not." She swallows and then says, "Thank you. I don't know what I'd do without you, Bet. I think I'm ready to try to sleep."

"Get your rest, Mama. Everything is figure-out-able. You'll be okay—better than okay."

IT'S NOT SPRING, but I feel congested with everything going on. It's like an allergy flare that hurts your whole face, except my entire body is under metaphysical pressure. It's demanding all my attention, and I messed up an order at work for the first time. Okay, two orders because what I did was conflate them. Instead of a Harvest Basket with carnations and a vase of red roses and daisies, I create a basket of daisies and a vase of roses and carnations. Lily caught it, at least, but the mistake feels ominous as I drive to Noble.

My original plan was to tell Lily about taking the job at Casa de Pan today, but I simply couldn't. I didn't say much today at all. The conversation with Emma, not knowing what will happen to Ted, and the Fall Festival being two short days away all have a shoving match inside me.

I don't like to admit it, but the phrase *it's not fair* keeps cropping up when I think about Ted. I've lived long enough to know that fairness is not really a thing when it comes to living at large, but goddamnit the timing. Falling in love should be so simple (and there's the other phrase that keeps emerging). It feels cruel how everything is happening at once. Why should I love Ted now when he might have to move and I can't? Why did Chuck have to make me such a ridiculous offer before we know the festival's results? What is Mark's problem, anyway?

Ted wouldn't tell me how the call went with him over text this morning. Not a positive sign, but he's teaching classes, so he at least wasn't fired.

Something is different at Noble. As usual, I hurry into class at the last minute and race to the bathrooms to change into my uniform. There isn't much time to assess. Maybe I'm imagining it, but the energy of the class feels off.

Nope. Not my imagination. When I join the line, several things become apparent at once. Cooper is here for the first time in weeks, looking smug. The black belts on either side of me are stealing glances my way.

Ted calls the class to our positions on the floor. I catch his eye, and he smiles. Does he not detect anything? I doubt myself again. I'm so worried, and even my bones are tired. It is probably me seeing things that aren't there.

As the class progresses, I lose myself in the movements. We're doing a jump round kick followed by a jab and cross, and the bag tips each time I hit it with the cross. It feels good, like a brief reprieve. Hitting it so hard hurts, but in a cathartic way.

I'm a little disappointed when Ted tells us to put on our sparring gear. I want to hit that bag until it falls over. Maybe we could stay late and practice tonight; even a little more time would be nice.

When everyone has their gear on, Ted asks us to get back into our original line along the back of the room, by height. I watch him make pairs from the far side of the room until I hear mumbling behind me. It's hard to understand what's being said because everyone has their mouthguards in, but it's unusual for there to be talking during instruction. I turn to see what's going on.

It's Cooper. He's not in line, and he's moving from one person to another, saying… something or trying to. Some of the people appear confused.

"What's going on over here? This isn't a line." Ted has worked his way to our side.

My stomach sinks as Cooper takes off his helmet and removes his mouthguard. "I was just telling them they don't have to take instruction from you. At least not for much longer."

Ted pauses for a second. It's so fast I don't know if anyone else will notice he's caught off guard. He speaks softly and intently, "We are Noble. We show honor. We live with integrity. We respect all people. In this way, we are strong. You could be right, Cooper, but I'm still here today, and we'll treat each other respectfully."

The class is eerily still. Every eye is on Ted and Cooper. Ted reaches his hand to the following persons to be paired up for sparring, and I think the intensity is over until Cooper spits, "You can't be noble if you're a slut." My jaw drops, and the mouthguard threatens to fall out. Cooper is looking right at me. "That's right. We all know about you and Three Points. Sorry, you picked the losing team."

I'm suspended, but Ted isn't. He's between me and Cooper before I can unstick myself. He's smiling, yet this is not an expression I've ever seen on Ted. He could eat Cooper one bite at a time, and I wouldn't be surprised. "I think everyone else has been partnered up. That leaves me and you."

The other students behind Ted and Cooper exchange looks. They've been here long enough to know the history. Cooper's face changes from stunned to satisfied in an instant. "Let's go."

Except the only two people who move to the floor are them. Everyone else is under a spell. Ted doesn't correct anyone, but he holds his hand out to Cooper to touch gloves, a sign of respect before a match. Cooper bats his hand away, and his movement gives me a momentary clear line of sight to Ted's face. Even behind the shield of his helmet, I see something flash in his eyes. He winks at me and immediately throws a reverse side kick. It's so fast and unexpected that Cooper doesn't block it. The force of the kick to his chest makes him stumble backward, and I feel sure if he weren't wearing the chest gear, he'd have several broken ribs.

Cooper doesn't make the same mistake again and launches himself toward Ted. He throws a combination of punches that Ted mostly blocks.

They're moving so fast it's hard to register whose limb is whose.

Cooper tries for a headshot, but Ted jumps back, and the momentum of his unchecked crescent kick swings him around in a circle. Ted meets him on the other side with what I recognize as one of our combination patterns: jab, cross, hook. He deflects the punches.

Around me, the other students relax and comment on the fight. Ted lands a front kick, and the crowd oohs. Cooper attempts an uppercut, and a great intake of breath through teeth fills the air.

The men circle each other, still throwing fast and furious moves. It's unlike any fight I've seen. This isn't to learn or make your partner look good, as I've heard Ted say many times. They're trying to hurt each other. I'd be lying if I said it wasn't the hottest thing I've ever seen. Ted is a work of art. The strength and precision of his movements are impossible, as if he were using movie magic to attain them. His violence is laced with grace. But how will this end? Nobody is adjudicating; nobody is keeping score.

Just as I wonder how long they can keep this up, Cooper spins so I see his face, which is riddled with surprise. His brows are permanently up, and his mouth is turned down and determined. He feints a left cross, Ted blocks, and Cooper sweeps in from the right, landing another hook below Ted's arm.

Ted stumbles back a couple of steps, gripping his ribs. Cooper prowls toward him like a jungle predator, but Ted suddenly lunges forward with a number one side kick. He connects, causing Cooper to wince and fold forward. Ted launches from the floor into a number two round kick. His body is a beautiful twisting arc, and the person beside me breathes, "Oh, shit." His foot slams into the side of Cooper's face. Cooper falls to his knees, hand on his helmet above his right cheek. Ted stands over him, observing Cooper for a few moments. When he doesn't rise, Ted takes off his helmet and mouthguard. Sweat pours from the helmet onto the mat. He snarls, "Never talk about Bet again." Then, he snaps his arms to his side and bows at the waist.

Ted returns to the front of the classroom as if nothing unusual occurred. "Everyone back to your places." The students, who were watching, stunned, run to their spots on the mat. Cooper slowly rises, surrounded by people in position, everyone secretly observing him. He takes off his helmet and removes his mouthguard. A bloody string of saliva pulls between his mouth and the silicon. Cooper walks to the side of the room, angrily shoves his gear into his bag, and leaves without a word.

The people around me murmur at each other, but Ted again pretends there is no disruption. "Everyone set!" People snap to attention all around. "Noble is more than the name of our school. It's more than part of our creed that we repeat. It's something each of you should have in your hearts. It should guide all your actions here and throughout your lives. As we close today, really listen to the words and take them with you." Ted breathes and, with frightening solemnity, says, "We are Noble."

Now I know where I've heard this before, not inside the school, but on a hot day at Grant Memorial Park.

Voices rise from all around me, firm and emotional, just as they were when they recited these words at Phil's funeral wearing their white doboks. "We show honor. We live with integrity. We respect all people. In this way, we are strong!"

"Thank you. You're dismissed."

There's a sense of hesitation. Some people shuffle off to pack their bags, but some crowd around Ted before I reach him. I join them, and to my relief, they're saying positive things. An older man, Carl, claps Ted on the shoulder and says, "Well handled." One of the teens asks if Ted can teach him the side kick to jump round combo.

I'm waiting my turn to reach him when someone taps me on the shoulder. It's Roy, Brian right behind him. Roy says, "Hey," but struggles with whatever else he wants to say.

"Hi." I get it. I don't know what to say to them either.

"Um," he clears his throat, "I just want to say it was not cool of him to call you a name like that."

Brian nods fervently and adds, "Yeah."

I feel Ted step up to my side. Roy and Brian's eyes sweep left to him. Brian is the first to act this time. "That was... impressive." Roy whistles his agreement.

"Thank you." They nod at each other, and Roy and Brian retreat.

Ted follows me to my bag and sits in a chair next to me. I scan the room to confirm we're alone. My heart starts beating heavily in my chest. "Are you okay?"

He doesn't answer immediately. When I look at him, his eyes are washing over me. "Are you?"

"I'm not the one who engaged in mortal combat!" The right side of his mouth quirks up, dimpling his cheek underneath his beard. "And with Cooper!"

He leans back into the chair and puts his arms behind his head. "Yeah. I guess that did happen. I didn't think about the part where it was me and Cooper until it was over."

"You were amazing. I've never seen anyone do anything like that before. It was so fast." I toss my bag aside and approach Ted. He's still in the chair, and I'm standing between his legs. He straightens and runs his hands along the back of my thighs. "I don't know what will happen next."

My voice comes out a purr, and I stifle my own surprise at its sound. "I do." I straddle Ted, lowering into his lap. He looks up at me, and I kiss him. His hair is drenched with sweat when I run my hands through it. Our kiss deepens, and I can't stop myself from grinding into him.

"Ow!" Ted's cry of pain stops me. "I'm sorry." He resumes our kiss, and his hand makes its way beneath my shirt. My panties are wet, and I wonder if he'll agree to fuck me right here. It'd be a wild location for our first time, but I am living in this moment. I grab the hem of his shirt and tug up but stop when Ted pulls back, wincing.

"You're hurt." I get off his lap.

"It's not too bad."

"What isn't?" I demand. I grab his arm and pull him to standing. He winces again. I don't remember him limping after the match, but he is now as we walk toward the bathroom. In the back, Ted takes his shirt off. Bruises are erupting all over his chest and side, but his arms... His arms are changing colors in real time. I can watch the bruising spread and deepen. "What's happening?" I point to his deep brown forearms.

"From blocking."

There isn't protective gear to cover arms. Even so, sparring doesn't typically leave injuries like these. Partners are not usually striking at full force; that's not the goal. "We're going to need a hell of a lot of ice. What else is hurt? Why are you limping?"

"Pretty sure there are some bruises on my hip. I might have pulled a hamstring. I'm okay, though, really."

"You didn't act hurt at all after."

He shakes his head. "Adrenaline was still doing its job."

I steady myself with an inhale. "You're too hot to be this injured." Ted tries to say something, but I talk over him. "You're going to let me close shop tonight, and then we'll take you home and get you cleaned up."

Ted looks like he'll protest for a moment but gives a single nod, "Yes, Ma'am."

34

TED

I can hear Bet working in the kitchen from my bathtub. When we got here, she drew me a bath, filled several ziplock bags with ice, and let me have some privacy while she got started baking. "Screw the plans. Tonight is chocolate chip cookies."

Remembering the declaration makes me chuckle, but I stop because laughing hurts. Smiling hurts. Everything hurts, actually. I *am* fine, but I've never been in a fight like that before, and I hope I never am again.

It's an interesting thing, though; unlike last time, I don't regret it at all. I have no idea what's going to happen now. Mark could call at any moment and fire me. Cooper could quit. Nothing could change at all. The wonderful thing is… I don't care. Whatever happens, I'm ready for it, and it's not that I'm deluding myself. I know things could go wrong, but I also know I'll pick myself up if they do. And I know another thing, too.

I let the tub drain and gently dab myself with the towel to dry off. My arms are the worst of it. They're purple from wrist to elbow and ache even when undisturbed. I consider my options and decide to wrap the towel around my waist.

"Am I still too hot to be injured?" Bet jumps. The oven fan allowed me to sneak up on her. When she sees me in nothing but a towel, her expression changes instantly from startled to coy.

She slinks to me and gently runs a hand down my front. "I mean, yes. Have you looked in a mirror?"

"Yes, and I don't think I'm too injured... for everything."

"Mmm. Let's see." Bet whips the towel from around my hips. Her pupils dilate, and we speak simultaneously.

"Whoa."

"That's not what I mean..." Only I can't finish the sentence because her hand is grasping my cock, and she's kneeling before me. I lean against the kitchen entry for support. My confidence wanes at my ability to last. It's been a long time since I've been with anyone.

Bet pumps slowly. There's a streak of flour in her hair by her temple. She looks up at me, hand still gliding up and down my length, "You're... beautiful." The word choice is so unexpected that I huff a laugh, which hurts my ribs. "No, I'm serious. You're body is... I don't know, Grecian? You're gorgeous." She runs her other hand up my abs, so gentle it's the whisper of a touch, then devours me.

I moan some animalistic sound. My legs weaken at the sensation, and I lean harder into the wall. When she pulls away, her tongue lingers around my head, then she circles my cock with it slowly and takes me in again. All the while, her hand pumping. "I, ohhh, I might not last long."

"That's okay. Should I go slower?" Bet doesn't wait for a reply but slows all her movements. She flicks her tongue on my frenulum, almost pushing me over the edge. Bet hums her approval. "When you're ready, grab my hair."

It's never been so hard to focus, but I need to understand. "Grab your hair?"

Bet pulls off me again. "Yeah, grab it hard. You can thrust if you want."

The mere suggestion has me ready to explode. She takes my entire length in and twirls her tongue around me like a candy cane as she backs up. Her hand cups my balls. Energy is building behind my naval and in my pelvis. I won't be able to resist. I weave my fingers through Bet's hair and tug. She responds by quickening her pace. She hums, and the vibration of it joins the other feelings building up. I can't stop myself. My hips thrust forward into her mouth, my hands still gripping her hair. A wave of sensation rushes through my body, and for a moment, all I see is blinding white. An ecstatic sound escapes my lips.

When I open my eyes, Bet is still kneeling, watching me with a pleased expression. The flour in her hair is gone. I breathe for a moment, mind reeling with all the things I want to do to her. "That was, phew, incredible, but it's not what I meant." I grab her hand and help her stand, ignoring the pain shooting through my side.

Her lips curl slowly, "Oh? Then whatever could you have meant?"

I suppress the urge to limp, leading her to my bedroom. "I'd usually carry you here and undress you, but forgive me a modification due to current conditions. Have a seat."

Bet plants herself on the foot of the bed directly in front of me. I stoop to kiss her and grab the hem of her shirt to lift it over her head. Her body is all long, elegant lines. I unclasp the black sports bra, and as it falls away, it's all I can do not to gasp. Her breasts are perfect: petite, her nipples dark pink and turned up, and a dark freckle on her lower sternum that was no doubt placed there like a gift from some artistic deity.

Our lips meet again, and this time, I lay her back on the bed. The scent of her as I kiss down her neck makes me feral. I suck at the perfect pink buds of her breast before letting the back of my tongue trace down, down, down her torso. "These pants won't do."

"Mmm, I couldn't agree more." She grabs the waist and pushes them down below her butt. I take them the rest of the way off with her panties and discard them on the floor. A thatch of black hair is beneath. The crests of her hips arch gracefully on either side. I let my fingers trace them, the natural conclusion leading me to her center. She's already wet, and I can't wait to taste her.

"May I?"

Bet's breathing is shallow, but she says, "Please."

I part her lips. She's gorgeous, splayed out like a flower, all shades of pink and life. I exhale warm air onto her before slowly running my tongue up her center. She inhales sharply. Noted. I want to memorize every reaction. Understand what she likes and become her personal pleasure servant.

I make my tongue wave against her clit, and she grabs a fistful of sheets. I experiment with different movements. Gentle and pushing. Flicking and sucking and circling. It's no surprise that she enjoys clitoral stimulation, but I make the tantalizing note that she seems to like it rough.

My beard is wet with her essence. Bet is writhing on my sheets. It all feels like a dream, but I want more. "Can I finger you?"

She opens her eyes and nods—all the invitation I need. I dive back in hungrily. Eager to be touching her, pleasing her again. My tongue dances across her, and I slowly slip a finger inside of her. Bet is wet and warm and inviting. She arcs her long spine when I curve my finger upward and press gently at first, but at her response, I insert a second finger and pulsate on that spot. Her muscles tighten around my digits, and I know she's close.

Bet's hips thrust forward rhythmically. I can't see her expression well, but when I catch glimpses, her eyes are closed, and she's biting her lower lip hard. "Mmm… How are you doing this?!"

"Simple," my voice rumbles into her between caresses, "I've imagined this, exactly this, for months. It's everything I've envisioned, except I've always wondered… What your face would look like when you come."

I keep humming the end of the word, and her rhythm shudders. She cries out. Her face tenses, brows down, and then relaxes. Her skin radiates with the wash of pleasure, and I have never seen anything more resplendent in my life.

She laughs with ease but then suddenly shoots out of bed and runs out of the room. "The cookies!" How long had the timer been going off? I roll back onto my feet carefully and stand slowly, my ribs aching. I follow her as quickly as I can. When I round the corner, she's nude except for a single oven mitt and tossing the cookie sheet onto the stove. They're burnt.

My lips clamp together to suppress laughter, but when she looks at me and chuckles, I lose it. I limp over to her and remove the mitt from her hand. "We'll have to make some more."

"There's never been a better reason to restart a batch of cookies. That was…"

I finish her sentence, "something otherworldly."

She lays her head against my chest. "Exactly."

AFTER THE COOKIES were successfully baked, we lay in bed, our hands brushing each other's bodies. Bet tries to avoid all the purple splotches on mine until her expression turns serious. "So, what was the call with Mark like?"

Was that this morning? How do I explain the difference I feel now versus then, or should I even try? I play with her hair and stare at the ceiling fan above us. "He said he was surprised I was still here and basically confirmed he's trying to replace me with Cooper. He said the festival is my last chance."

Bet props herself up on her elbow. "Wait, he said he's surprised you're still here?"

"Yeah."

"That's telling."

I can't lie on my side but turn my head to see Bet's look of concentration. "How so?"

"There's no reason it should be a surprise. Think about it. You've worked here practically since you were a child and haven't shown any indication of wanting to go. You said he knew you were supposed to inherit the school, which implies you'd be sticking around a long time. The only reason for it to be surprising you're still around is if he's *trying* to run you off. What else did he say?"

I bring her through the entire conversation as best as I can recall. "The end was hard to hear. He was more talking to himself than me, and the next class was coming in, but it sounded like it was something about me being a risk. I could be wrong, though. I thought about that a lot during the day, and it doesn't make much sense."

"Huh." Bet rolls back over with her hands behind her head. "Yeah, I can't imagine how you could be a risk, but do you believe me now? About him wanting you gone in particular? That's why he's been such a dickbag, and why he set that impossible goal and clings to it!"

It does all add up. "It's why he'd present Cooper as a partner if he's found out anything about our past… but why?" We're silent for a while, both staring somewhere past the ceiling. "I think if the festival isn't a success, I'll be out of a job. I'm not sure what I'll do if that happens, but I don't want to do anything without you."

Bet doesn't reply. I look toward her again to find she's asleep.

35

BET

The energy in the Haven Cove Mall parking lot at five in the morning is, for the most part, chipper. I can tell who is used to rising early and who isn't. Since I'm always up, I volunteered to pick up the coffee. A huge box of the stuff, along with cups, creamer, and sugar packs from Dunkin' Donuts, is beside me on a bench.

Mitch is his usual self, and PJ seems downright ready to get started. He's printed out the plans for the lot and is describing them to Mitch, pointing to areas he references as if he's been setting up fairs his whole life.

Ted is brimming with nerves. He's leaned back against the wall next to the bench, tapping his foot and checking his watch every few seconds. "Any time now. I told Melissa we wouldn't start until she was here."

"She'll be here soon. It's going to be worth it to document the entire process." Abby stretches and yawns beside me. She's the only one showing signs of tiredness, but at least she's in good spirits.

I know Abby's right, but I feel for Ted. There's so much anticipation about today, and if getting going would help take his mind off things, then we should. "How far away does Melissa live?"

My question goes unanswered as her jeep comes into view. She tries to pull into the lot, but we've already roped it off for the event. Mitch says, "I'll help her find the back parking," and trots toward her.

Abby refills her paper cup and says, "Told you she'd be here soon."

"I'm just glad to get started. PJ, you seem to have a plan. How can we help?" I ask.

PJ winks and clinks his tongue. "I started thinking about it like a big science fair. I've helped set those up for years, and this is no different. If we start marking the food area first, that will make the most sense. Or we could divide and conquer; I have a couple of copies of the layout."

Footsteps draw our attention, and I turn to greet Melissa. Mitch is walking two steps before her, and his eyes are severe. He shakes his head the tiniest bit and makes a cutting motion across his throat, but then his mouth splits into a devilish grin. I have no clue how to interpret him. "Hi Melissa, good to see you."

Melissa doesn't smile. "It's not good to see anyone this early. Humans shouldn't be awake before the sun; it's unnatural, and we're not splitting into groups. PJ, how stupid would that be? Then I'd have to run back and forth across this wasteland of a parking lot to take the pictures instead of staying in one place."

Knowing eyes dart to each other, and Mitch stifles a laugh. It's a good thing because I'm pretty sure Melissa would kill him. PJ smiles and makes a big checking motion in front of him, "No divide and conquer. No problem."

"Can I get you some coffee, Melissa?"

She whips her head toward me, blonde hair lashing with the motion. "Yes." She pauses and then adds a clipped

"Please" before walking to the next bench and unloading her camera equipment.

Ted and I lock eyes on my way to the coffee box. I mouth, "Wow," and he grins.

"Yeah. Not exactly a morning person."

"No kidding! She's usually so soft-spoken." I squint at the black coffee in the cup and spin to face the group again. "Does anyone know how she takes her coffee?"

Mitch steps forward and takes the cup from my hands. "I've got this."

All my suspicions about them return and I can't wait any longer. I point between them and whisper in Ted's ear, "Are they?"

He shakes his head but says, "Abby and I have always thought so." Abby is watching closely and must suspect what we're talking about because she gestures to Melissa and Mitch at the other bench and raises an eyebrow.

I nod to confirm, and she steps closer and leans toward my ear. "Right? What's the hold up with them?"

I jump at the hiss in my other ear, "What are we whispering about?" PJ has stepped into our small circle. We all laugh, earning a pointed glare from Melissa.

Abby fills him in. "Same old, same old. Bet sees it, too." She indicates Mitch and Melissa behind her with a swift thumb point.

PJ rolls his eyes. "Melissa is just too quiet, and Mitch, despite being brazen about everything else, is a shy guy when it comes to women. I can't recall him ever asking anyone out, can you?"

"She isn't quiet now."

My observation is met with snickers, but Abby pushes my shoulder. "You're right, though!"

Our talking comes to a sudden halt as the topics of

conversation join us. Melissa sighs heavily. "I'm ready. Let's go."

"Lead the way, PJ." Ted pushes off from his place on the wall. His arms are still a frightening sight, dark and tinged with green, but he stopped limping yesterday, and I know the bruises on his body have lightened.

As we tramp to the far side of the lot, I can't help but think that if one of us asked Melissa the right thing at the right time (now, apparently, before the sun is all the way up), she might ask Mitch out. But what is that thing, and how could we ask it innocently?

PJ takes the duffel bag from his shoulder and unloads it on the grass. "Each booth has been issued a number, and the vendors should know their assigned number. We will use these stakes, tape the booth number to each one, and mark the center of the area with it. This chalk is to outline spaces on the cement. I've also color-coded the different alleys to make it easier for vendors to find their spot when they arrive." He then references his map, labels one of the stakes, and drives it into the ground to demonstrate.

Mitch shoots his hand in the air and waves it around frantically, "Ooo, me! Pick me!"

One murderous look later, PJ points to Mitch, "Yes, Mitch?"

He steps beside PJ and adopts the speaking patterns of an infomercial, "You may be thinking, these stakes look awesome, but how will we use them in the parking lot?" He picks up a stake and tries to drive it through the cement. "Don't worry, we've thought of everything. PJ, show them the string."

PJ rummages in the bag and draws out thick spools of twine. He high-fives Mitch. "We have more than enough to run back and forth across the lot, and we can affix the number signs along them. The hardest part will be picking which trees to use."

"Great job, you two!" Abby turns her lips down, impressed.

Melissa grumbles under her breath, and when attention turns to her, she says louder, "Can you do something worth photographing already?"

"Let's get started," Ted says as he affixes the following number to a stake while Mitch uses a tape measure to determine where to place it.

The six of us fall into a groove, measuring, taping, hanging, staking, and marking spaces with chalk when we get to the cement. Melissa buzzes around us, snapping photos with a frown and occasionally changing lenses.

Daylight is growing stronger around us when we're about half done. Melissa blows her hair up her face to displace the bangs that have fallen over her eyes and announces she needs more coffee. This is my only chance to talk to her privately, so I follow her to the bench.

"Hey, Melissa. Um, not much of a morning person, huh?" I laugh nervously as she returns what I swear is a snarl.

"No. I hate being up early. Sorry. I know I'm not pleasant to be around when I have to be."

My head moves back and forth, weighing her statement. "You know, one good thing is that you're so much more talkative than usual."

She sips her heavily sugared cup. "Ugh. It's embarrassing. It's like my filter is broken in the early hours. It happens when I'm angry, too."

"Can I, um, ask you something?" Melissa is still not her usual self, but I'm heartened that she's talking to me. It's now or never.

"Hmm?"

"It's about Mitch. Errr, what do you think about him?" I

am not good at this. Melissa narrows her cat-like eyes at me but says nothing. I continue, "Like, you think he's handsome?"

She turns from me in what looks like disgust. "What, like Ted isn't good enough for you?!"

No. I'm speechless. How could she think that's what I meant? Melissa's absence jolts me into action. "No. No, no, no." Melissa speeds back toward the group. "Melissa, NO! NOT LIKE THAT!" Ahead of us, I see PJ, Ted, Abby, and Mitch pull away from a cluster they'd formed and get back to work. Melissa is nearly running toward them now, camera in hand. I'm not far behind her, but she's going to reach them first.

"Ted, you need to seriously reconsider the people you bring into our circle. I knew Bet was too good to be true, but she's just told me she thinks Mitch is handsome!" She screams. There's no way to undo this. I stand five feet behind her, shaking my head, fighting tears, looking at each of the faces in front of me.

All of them burst out laughing, and relief plunges through my veins. PJ keels over, bracing himself on his knees. Abby approaches Melissa, puts a gentle hand on her shoulder, and starts to explain, but before she can do so, Mitch interrupts. "Melissa. Bet doesn't like me like that, but everyone thinks you might… And," He grabs the back of his neck and looks down at his feet. "And, I like you too. That's what all these people were saying." He points at Ted, Abby, and PJ, who is now lying on the ground. "So, you know, if it's true, do you want to hang out sometime?"

A Disney Princess transformation scene occurs before us. Melissa's bad mood melts from her, a smile brighter than the sun replaces it. "Really?" She only has eyes for Mitch.

Mitch grins back at her and nods. "Yeah. Really."

Melissa squeals and jumps, kicking her heels up behind

her. She lands and spins toward me as if the impact jarred her memory. "Oh my God, Bet. I am so sorry. I'm so, so sorry! That wasn't the true me; that was sleep-deprived Melissa!"

I put my hands up to stop her. "It's okay."

Melissa and Mitch flirt nonstop throughout the setup, and I notice that even late into the morning, her shyness doesn't silence her as much as I'm used to.

36

TED

My heart has been all over the place today. It was in my stomach as soon as I woke up, in my throat, making talking difficult during set-up, and all the way down in my feet as vendors started arriving, and I was on the lookout for any problems. Thankfully, now it seems right back where it belongs, beating happily in my chest.

The Fall Festival is here. It's happening all around me! Hundreds of people mill around, playing games, getting their faces painted (not entirely yellow), shopping, eating, and watching the stage. Currently, a Pre-K dance class is performing a routine, if you can call it that. Three-year-olds in tutus twirl and leap, but their choreography falls apart after the first move. Even the instructor running on stage and dancing with them doesn't correct it, but it's so adorable none of the audience cares. It may even be better this way.

Aside from short touch bases, Bet and I have been pulled apart all day. We've both worked the entry table, selling tickets and giving people directions with PJ and Mitch while Abby runs the stage. Bet has balanced her time between there and helping Lily while I've been pulling double duty practicing with the Demo Team and was even pulled aside for an interview with the Haven Cove Herald. That was unexpected, but talking about how we built this thing from my mom's idea to seeing all these happy faces put it in perspective. We've really accomplished something.

I start wending through the crowd toward Daisy's Daisies & Other Flowers booth to fetch Bet. I'm to get her before the Demo Team goes on so she can watch. Kids race in front of me, and I'm forced to dodge to the right so I don't trample them. A resigned-looking dad donning a jester hat follows them and mouths a half-apology before he's out of hearing range again. A large group of teenage girls walk by, holding some ice cream topped with fresh strawberries. Behind them are several guys of similar age in football jerseys, jogging as best they can through the crowd to catch up.

I stealthily join one of the small lines queueing in front of Daisy's Daisies, ensuring to stay hidden behind the other customers. Judging from the nearby people, the flower crowns are a big hit. Bet is making change across the table, chatting with the lady as she does so. She's in a beige shop t-shirt with a massive daisy on the front tucked into dark blue jeans. I know a lot of socializing drains her battery, but she looks like a professional extrovert right now.

Has she told Lily about resigning yet? It's weighing on her, and she'd considered having that conversation today, but I can't tell. Lily also looks pleased and is chatting away, working her line. She somehow manages to spot me and winks in my direction.

When the large gentleman I was hiding behind collects his two roses and leaves, Bet finally sees me, too. "I'd like a flower crown, please."

"A flower crown, eh? Are you buying it for someone special?"

As I count out the cash, I quip back, "I like to think of

myself as special. You think those little green ones will bring out my eyes?"

"The chrysanthemums?" Bet puts on a show of inspecting me from each angle. "Yeah, this crown is going to be perfect for you." She takes my seven dollars and places it on top of my head.

"We're about 25 minutes out from Demo. I've got to run back and get them prepped, but I wanted to let you know."

"Yep! About on schedule, that's pretty good." She asks Lily, "Is it alright if I go with Ted? I'll come back in about an hour to help again."

Lily shakes her head. "We'll be out of supplies in an hour. Yes, go, but don't worry about coming back. I figure we have about 15 minutes left before I break down."

I ask, "I hope that means you've had a successful day?"

"Oh, yes, dear. Very lucrative and fun. A job well done by you and your team."

"Wonderful! I hope everyone else feels the same and that my Demo Team recruits a whole lot of people, too."

Lily smiles, and the wrinkles on her cheeks intensify. "Me too." She turns back to Bet. "And you. I am so happy for you and regarding your suggestion earlier… There are a lot of unknown pieces, but I will consider it."

Bet moves so fast to hug Lily that she catches her off guard. Her wispy brows shoot up, and she laughs, patting Bet between the shoulder blades. "Thank you. For everything." Lily waves her off, as I've seen her do before, and returns to tending to customers.

Lily calls, "You two have fun. Good luck, Ted!" as we walk off.

It's a short distance to the stage, but moving through the hordes of people takes time. I grab Bet's hand and weave us through as quickly as possible. "So you told her?"

"Yep! You called it. I was scared, but her immediate

response was to be happy for me. I swear it's like she doesn't worry about herself at all. She thinks everything will just get done. I'm baffled by it."

"Ha! I knew it, and I'm so happy for you too. It must be such a relief to have it off your chest."

Bet agrees. "Yes, I feel like a million bucks! I can't wait to start at Casa de Pan! We'll iron out the details later for my last day."

"Is that what she was going to consider?" I ask as I round a family of five.

"Mmm, not exactly. I'll tell you later." We'd arrived behind the stage, and the Demo Team was helter-skelter around the area. Their bright white doboks stand out and make them easy to spot.

I squeeze Bet's hand in thanks. We're scheduled to go on in ten minutes. "Noble Demo Team!" I wave my hands above my head to signal them to join me. Everyone in uniform draws toward me, and I count to make sure nobody is missing, but we're all here.

"Some of you have asked me if this performance is our last together, and the truth is I don't know. I hope not because I love seeing each of you grow in your art. What I will ask you to do is treat this like every other demonstration. You know the routine flawlessly and are about to blow people's minds out there. Remember to perform as a leader, and for crying out loud, have fun!" I pause to take in all the faces, try to lock them into my memory, and get the impression that some of them are doing the same exercise back at me. "We are Noble."

The team ends our mantra just as Abby ushers the previous performer, a guitarist, off stage. She waves for us, and I lead the team up the stairs. They follow in a tight line until they assume their initial formation centerstage. A brief tap on the microphone indicates it's still on. "Hi everyone,

I'm Ted Dawson, the lead instructor at Noble Martial Arts. Is everyone enjoying the Fall Festival?"

Applause and "Woos" answer back.

"Excellent! Noble and all the businesses here in the Haven Cove Mall are the sponsors for this event. Now, I don't want to take much of your time, but I want to introduce my Demo Team." I slide to the left and indicate them before returning to the mic. "These are some of my top students. You'll see them around town at events, and we come to schools to teach about martial arts; this team also competes and has brought home many trophies over the past 15 years. If you've ever been interested in martial arts, enjoy this demonstration, and if you'd like to start learning, please come talk to me. I'll be enjoying the show with you right in front of the stage." I hop down to the ground, give a thumbs up to the team, and Abby presses play for our music to start.

In perfect unison, all eight members take three steps forward, assume a wide stance, then bring their feet together and snap their arms down. "We are team Haven Cove!" They bow and step back to begin the routine. In most demo team routines, everyone makes the same moves at precisely the same time. The discipline to be so well-tuned to the people around you, even when performing eye-catching moves like hurricane kicks, is impressive.

This routine is different, new. My nerves and excitement suddenly go from 25 to 100, and I wonder if I'll throw up. Have I eaten today? Maybe throwing up is impossible.

The team starts together, hitting a front stance left block into a butterfly kick. Eight bodies are parallel to the ground, black and red belts dangling to the earth for a moment as they twist around to land. They're in such perfect unison I gasp, and I'm not alone. People from behind me make a variety of awed sounds, but the team is still executing a combination of punches in flawless timing with the music and each other that the snap of their doboks is amplified.

I know what's next and hold my breath. The back row performs a triple push side kick, and the front row performs the same, but they push backward to change positions, weaving through each other at an angle. After the third push side, they launch from the ground into a jumping hook kick, the front row to the right and the back row to the left. They nail it, and I exhale. All of them are performing with looks of determination, but I can tell they know they're hitting every mark; the excitement is radiating from them.

Next, they do a series of blocks and knife hand strikes demonstrating different stances in a square shape, ending on a hammer fist in a rear cross stance. They freeze here, breathing heavily, before snapping into an attention position, bowing, and lining up at the back of the stage.

The crowd loses it, and I dare to look over my shoulder. A huge swath of people has gathered to watch—so many that the walkway behind us is obstructed. People whistle, shout, and applaud, and it's not over. Our weapons demonstrations are starting.

I barely pay attention to my soloists who are demonstrating choreographies featuring bo staff, nunchuck, and katana because of all the people who want to talk to me about classes. It's unorganized. Instead of a line, I'm surrounded by a group of people asking different questions. What's the cost of lessons? When are classes held? What's the best age to start? How fast can we get *that* good? Do we have other branches in the area? Where'd the flower crown come from? I answer the questions as best I can while feeling like a celebrity mobbed by paparazzi. Fortunately, they all show interest in the answers to all these queries, and the person who asked about the crown scurries off to find Daisy's Daisies booth.

More and more people come to speak to me, even after our last performer is done and a drumming troop has begun. I end up scheduling six formal meetings to discuss enrollment further and giving my email and phone number to so many others I can't keep track—I'd guess at least ten.

The amount of interest far surpassed my expectations, but there goes my heart sinking low again. Not all of these families will join. Typically, about 30% of the people I meet with become students, and there's a high level of loss after the first year. I've heard people say only 1% of beginners make it to black belt. Noble does a little better than that, but it doesn't matter.

"They were amazing!" Bet has been patiently waiting for me to get through all the questions. "The performance was insane, and all these people wanted more info! That's awesome!"

I should be happy. She's totally right, and I do even feel some excitement, but it's tempered with… I don't know. A letdown that I knew was coming. "That's the best performance I've ever seen the Demo Team give, which is saying something."

Bet searches my face and starts to say something, but she changes her mind and says, "Should we go help with the tickets some more? There are only 30 minutes left until we shut down."

"Yeah. Let's go." When we arrive at the entrance, there's no longer a line waiting for tickets. Mitch is leaning back in his chair, feet crossed on the table. There's no sign of PJ. "How are you holding up?"

Mitch lets his chair fall back on all four legs. "Ready to get outta here," he chuckles.

Bet asks, "Where's PJ?"

"He's counting the till. Couldn't wait until we were officially done. When we stopped having a line, he went to his car and locked himself in there with the ledger."

"You think we made out alright?"

Mitch shakes his head, eyes wide. "I've never seen so much money in one place, and that's just the cash. Look at all those people behind us. They all paid to get in!"

I've been experiencing the volume of people all day, but I let my eyes focus on the crowd. It's not as dense as it once was, but hundreds of people are still present. "I can't believe we did this." Bet squeezes my shoulder, but a disconcerting thought pops into my mind. "Um… I haven't considered this before, but how do we get them to leave?"

"Easy." Abby sits in the chair next to Mitch. "The last performer wrapped up," she explains. "Don't worry about closing, though. It'll happen on its own. Vendors will shut down, and then there'll be no reason for people to hang around anymore."

"Oh! Makes sense."

The total weight of my exhaustion sets in all at once, and I sit on the table, Bet following suit. Abby tells us about some of the more interesting characters she encountered running the stage, and after a few minutes, PJ emerges from behind the mall. "You won't believe this, but I counted three times." Everyone sits up straighter. "We had over 2,000 people come through. Between the $7 for adults and $5 for kids and less the card service fee, we made $11,875."

I do some rough math. "Subtract out the cost of the permit, and it's about 1,500 for each of the businesses in the mall—almost a third higher than we anticipated."

Bet snarks, "Connie should be pleased. That also means Noble pulled in more than we thought from ticket sales."

"Yeah." Still not enough. I can hardly bear it. My friends all worked so hard for this; now their efforts will be for nothing. "I don't feel well."

Abby narrows her eyes at me. "You don't *look* well. Go lie down. You go with him." She points at Bet, who nods in agreement.

I start to protest, but before I can speak, she says, "Tear down is nothing. It takes less than ten minutes. We'll see you in a few." My mettle is lacking, and I let Bet tug me up from the table and lead me to Noble.

37

BET

Ted unlocks the door to Noble and goes straight to the chair behind the front desk. It's a rare occasion that I've seen him sit in this chair, even when behind the desk he usually stands. "What feels bad?"

He leans forward and rests his head in his hands. Dark curls wrap around his fingers. "It didn't work."

I know what he's going to say, but I place my hand on his back and ask, "What didn't?"

"You and Abby, PJ, Mitch, Melissa, and even Lily and Connie and everyone else… We all worked so hard for this, and we did it! But it's not enough. Nothing would've been enough."

"So you feel guilty? Or like we failed?" I swirl my fingers gently around his muscled back.

"Both." He still doesn't look up.

"Do you think any of us regret putting forth the effort?" Ted stills even further but doesn't reply. "We love you, Ted. None of us would have done anything differently. None of us think this was less than a success. You stay here. I'm going to get you something to eat."

I let my fingers fall from him as I round the counter and walk to the back rooms. While we haven't been together the whole day, I can't recall seeing Ted eat anything, and I know there are snacks back here. Finding a box of protein bars and miniature water bottles doesn't take long.

When I round the corner, Ted is upright in the chair again. I toss him a bar and set a water down on the desk. He says nothing but eats slowly, taking swigs of water between bites. He looks better immediately after he eats. I smirk and ask, "Forget to eat today?" Ted shrugs, but there's something in his eyes. He looks mischievous as if he knows something I don't. I have to understand where this newfound energy is coming from. "What?" I demand.

His shoulders are back against the chair; he's pleased, but nothing could have changed in the time it took me to fetch the snacks. His throat bobs. I wonder if he will tell me at all since he's taking so long to reply, but he finally speaks, not as confident as he looked: "You said you love me." He shoots his eyes sideways and amends, "Sort of."

My brows shoot up, and I purse my lips. "Well…" I slowly approach him as I speak, "It's something that's been in my head for quite some time, actually." He grabs my hips, and I straddle him on the chair. Ted is not so malnourished that he has any issue with an erection. I lock eyes with him. "I do love you, Ted."

His breath hitches, and a tear slides down his cheek. I wipe it away. "I love you, too. So much." We pull each other close, and I breathe him in. The future for us is hard, but at the moment, I let that knowledge go. He kisses my neck up to my ear and whispers, "I love you," again. My back arches as he nips my earlobe. Hearing him saying it - hearing me say it after ignoring the urge to for days, is a release. I grind against him. As close as we are, I need more. Ted returns the movement, and we kiss like we're starved for them.

He unbuttons my jeans and eagerly slides his hand beyond the waistband. I couldn't agree more, except our position is still not working with the stiff fabric. I stand to strip them off, and Ted rises, too. "One sec." He jogs to the windows and lets down the rolled-up blinds.

"I didn't know we had those."

"I haven't put them down in years. No need for them."

I smirk and add, "Except maybe this."

He hums an agreement so low it sounds like a growl. Then we're upon each other again. Ted strips off my shirt, and I grab his from between his shoulder blades and tear it over his head. I slide down his joggers and briefs together, and the sight of him, the size of him, still stuns me. He tries to peel my jeans off, but they're snug fitting, so it becomes a team effort. Finally free of all restrictions, Ted looks at me fiercely but then blinks and says, "I don't have a condom."

"I'm on birth control."

His eyes darken. "Thank Fuck."

We're at each other again, but now our hands are busy. Sliding and twirling and pumping. Ted slaps my pussy, and I let out an "Oh" of shock. I have to have him inside of me. "Take me against the wall."

He pins me against it, lifts my hands over my head and holds them there by the wrist with one hand, and uses the other to guide his cock into me. Our similar heights work out perfectly for this position. The first movement is slow. Almost gentle, except that word doesn't capture how hard he is. I whimper as our pubic bones touch. "Is this okay?"

My words are stolen, but I eke out an mmhmm, and Ted thrusts in and out, still unnervingly slow. The barely there light coming through the side of the curtains reveals how perfect Ted's ass is. His glutes hallow on the sides when he pushes into me, round and firm when he retracts. I take my hands down to explore his body.

When my touch travels down to his carved gluteals, Ted increases the pace, and a moan I have no control over spills from my mouth. I'm full of Ted and still want even more. I bite his chest playfully, then kiss over the place. "Can you pick me up in this position?" I blurt the question without thinking.

Ted answers with action. It's seconds before my legs are wrapped around his hips, his hands under each thigh, and he's leaning into the wall with me. It's perfect. The change of angle has his dick pushing into me as far as possible. He hits my G-Spot again and again.

We're grinding at a frenzied pace. I'm returning what movement I can to him using the wall for leverage. Behind us, papers fall off the desk, and I realize we're shaking it. The wall and the chair and desk are vibrating. The whole world is vibrating, and I'm coming harder than I ever have in my life. A crashing sound comes from our left. Ted cries out seconds after I do. A moment passes when we're both still, enjoying the afterglow. He sets my feet back on the floor and kisses my chest. "You're all pink." He points at my chest, which has taken on a rose color. "Gorgeous."

"I think we made a small earthquake." I bend over to fetch the papers and straighten them on the desk.

"Seismologists will scratch their heads at this one, but we'll know the truth," Ted winks at me.

"You know, I never imagined the first day I came in here and talked to you that you'd rail me against the wall. Now that it's happened, I can't help but think of all the other positions we might try here. The padded shield things?"

"Hah! Could be fun. The tumbling mat is practically a bed."

My imagination runs wild as I hop back into my jeans. I look for more inspiration when I see that several things hanging on the wall have fallen. I point over to the blank wall and say, "That'll be what made the crash."

Ted frowns. "I didn't hear it for some reason." I push his shoulder, and we inspect the damage.

The framed placard containing Noble's mantra is in pieces, and one of the swords is next to it on the ground. I pick up the frame to inspect it. "It's not broken. The back just came loose," I note.

Ted still frowns slightly. "It's a good thing we weren't beneath them, though." He picks up the sign.

"What's that?" I point to the back of the sign, which has a small manilla envelope taped to it.

38

TED

The tape releases from the placard with a *thech*, and I turn over the envelope. "That's Phil's handwriting." His unmistakable scrawl reads, "Just In Case" across the center. My hands shake as I bend the metal tabs to open it. There's a note and another white letter envelope.

"What does it say?" Bet is several feet in front of me, watching. Giving me space.

Mr. Ted Dawson,

How do I explain what led me to hide the contents of this envelope in our studio? How can I forgive myself for suspecting what might go so wrong and not clueing you in? Hope is sometimes misleading.

My greatest wish is that you find this many years from now, perhaps when you are retiring or when you finally decide to remodel the school. You'll read it and laugh at an old friend's paranoia. My fears won't even make sense to you, as I've kept you at arm's length of certain more complicated parts of my life.

Yet, I do fear.

I have barely spoken with my brother, Mark, in the past 43 years. That has changed in the past six months when he sought me out to make amends. You see, our history has not been one of kindness. Even when we were children, Mark was jealous of me. My successes seemed to taint his own. We were different people, always. I excelled in art and language in school, and Mark was an incredible mathematician. Our parents celebrated our accomplishments equally (or so it seemed to me), but Mark didn't see it that way.

It was a poison over time, envy festering in him such that he began to attempt to frame me for inconsequential wrongdoings. I could never prove it until one day when things escalated. I was 23 and competing for my third degree. Mark is older than I and had never attended a testing or competition before but asked to attend this one. While I was performing our forms, Master Gutierrez caught him tampering with scoring sheets. We do not look dissimilar, and when Master Gutierrez asked him to identify himself he gave my name. Luckily, I could prove my innocence thanks to the technology of video recorders, but it still shamed my name and broke my heart.

His actions drove a wedge between us, and as I

say, we only spoke in passing at holiday gatherings until recently. Because I am sick, I am sure, he reached out to make amends. I have found it refreshing to speak to him openly and frequently. Forgiveness is a type of magic.

We are still different people, and although I yearn to believe his intentions are pure - I will believe they are - there is a black seed of doubt in my heart. This is a very hard letter to write. If I have been foolhardy, please forgive me. I pray you find this at an auspicious time.

Ted, you have been the son that I never had. You are the most Noble of anyone I've had the joy to teach.

Love,
Phil Daughtry

HOT TEARS TRACK down my cheeks as I hand the letter to Bet. Her eyes travel to and fro across the page. She whispers, "Son of a bitch" and I'm sure I know where she's at. She lays the letter on the desk reverently. Her eyes are misty as she points to the white envelope. "It has to be, right?" I know what she's thinking.

I'm holding Phil's last will and testament.

39

BET

The envelope flap isn't sealed, just tucked in. Ted gently lifts it and removes the tri-folded papers, laying them on the desk next to the letter. I've never seen a will before, but this one is short, only two pages long, and mostly legalese establishing identity and the witnesses. I scan down the page until I see the title "Disposition of Property," directly beneath it is a subtitle reading "1st Beneficiary." I take a sharp breath in. "You're his sole beneficiary." Ted shakes his head. "Look, down here, it specifies the proprietorship of Noble!"

Ted's voice wavers, "I… I can't believe this."

Me either. "Auspicious timing, indeed!"

Ted shakes his head again, and concerns rush from him. "What does it mean, though? Did Mark hide the original will? Forge one? If he did, how could we possibly prove it? Phil passed five months ago. Is it too late? I don't know where to start."

I wish I had answers or even an inkling. I don't, but I know someone who might. "This might be a little awkward, but I went on a date once with a guy who's an Estate Attorney. I don't know if this is in his wheelhouse, but he might be able to help."

It takes a lot of scrolling through messages to find his contact information and remind myself of his name, which I feel a little bad for… David. Okay.

"Hey, David. Um, it's Bet. I know we haven't spoken since our date and all, but, well, it's complicated. I'll explain better on the phone, but could you look at a will for me? Call me back. Please." My call went directly to David's voicemail. Hopefully, he's out fishing and not ignoring my number.

We'd picked up some take-out on the way to Ted's place and had already eaten an entire carton of rice and General Tso's Chicken. It was the most delicious food I've ever tasted, but that may be an indication of how hungry I was rather than the quality. We'd been speculating and googling throughout the meal, but our hopes were tied to David.

Ted returns from taking the now-empty cartons to the trash and flops face-first into the bed. "No matter what Mark did, there's no way to prove it."

I hum in disbelief. "There has to be a way. We're so close, and we have Phil's own words!"

Ted rolls onto his side, facing me. "Yeah, maybe. My brain hurts." He yawns and sputters, "I'm so tired!"

"Me too. I don't think I can keep my eyes open much longer."

My phone alarm goes off at 4:30 am. I curse myself for not remembering to turn it off and fumble for it effectively enough to dismiss it before Ted wakes up. The bed is too comfortable, and I am still too happy to be in it to rise, so I go back to sleep.

The fucking alarm starts going off again! I don't know what time it is, but there's no reason for it to be sounding, and I angrily search for the phone again.

Except it isn't the alarm. It's 10 am, and David is calling.

I reach out my arm and nudge the lump next to me, which is Ted. "It's David! Wake up!" Ted inhales sharply. "Wazzit?"

"It's David!" I clear my throat and answer the phone. "Hey David. How are you?"

"I'm good, thanks. I was surprised to see your number. You said something about a will?"

I give David what I consider the essential, need-to-know information. Phil owned Noble and had always told Ted he would leave it to him. When he passed, it was a surprise to find his brother, Mark, was the apparent heir to the school instead. We found a letter from Phil and a copy of his will last night hidden in the school, and we have reasons to believe that Mark may have manipulated information to come into proprietorship. The details can wait until later *if* David will even help us.

David takes a second to digest, then asks, "This is an unusual situation. Is it a standard will?"

I frown. "Um, I've only ever seen this one, so…"

"Has probate ended?"

I put my hand over the receiver and ask Ted, "Do you know if probate has ended?"

Thank goodness this makes sense to Ted because I don't even know what probate is. He shakes his head, "I don't know. I wasn't included in anything after his passing."

"We don't know."

David is momentarily silent before saying, "I guess it doesn't really matter. At least, if there was funny business, we could open it back up."

"What does that mean?" I ask.

"I need to see the will and do some research to determine what, if anything, can be done."

"So you'll help?"

"I'll try."

"Oh my God! Thank you so much."

We plan to meet in two days because David has business that will bring him closer to Haven Cove, and I text him pictures of the will and letter.

Ted and I are wide awake now, looking at each other in disbelief. His morning bedhead is comic book quality adorable.

He breaks the silence with a laugh. "It's going to be a strange two days waiting. I guess we pretend everything is normal?"

"I guess so. Geez, Cooper starts today."

"Oof, and remember, Mark said the Fall Festival was my last chance, so I'm counting on him calling me. I might even get fired!" The situation is so ludicrous that we both start laughing in a fit. When we finally slow down, Ted half-whistles, "Just act normal," and renews the hysterics.

JUST ACT normal became the rallying call for us the next two days, but we somehow did it. It was much worse for Ted than it was for me. Cooper did show up and asked to split the teaching schedule. Ted insisted on having a week of shadowing time before Cooper took a class alone. It was a tense conversation, but ultimately, Cooper acquiesced when Ted pointed out that all jobs involve training. He also did have to take a call from Mark. Fortunately, it was a short one. He seemed pleased despite himself at the festival's results and ensured Cooper had been in touch.

Now we're in my apartment, waiting for David to arrive. I'm keeping us busy in the kitchen making vegan cinnamon rolls. "Is it vegan if it has yeast?" Ted screws the lid back on the jar of yeast and returns it to the refrigerator.

"I've never known a vegan to take issue with yeast. Why do you ask?"

Ted shrugs. "It's a living organism. Sugar is like its nutrition and makes it reproduce, I think."

"Huh. I never thought of it that way. It probably depends, then. People choose their diet for a ton of different reasons." I jump at a knock on the door. "He's here!"

David is dressed more casually than he was for our dinner, which suits him. He's wearing a white and blue striped collared shirt tucked into jeans. I remember him as being awkward. Sweet if bumbling, but he defies those recollections as well. He comes in comfortable and confident. "Bet, good to see you again." He shakes my hand firmly. "You must be Ted?" He shakes Ted's hand, too. I pull him out a chair and he asks, "Any vegan Key Lime Pie?" I search my memory, but before I think of how to reply, he says, "Kidding," and retrieves papers from his briefcase.

"Thank you so much for helping us, David." I could not be more sincere. It would have been understandable if he never answered my call.

Ted adds, "Yes. I know we're out of your way, and we've never even met. I appreciate your help more than I can say."

David smiles blandly and strums his fingers across the table. "Don't worry, guys. This is what I do- well, it's actually not usually what I do because this doesn't happen often, but I am an expert in this arena. Plus, this is all mighty interesting. Are you ready?"

Ted nods and lays his hand on my knee beneath the table.

"Good. Here's the easy part. The will you found is absolutely standard, and the signing attorney verified it to be authentic and the most recent version he knows of. In other words, I believe this is Phil's true will."

The grip on my knee intensifies, and I squeeze Ted's hand back. "That's great news. So Ted is the rightful owner of Noble?"

"Yes, but it's complicated. Unfortunately, probate closed in September, so it's not as simple as submitting the will. The other complicating thing is that no will was considered during probate. In this case, next of kin was determined to be inheritors, so everything officially moved to Mark already."

Ted sits back in his chair; his hand whips from my leg and goes to his chin. "There was no will? I kinda thought there would have been a… I guess, a modified one."

David nods. "A forgery would have been better for us. If there were a forged will, proving the document was tampered with would be simple. Comparing the physical documents, consulting the signing attorneys, and determining who would benefit most from the lie makes this easier than you might think. However, with no will, we don't have anything to compare.

Ted concludes, "Mark must have hidden it or destroyed it, then."

At the same time, I ask, "Surely there's a way to introduce a will that was found late, right?"

"Bet, yes, you're right, but let me ask Ted first. Why do you think he hid it instead of not knowing about it in the first place?"

"You don't know Mark," Ted says darkly. "He's… a level of unpleasantness I've never encountered and impossible to work with. He's been blatantly, greedily, doing things with the school to funnel more money to him at any cost. Plus, he told me he knew I was supposed to inherit Noble!"

David's face is unconvinced. "There are a lot of unpleasant, greedy people in the world, and Phil could have told him that he planned on you taking the school."

"But, David, he also has been gunning to make Ted quit and even preparing to fire him. When Ted asked about it, he basically admitted it, then said something about Ted being too big a threat to keep around."

David put his hands up. "Hey, I'm not saying you're wrong! In fact, I'm sure you're right. Phil's letter and Mark's behavior you're citing do paint a picture. What I'm saying is we have no hard and fast proof. I don't think we could sway a judge if we tried to take this course, which brings me back to what you asked, Bet. Yes, reopening an estate after probate is possible because of a recovered will. It's a messy business, however, because the estate has already been distributed and the inheritors have presumably utilized those items or funds, it may be impossible to recoup. I should also mention there are costs associated with re-opening probate. You'd be looking at $4,500. Maybe more, it's 3% of the estate value."

Ted's face falls. "How is that figured, exactly?"

"I get that you're focused on the business, but you know he left you a house, too? Phil owned a small, older house in a prime location along the bay. They don't make them like that anymore, so I'm only going to guess the value for now. I did drive by it on the way, and someone is inhabiting the home. At least a car was outside, and the grass was mowed."

"He can keep the house! If we reopen the estate for just Noble, would it still cost the same?"

David nods. "I'm sorry, I'm afraid it would. We can't pick and choose what parts are reopened. Now, you and Mark could agree on your own, and the house would be an excellent bargaining chip. Did you know Mark hasn't yet filed for a new business registration for Noble? I'm getting ahead of myself, though. Obviously, the cost is a concern, and we can't guarantee the outcome, but I have an idea. Are you open to trying something a little roguish?"

40

TED

The plan is farfetched, but I take solace in knowing nothing is lost, even if it doesn't work. We'd just be back to our original options. Do nothing, or come up with a bunch of money and take a risk on reopening probate. If it does work… I've been afraid to dwell on it too much. Bet does enough of it for the both of us in any case. It's new for her to dream about the future. I know because she told me, and I have never felt more privileged. Not even when she says she loves me, which still blows me away. Knowing that she dares to dream of a future with me, whatever that might entail, has me dreaming right back despite myself.

Bet and I are hidden in an empty office across the hall from another, where David is set up. The Law Offices of Parish & Parish agreed he could borrow space to meet with a local client after hours. Being so close to Noble makes it convenient for me and, I guess, Mark, too. I even got to give David a tour of the school.

A door opens, and footsteps sound down the hall. "I don't remember your face. Were you one of the assistants or something?" I'd recognize Mark's voice anywhere.

David's voice is chipper, "Oh, no, sir. We must not have run into each other is all. I was available to meet with you; this shouldn't be too difficult."

"Good. I thought everything was taken care of already!"

The door closes across the hall, our cue to move so we can listen to the discussion. Bet and I open our door, holding the handle so it won't click when we close it again. We press our ears as close to their door as we dare without touching it.

I hear leathery chairs being occupied, and David asks, "Is it alright if I record our conversation? Standard procedure."

Mark hesitates but agrees, "I suppose. Don't remember doing that before."

"Thank you." David's tone changes with his following words, and a chill runs down my spine. "I can tell you're a man who appreciates the blunt truth, so I'm going to give it to you. I know about your brother's will. I have a copy of it and have verified its authenticity with the signing council."

After his statement, silence stretches on and on. My heart is pounding. Bet grabs my elbow as we wait, but neither man seems to want to be the first to speak. After what feels like an eternity, Mark says, "I wasn't aware…"

David interrupts him, "Oh, I think you were, and here's the thing." I don't hear it, but I imagine the slight click of him turning off the recorder. "I want in."

"Hah! Want in on *what?*" Mark is still playing ignorant. If he continues, we have a plan for that, but it isn't our first option.

David's voice is cool and hard. "You know what. This happens more often than you might believe, and I respect it. You're smart. This isn't an estate with many dependencies; it's easy and clean, plus you've got a perpetual income machine of the business that's already established. It's the perfect opportunity, and you saw it. Had the balls to do it. I respect that. We're a lot alike." He pauses, either to give Mark a chance to talk or for dramatic effect, I don't know. When Mark doesn't reply, he continues, "The thing is. I have this will. So you have two options. Whether or not you knew about it or not, it's here now. I *could* contact this… Ted Dawson. He could reopen probate and make life real hard for you, expensive too. Or, I could ensure nobody ever sees this document again and help you out. Smart as you are, you're making some big mistakes."

Mark breaks his silence with a snarl, "What fucking mistakes?"

"Oh, those are something I'd tell a business partner. Are you ready to make a deal?"

It's barely audible, but Mark asks, "What do you want?" Bet catches my eye. This is what we hoped for.

"I'm not asking for much. It's a steal for my expertise, but I understand we're also talking about a small estate. Are you selling the house?"

"Yes."

"Five percent of the cut from the house sale since it's a one-time event. Three percent a year from the business." More silence. "I can tell you aren't pleased but can't find a way out. Otherwise, you'd have left. I'm a businessman; talk to me."

"Three percent in perpetuity is too much." I hold back a scoff. Noble isn't a cash cow; most of its income goes back into operating costs. It's possible to make a modest living from it, but three percent would not be much.

David backs down right away. "I have no idea what the financials are for your business, so I don't have much of a bargaining chip here. To show my good faith, let's say two percent?"

"Fine. You've got a deal *if* you tell me what you think I'm screwing up. Demonstrate some of your supposed expertise."

"Easy. You're botching up the business ownership. Why

haven't you renewed the registration under your name as the new owner? And don't tell me it's some sort of tax dodging. I said you were smart before, but that would be pathetically idiotic."

To my surprise, Mark's tone changes to something that might be conversational. "Now, why would you say that? Saving a little money never hurt anyone."

"Friend, this was all so clever because nobody will catch you. Taxes are a much bigger deal, and frankly, what you're doing will be obvious. Not to mention, when you do file to transfer the business to your name, you'll have to put the effective date as the one on the death certificate and submit a copy of said certificate. You're already suspiciously late but put it to a brother grieving, and you'll be fine."

"Hmph. Alright." The last word is a drawn-out concession.

"You've got someone pro at paperwork. Let me know if you need a second eye on the filing. Now, the last thing. About this Ted guy. You know him? Is he going to show up claiming anything?"

Mark laughs, and my blood boils. Bet squeezes my elbow again, anchoring me. "He won't be any trouble. He's just some boy with his head in the clouds. He doesn't expect a thing and is about to be unemployed."

"Wait, what do you know about his employment?"

"Ugh, there was potential for this to go sideways with him because he's the teacher at the school; that's the business, a karate school. Anyway, I knew keeping him around would be bad news, so I started managing him out from day one. Made some lofty goals he'd never reach so I had a paper trail. Last week, I had another teacher start, so I can finally cut the pain in the ass loose."

David is impressed. "Wow, you did well getting him out

of the picture. You were right to do so, too. Having him around is dangerous."

"You have no idea." Mark is bragging now. "These young people don't know anything. I thought for sure I could make him quit at first; that would've been even better. Good ol' Ted and the new teacher are rivals—like the same girl or something. I even had Cooper, the new guy, follow Ted and the girl one night. That got him all riled up!"

David knocks on the desk three times, our sign. "He still didn't quit?"

"Nah. Doesn't matter though, he's on the way out."

Bet is shaking with rage. This time, it's my turn to be an anchor for her. I put my hands on her shoulders and barely whisper, "Deep breath. Are you ready?" Her hand is already on the knob. She twists it so slowly it's silent as we enter.

We're supposed to stand there until noticed, but Bet interrupts the conversation, her voice pure venom, "When?"

Mark jumps and spins in his chair. His face contorts from shock to rage. "What?!"

Bet repeats, "No. When? You made Cooper spy on us. When?"

"What is go…" Mark stands from his chair.

Bet screams, "WHEN?!"

David slams both hands on the desk and says with such authority, my hair stands on end, "Mark, sit down. Answer Bet."

Amazingly, Mark sits. "You think I fucking remember when? It doesn't matter. It was nothing."

David holds his hand up to silence Bet. He could be addressing a naughty toddler for his inflection now. "It does matter, Mark. It matters to the people you manipulated. Think hard."

Mark looks like he's taken a bite out of something sour. "It was the night after I visited the school. He followed me out to the parking lot, asking to help. He practically volunteered to do it."

Bet turns to me now. "Those flashes of light during our first kiss… His weird text was the very next day!"

I know what she's saying, but my attention is on Mark. His face is bright red, and just as I think he can't flush more, he screams, "What is all this then? A fucking set up?"

David leans back in his chair, the picture of relaxation and the antithesis of Mark. "When we started this meeting, I explained you had two options. You still do. You could hand over all the assets you've taken wrongful ownership of to Ted." I narrow my eyes in question at David, and he meets them for a fraction of a second. "It's by far the best outcome for you. The second option would be for us to reopen probate and sue for damages. It would be much more expensive and probably include jail time for interference with estate administration, fraud, and theft."

Mark is furious, but he controls his volume. "I don't know about that. You turned your pretty little recorder off, remember? You can't prove anything!"

"Did I?" David asks.

Mark snatches the recorder from the desk and throws it on the ground. He stomps on it violently until the plastic splinters and pieces fly in different directions. David watches calmly. When Mark is finished, out of breath, he looks back at David with apparent pleasure. David slowly pulls a small black device from his coat pocket, then tucks it safely away. "That's not. That can't be. THAT'S NOT LEGAL!"

"I assure you it is. I attained your consent to record, and you never revoked it. The recorder on the desk isn't even functional. It's an outdated children's police kit toy. I'm curious, did you really believe recordings were still done with a tape cassette?" Mark is beyond words, and I prepare for him to get violent. "Something fortunate is that I happen to have all the paperwork prepared to right this wrong." David unzips his case and then slides a hefty stack of papers and a pen across the table. "Would you like me to take you through these so you know what you're agreeing to, or simply point out where to sign and initial?"

To my amazement, instead of flipping the desk, Mark wordlessly picks up the pen and starts tearing through pages, signing without reading. The only sounds are of fluttering paper and David's instructions when Mark misses places that require initialing. When he finishes, Mark pushes his chair back so hard it falls over. He stomps to me, his face so close to mine that I feel the spittle fleck against my cheeks as he promises, "This isn't over, boy." Then he's gone.

We hear doors close, but Bet follows him after a moment and returns swiftly to confirm he's gone. She takes both of my hands, "Are you okay? You haven't said anything this whole time."

Shit. She's right. It's hard to break my silence because I don't know what to say first. "Yes. I can't believe that happened. I can't believe it!" Bet starts to cry, and I hug her close. "And you! David, you were incredible! You could be an actor! I... I felt like we were in a movie!"

David hasn't risen from his chair yet but smiles kindly and gestures for me to sit. Bet turns the fallen chair upright. "You'll need to sign some of this stack, too." He doesn't let me sign mindlessly as he did with Mark; instead, he explains everything on the page and answers my questions.

At the end, he stands and extends his hand toward me. I shake it. "Congratulations. You're the new owner and operator of Noble Martial Arts and a homeowner."

"Yeah, why did you go for the home? I thought it was our bargaining chip."

David shakes his head. "I knew we had him. There was no

reason not to include it. On a serious note, you absolutely have to renew Noble's business registration in your name."

I laugh. "Believe it or not, I know how to do that. Phil taught me how to renew when it came up. This time will be a little different, but I can figure it out."

Bet blurts out from beside me, "How is this you?!" David and I turn toward her, and her face turns pink. "I mean, when we met, you were so shy and nervous. Now you've hustled a criminal like it was nothing!"

David laughs now. "Whelp, I'm not very good at dating, but I am excellent at my job."

Bet shakes her head. "You should be excellent at both. Confidence like that will get you anywhere in the dating world."

David walks us out and locks the door. I thank him at least a dozen more times. I need him to know he's changed my entire life, and I can't seem to put it in words.

Later, Bet and I lay under the covers; Hitch planted firmly between us. She asks, "What are we going to do now?"

I don't hesitate to dream with her freely.

EPILOGUE

BET

SIXTEEN MONTHS LATER...

Phil's home was in a decidedly medium state when we inspected it. We figured his age, in conjunction with being sick, led to missing some of the upkeep needed those last couple of years. It took a lot of hard work and finding time, but now it's a quaint little bay-front oasis.

Even this morning, the transformation takes me aback as I walk up the path. It's early, still dark out, and the solar panel lights lining the way are down to a flicker. I smile at the bright green door. The bold color was a certain someone's decision, and I wonder if he'll be sleeping or bright-eyed and bushy-tailed today. Time to find out. The bell chimes, but the door opens before its song is completed. "Good morning. The coffee is almost ready." Emma has her sandy hair pulled back into a braid, but pieces of it wisp out to frame her face.

She leads me into her small kitchen and starts filling two

travel mugs. Charlie's feet thump quickly from the bedroom, and he barrels into my legs, "Aunt Bet!"

"There's my little ninja! Are you ready to have a great day with Mr. Ted?"

"Yeah!" He throws his hands up but then brings them down into a fighting stance, demonstrating punches and kicks, which lead him right out of the room.

Emma pushes a mug toward me. "My dress came in. Do you want to see it before we go?"

I place the coffee back on the counter too hard in my haste to answer, and a bit of coffee splashes out of the lid. "YES! Ugh, I'm so jealous. Mine isn't scheduled to be here for another couple of days."

"I can't believe she asked me to be a bridesmaid. Or that I'm invited to a wedding at all! My life is so different than it was before." Much to Abby's chagrin, it had taken longer than she liked for Wes to finally pop the question. Their wedding will be in a gazebo right off the bay in April.

I follow Emma to her bedroom and plop down on the foot of the squashy bed. She digs into the closet, swishes a garment bag out, and hangs it over the door. "Okay, here we go…" She unzips the bag and stands back.

"Oh my God!" I'm up in an instant exploring the soft yellow dress. "I know bridesmaids' dresses are supposed to get a lot of flack, but bless Abby, this is beautiful. You're going to be gorgeous in this!"

Emma grins. "It fits perfectly, too. I just know yours is going to be so good on you! You've got the sea-foamy edition, Ms. Maid of Honor; it'll be perfect with your hair. I love it longer!" She twirls a finger around my shoulder-length hair. It's about the 105th time she's told me. "Maybe we should invite everyone over for a dress-up party when all of them are in?"

"That would be fun. What will Mel wear?" Melissa had

been offered the Maid of Honor position and refused because she couldn't do justice to the role and manage her photography staff simultaneously. I won't speak for everyone, but I was secretly relieved. She's become rather outspoken since she and Mitch got together, or maybe it's managing her photography assistants. Don't get me wrong, she is a wonderful friend, but I can see her being a Maid of Honor-Zilla.

Emma looks at her watch. "We better go. I'm on delivery today."

"Let's do."

On the ride to Daisy's Daisies & Other Flowers, the conversation flows from our latest D&D Campaign (PJ is DMing this round, and there are mimics everywhere we turn. The entire party checks for them incessantly, and it takes up 70% of our time) to my jobs. "I can't believe you finally got down to one job you love just to take up another job again. You realize you did that, right?" I feel Emma's side-eye.

I sigh. "Yeah. You have to admit it is different, though. I was already spending all my afternoons at Noble anyway. Ultimately, it made sense for me to be the Program Manager. Now, Ted gets to focus on teaching and doesn't have to worry about the front-end stuff as much. Goodness knows he needed the bandwidth to train Roy. He's such a good technician, but he can't explain how to perform a move with words yet."

"Charlie loves Roy, don't you, baby?"

"Rawr!" Comes from the back seat.

"I'm going to take that as a yes." We both laugh.

I pull into the lot, and Emma unbuckles and hops out. "Have a good day. Say hi to Lily for me."

"Bye, Mama!" Charlie calls from behind me.

"See you soon, you two. Charlie, you be good for Ted."

Emma waves, and I watch her unlock the front door. When it closes behind her, I back out and head home.

When we arrive at the duplex, Ted is making breakfast. The air smells delicious, with the scents of bacon and eggs reaching the front door as Charlie and I enter. He hears us and shouts, "Come fuel up, everyone!"

When I round the corner, he hands me a sandwich wrapped up to go and kisses me on the cheek. "It's interview day. Hire a good one!" I've been working at Casa de Pan since Emma moved into the house and started with Lily, and today, I'm interviewing for my first assistant. Our vegan goods have become such a demand that Chuck identified my being the only expert in the area as a business risk.

"Yes! I'll probably be late getting to Noble today."

Ted chuckles darkly. "Don't worry. I still know how to run the front if needed." He shivers.

I poke him in the ribs, and Charlie, who has scrambled up into a chair around the table, says, "Bacon, please!"

"Oops! You're right, Charlie. Coming right up." Ted spins on his heel to load a plate and slides it to him. Hitch immediately appears, prowling around Charlie's feet. Smart cat.

"Emma's dress came in. It's so pretty!"

"Yeah?" Ted asks.

"Mmhmm. Six weeks away, I can't believe it."

Ted wraps me in a hug. He whispers, "Can't wait to see you in a dress."

"I know, right? Mine should get here in a few days."

He rears back and looks me in the eyes. "Not that one." Before I reply or even get my brain in gear to interpret what he means, he says, "You better get going. Don't be late on interview day!"

AFTERWORD

Dear Reader,

Thank you for reading Petals & Punches! I hope you loved it as much as I enjoyed writing it.

If you'd like to read more, use the link below to access bonus material which includes a sexy sparring match and the story of Hitch's adoption.

ACKNOWLEDGMENTS

My husband (Tim) and I both studied martial arts growing up.

I enjoyed learning the forms but hated sparring and was too nervous to attend competitions required to progress. My school eventually graduated me to the yellow belt anyway, but I stopped attending soon after that.

Tim became a black belt at age 15 but eventually stopped practicing due to life events and injuries.

Fast forward to 2021. Our children expressed interest in learning martial arts, so we enrolled as a family at the local taekwondo studio. Tim is now a second-degree black belt, our sons have achieved their black belts, and my youngest and I are not far behind (even though I still hate sparring).

I'm grateful for the opportunity to learn together as a family and for the inspiration this experience gave me, which led to this book.

Special thanks to my family, who always love and support me. I'm so lucky to have you in my life.

Thanks to my beta readers for all your thoughtful feedback.

Thanks to YOU for reading Petals & Punches and taking a chance on a relatively unknown indie author.

ABOUT THE AUTHOR

Lori Thorn writes romances featuring realistic characters finding their way into healthy relationships and hosts Page Rebels, a podcast spotlighting indie authors.

She draws inspiration from her life, including living bay-side and attending a taekwondo studio with her family.

Lori lives in Florida with her husband, Tim, and their three kiddos. She enjoys playing clarinet (and bass clarinet and tenor sax) in the local community band and preparing scrumptious vegetarian meals.

tiktok.com/@glorylace
instagram.com/author_lori_thorn
facebook.com/authorlorithorn

ABOUT THE ILLUSTRATOR

Heather Balcerek is a passionate creative and lover of books. While her design experience has been born out of necessity in her past roles, she eagerly learns new programs and tricks of the trade whenever she can. Whether she is drawing Zentangles or noodling around on ProCreate or designing in Canva, Heather puts all her love and energy into each piece. Aside from visual creativity, she also hosts the Connect the Dots podcast, which focuses on career development.

Heather lives in Clearwater, FL with her husband. Together they run the food and travel blog, It's a Salty Life.

Connect with Heather
    @msheatherbdot
    @connectthedots_podcast
    www.thepolkadotdesk.com
    @saltylifefft
    www.itsasaltylife.com

ALSO BY LORI THORN

Remotely Love is a workplace romance for the modern world, taking place between telecommuters.

Locally Love is the Christmastime follow-up novella to Remotely Love.

Crescendo is a small-town romance between band directors.

All of Lori's works contain elements of humor, a focus on healthy relationships, and open doors.

Made in the USA
Middletown, DE
01 July 2024

56559444R00168